Fallen Grace

Also by Mary Hooper

Historical fiction

At the Sign of the Sugared Plum
Petals in the Ashes
The Fever and the Flame
(a special omnibus edition of the two books above)
The Remarkable Life and Times of Eliza Rose
At the House of the Magician
By Royal Command
The Betrayal
Velvet
The Disgrace of Kitty Grey

Contemporary fiction

Megan
Megan 2
Megan 3
Holly
Amy
Chelsea and Astra: Two Sides of the Story
Zara

Fallen Grace

MARY HOOPER

BLOOMSBURY

LONDON   NEW DELHI   NEW YORK   SYDNEY

For Richard, with love

Bloomsbury Publishing, London, New Delhi, New York and Sydney

First published in Great Britain in 2010 by Bloomsbury Publishing Plc
50 Bedford Square, London WC1B 3DP

This paperback edition first published in June 2011

Text copyright © Mary Hooper 2010
Illustrations copyright © Siân Bailey 2010

The moral rights of the author and illustrator have been asserted

A CIP catalogue record for this book is available from the British Library

ISBN 978 0 7475 9912 8

MIX
Paper from
responsible sources
FSC® C020471
www.fsc.org

Typeset by Dorchester Typesetting Group Ltd
Printed and bound in Great Britain by CPI Group (UK) Ltd, Croydon CR0 4YY

5 7 9 10 8 6 4

www.bloomsbury.com
www.maryhooper.co.uk

Contents

The interment of the late *Susannah Solent*
will take place on *Monday 8th June 1861*
at THE LONDON NECROPOLIS, BROOKWOOD.

*Those mourners wishing to accompany the corpse to its
final resting place should assemble in the Necropolis
Company's first-class waiting room at Waterloo.
The train will depart at 11.30 a.m.*

Chapter One

Grace, holding on tightly to her precious burden, found the station entrance without much difficulty. The Necropolis Railway ran, just as Mrs Smith the midwife had said, on its own special line from Waterloo to Brookwood Cemetery in the county of Surrey, and it was at the London station, just before eleven o'clock, that the newly bereaved gathered, all dressed in the first stage of deep mourning. The few women whose nervous tension allowed them to attend wore heavy veils, their black crêpe gowns unrelieved by any bright jewellery, buttons or fancy trimmings, while the men wore top hats with a mourning band, formal frock coats and black bombazine cravats. All were waiting for the train which would take them and their loved ones into the countryside, to the

1

great garden of sleep at Brookwood. Here, away from the fogs and filth of London, their dear departed could rest in peace among pines, roses and evergreens.

Grace stood back a little, watching as mourners approached the window of the booking office to buy their tickets. She had never travelled on a train before and, feeling timid and uneasy, wanted to make sure she did everything correctly. When almost everyone else had passed through the ticket office and gone to their relevant waiting rooms, she went to the window.

'Brookwood, please,' she asked. 'A return fare.'

The clerk issuing tickets looked up. 'First, second or third class, miss?' he asked in the solicitous tone that employees of the Necropolis Railway had been asked to assume.

'Third class,' Grace said, proffering the two shillings that the midwife had given her.

'You're not with a funeral party? It's just you travelling?'

Grace nodded. 'Just me. I . . . I'm visiting my mother's grave,' she lied.

The clerk pushed a thick, black-edged ticket towards her. 'Then kindly proceed to the appropriate waiting room. You'll be shown where to go,' he said. 'May I remind you that the train leaves at half past eleven precisely. Good day to you.'

Grace took the ticket, stammered her thanks and left the window.

There were three waiting rooms, one for each class,

and the people in them – although all in black, of course – were dressed according to their positions in life. Thus the people in second class were clothed neither as elegantly nor as formally as those in the first class, and some of those people in the third class, to judge by their patched garments and dishevelled appearance, seemed little more than paupers. Grace, her garments faded and mended, was able to mingle among the latter quite easily. Bearing their own grief as well as they could, none of the other mourners looked at Grace, a slight, pale girl looking younger than her fifteen years, who kept her eyes to the ground and held a small, linen-wrapped bundle under her arm. If anyone had wondered what it was she carried so close, they might have guessed it to be a spare pair of shoes in case the grounds of the cemetery were muddy, or an extra shawl against the sky suddenly clouding over.

At twenty past eleven precisely, the various parties started moving out of the waiting rooms to board the train, with first-class passengers being bowed to private carriages by representatives of their funeral companies. They boarded first, so they wouldn't be offended by having to mingle with – or even see – third-class passengers. The coffins of their relatives would also travel apart from the others, so they wouldn't have to suffer the ignominy of being placed with lower classes.

Once all the live passengers were safely on board, the matter of loading the coffins into the hearse-carriage was dealt with in as discreet a manner as possible, so as not to cause undue distress. Those not travelling with a coffin but who were going to the cemetery to tend a grave or mark an anniversary filed into a separate carriage, and Grace joined them. Someone made a remark about it being pleasant that the sun was shining that day and there was a murmur of agreement all round, but Grace didn't look up or even think of contributing a comment of her own, so occupied was she with her own devastating circumstances.

After all, what difference would it make to her if it rained or snowed – or indeed, the world were swallowed up by fog and no one ever saw sunlight again? She had given birth to a child, and the child had died. At that moment, nothing else was of the slightest importance.

The train started right on time with a tremendous roaring noise and rattling, amid gusts of steam and smoke which enveloped the carriage like a cloud. From further down the train a bewildered shout of 'What the devil?!' was heard, and some women screamed in fright, for Grace was by no means the only one who hadn't travelled on a train before. Startled by the hissing steam and noise, she jumped to her feet, only to find herself the centre of attention. She sat down again quickly.

She knew that the journey would last about an hour and had been told exactly what to do: once the train was under way, she was to go into the van where all the coffins rested, choose one (not a pauper's coffin, the midwife had instructed, but one in the first-class section, made of good wood with brass handles), lift a corner of the lid and put her precious bundle inside. That was all. Once the train reached the cemetery, the coffins would be unloaded from the train and their lids screwed down permanently before being carried to their final resting places, where private services and ceremonials would be held.

If Grace was quick, the midwife had said, then no one would know that there had been a small addition to one of the coffins – and treating the dead child thus would be far, far better than taking it to a paupers' burial ground in London.

'I always recommend it for young girls like you who've suffered such a loss,' the midwife had gone on to say. 'And afterwards you must forget it ever happened. Never tell a soul about the child – no, not even if you marry. You are a fallen woman, and no one can forgive such a sin.'

Grace had tried to protest that it had not been a sin on *her* part; she had not wished nor invited the incident which had caused her to have a child, but Mrs Smith had told her not to speak any more about it, said that she would forget about it quicker that way.

As the train settled into a rhythm and the stink and mire of London gradually gave way to the sweeter green of the countryside, Grace looked out of the window, unable to stop her thoughts turning to the events of the past few days.

*

The last stage of her labour, though painful, had been blessedly quick – but that was mostly because for hours she'd denied to herself that she was in any real pain. For months before *that*, she'd denied being with child at all, and indeed no one looking at her could have guessed it until the last couple of weeks. Only then had she seen people exchanging glances and winking at each other, or heard catcalls of 'There's a gal as wants a husband in a hurry!' or 'That's not beer what's made her belly swell!' when going past a tavern on a Saturday night. She'd told Lily, of course, but had no idea how much someone like her sister could understand about babies and the process of getting them.

Coming close to her time (how she knew this she couldn't say, for she had no idea how long a pregnancy should last), Grace began to search for someone who would help her with the birth, for she knew it to be a matter involving not only a deal of pain, but also blood and linens and bowls of water. Earlier on, she'd asked advice from a girl who was obviously in the same situation and had been given the name of a midwife, but the woman had turned Grace down, saying she was too young and the whole matter was distasteful; she wouldn't have anything to do with bringing a bastard child into the world. She'd also gone to enquire at the big lying-in hospital at Westminster Bridge, but had been faced with a notice stating that only married women would be considered for admission, and they should bring in their marriage certificates as proof of status.

Grace, therefore, had to leave it to fate to decide how and where she would give birth and, very early the previous morning, the pains coming ever more frequently, she'd given Lily instructions for the following day, then managed to walk to the nearest hospital at Charing Cross. She was turned away from there, but was fortunate enough to speak to a sympathetic nurse who told her to go to Berkeley House in Westminster. 'Where they will take those who are fallen,' she'd been told in a whisper.

Berkeley House – an ugly building of grimy stone and shuttered windows – was only a short distance away, but by the time she'd reached there, the pains were coming so close together that, had they not agreed to accept her, Grace thought that she might have given birth on the doorstep. A notice outside stated that only unmarried women about to deliver their *first* child would be admitted, and gave a stark reminder of how perilous an undertaking childbearing was by adding:

Patients being admitted should ensure that, in the case of tragedy, they are able to pay for a funeral. No responsibility will be taken by the hospital for burial fees for mother or child.

Without, thankfully, any questions being asked, Grace was taken to a ward with six beds, each separated from the next by a limp cotton curtain and each with a wooden box standing in for a cradle at its foot. Save for these, there was no furniture or decoration in the room, bar a large monochrome picture of Queen Victoria.

Grace sank on to the end bed, hearing two babies crying, someone moaning and a woman calling upon God to help her in her hour of anguish. Mingled with these was the calm voice of a midwife going from bed to bed admonishing, commanding or speaking persuasively to the women in labour.

'Now, Mary, we are not far off,' she'd said on examining Grace. On protesting that *Grace* was her name, she was told that they called all their girls Mary. The midwife, in turn, had to be called Mrs Smith.

'Have you things prepared for the child?' Mrs Smith had asked. 'Have you a sleeping space out of the way of draughts and some clean cotton sheets that can be boiled?'

Grace had merely shaken her head.

'Have you clothes for it? Napkins and shawls? Vests and gowns?' Mrs Smith persisted. 'These things don't just arrive with the child, you know! Haven't you given any thought as to its wants and needs?'

Grace turned her face to the wall. She had not, in spite of her size, in spite of her rudimentary knowledge of bodily functions, in spite of what had happened nine months ago, *really* believed that she was expecting a child. How had such a thing happened? Surely she should have had some say in the matter?

The midwife tutted. 'Where do you live, child?'

'I have a room in Mrs Macready's lodging house at Seven Dials,' Grace had answered between pains.

'God help us – *there?*' Mrs Smith had shaken her head. 'In the rookeries?'

'It's a clean room,' Grace said defensively. 'I share only with my sister.'

'Have you any family? Are your parents aware of this coming infant? Have you applied to any charities to take you in? God help you, child, have you enough money to pay for a funeral if the worst happens to either of you?'

Grace, not wanting to reply to any of these questions, anticipated a pain and screwed up her face in readiness.

When it passed, the midwife asked, 'Does the father of the child know about it? Will he aid you? Is he – may God spare us – *married?*'

'He doesn't know,' Grace whispered. 'Nor will he ever.'

'So you have no one to tend you after lying in, and no one to welcome the child, nor to help you with its upbringing?'

Grace shook her head. She had never thought of it becoming *real*, one of those red-faced and screaming bundles that poor women tied on to their backs when they went out working.

'For the Lord's sake, are you just having this child as a prop to go a-begging with?' asked the midwife suddenly.

9

'No, I am not!' Grace replied with as much indignation as she could muster.

The pains grew stronger then, and closer together, and at one stage Mrs Smith gave Grace some strong salts to sniff which made her feel so lightheaded that she swooned into a state close to unconsciousness, although the pains still wracked her. When the effect of these wore off and she properly came to herself again, the room had darkened and the midwife had gone to tend a girl lying two beds away. Wearily, Grace heaved herself forward to look into the box at the foot of the bed.

It was empty.

Grace called out to Mrs Smith and after a moment she left her other charge and came over. She had a soft, conciliatory look on her face, and stroked Grace's hair as she spoke. ''Tis a sorrowful thing, but for the best,' she said.

'What happened? Where's the baby?'

'Ah. 'Tis sad to tell you this, my love, but the child died.'

There was a long, long silence when, to her surprise, tears fell down Grace's cheeks unchecked. She had hardly imagined it as a real, living baby, she thought wonderingly, so why was it so devastating that it was dead?

'What was it?' she asked at last.

'A boy, bless his heart.'

'Did he live at all?'

Mrs Smith shook her head. 'Stillborn. Never drew breath.'

Grace sank back on the mattress. 'Was it something I did wrong – when I was carrying him?'

'No, darling. 'Tis just a thing that happens sometimes with young girls – your body wasn't ready to bear it. It's for the best, I'm thinking. You're but a child yourself, with no one to care for you. The baby would have died this first winter anyway. Seven Dials is no place to raise a child.'

'But *dead* . . .'

'Never lived,' the midwife corrected. She pushed a lock of hair behind Grace's ear. 'You're very young. You'll have other babies in good time. You'll forget this sadness.'

'Can I . . . ?' As she began the question, she wasn't sure what she wanted the answer to be. But the midwife had already anticipated her.

'Best not to look at him,' she said briskly. 'I always advise against it. Just think of it as a dream, a story . . . something that never really happened. It's easier got over that way.'

Grace had begun to cry again.

''Tis for the best, I say. Now sleep and rest yourself overnight and you'll be recovered and on your way in no time at all.'

And indeed, after a night's sleep and a bowl of meat and boiled potatoes paid for by the Society for the Rehabilitation of Destitute Women and Girls, Grace was asked to relinquish her space at Berkeley House for

11

the next inmate. But before doing so, she was handed a well-wrapped bundle and told of a wonderful garden cemetery in the countryside.

'I don't do this for all the lasses,' the midwife had said, handing over two coins, 'but I feel remarkably sorry for you.'

Grace stared at her.

'These shillings are the fare for you to take this little burden out of London, for nearly all the London churchyards are full up and closed now, and you wouldn't wish the babe to lie uncoffined in a pauper's pit, would you?'

Grace shook her head, unable to bear the thought.

'No. So you must go to Brookwood.'

'What's that?'

'It's like a wonderful garden, with trees and flowers and statues. When you think about your poor child, you'll be able to imagine him there with beautiful stone angels watching over him.' Grace managed to smile a little at this, and the midwife smiled, too. It was as she'd thought: the burial of the child, the ritual to be completed, would help the mourning process. 'And when you have buried him,' she added, 'then you must start your life again . . .'

*

'*Start again . . .*' Grace murmured, recalling this conversation. Then she realised that, becoming drowsy from

12

the rocking motion of the train, she'd spoken the words aloud.

'Are you all right, child?' There was a man sitting alongside her wearing a shabby frock coat and battered black top hat.

Grace nodded and clutched at her bundle.

'You're very young to be travelling on this train alone. Is it a member of your family who's passed away?'

Grace nodded and, making a gesture as if to say she was too grief-stricken to speak, stared out of the window as the countryside slipped by.

Start again, the rhythm of the train's wheels seemed to be saying. *Start again* . . . If she could just get over this day and begin anew, then she would try to make something of her life. She would endeavour to make a different and better life for herself and Lily.

The train shrieked as it went under a bridge and the noise brought Grace out of her reverie. She had to find a last resting place for her child . . .

Some might have recoiled from this duty, fearing the thought of entering a dwelling place of the dead, but Grace had suffered enough misery in her life to know that it was only the living who could hurt you; that one had nothing to fear from those who'd passed to the other side. Tying her shawl more securely about her head, she opened the carriage door and went into the corridor. All was quiet, for each unit of mourners was secluded within its own private carriage (while in the last, the representatives of the funeral companies were sitting together exchanging stories whilst enjoying a nip of whisky).

The train roared, shook and swayed as it rounded a corner, and Grace grasped the window frame and waited until it straightened on its course. Then she pushed open the door to the van containing the coffins and went in.

There were no windows and the only light was from two candles burning in a sconce on the wall, so it took a moment for Grace's eyes to readjust. When they did, she saw that the van was divided into three sections and each of these contained rows of narrow iron shelves upon which the coffins rested. Even in the poor light it was easy to distinguish between rich and poor, for the third-class caskets were of matchwood, with hand-written cards stating the occupier's name and date of demise, while those of the first class were of highly polished wood with handles, trims and engraved plaques in brass or silver.

Grace went to the first-class section and read some of these plaques, which listed the corpse's accreditations like a calling card for Heaven: *Sebastian Taylor, devoted Husband and Father; Maud Pickersley, worked to improve the conditions of those less fortunate; Jessy Rennet, lived a life of Piety and Hope.*

The train's brakes gave a squeal and it slowed a little as if it was nearing its destination, and Grace surveyed the coffins quickly and anxiously. How to choose? She

14

wanted her dead child to be placed with a woman, of course, someone who sounded kindly and was from a good family. She paused in front of a box of white oak containing *The mortal remains of Miss Susannah Solent, Defender of the Weak, Princess of the Poor.*

Miss Susannah Solent. There was no indication as to her age and she was obviously not a mother herself, but she sounded the sort of woman who would be kind to a child and give it shelter.

She must act quickly! She lifted a corner of the lid of the pale-wood casket containing the body of Susannah Solent and, without looking inside, slipped in her bundle.

She felt that some sort of formal farewell was called for and murmured, 'May you sleep content and one day may we be reunited', and then moved quickly back into the corridor, dabbing her eyes.

*Mr and Mrs Stanley Robinson are happy to announce the safe
arrival of their son, Albert Stanley Robinson.*

*Mrs Robinson will be pleased to receive visitors and
well-wishers from 1st July.*

Please send your card in advance.

Chapter Two

A young couple, Mr and Mrs Stanley Robinson,
were in a nursery painted all over with ships in
full sail upon a foam-tipped sea. They were
bending over a lavishly decorated bassinette with lace
curtains, a frilled quilt and pillow threaded with white
ribbon, in which slept their new baby. With every stir
of their treasure and heir, every sniff and snuffle, they
marvelled anew.

'I don't suppose he'll be like this all the time,' the
man whispered. 'They say that babies cry a lot.'

The woman laughed, but not unkindly. 'Do you
think I don't know that? I do! And I'm quite prepared
for crying.'

'Shall we hire a nurse? Mother said she'd pay.'

'Certainly not,' the woman said. 'I've waited too long to give over care of Baby to a stranger.'

'Just as you like, my sweet,' said the man. He put out a finger and stroked the baby's cheek, plump and pink under the prettiest of lace bonnets. The baby started in his sleep, and the couple froze in case he was about to wake up, but he fell still again. 'Dear Baby,' said the man.

'Dear, precious Baby,' said the woman, and she and her husband smiled at each other fondly. 'At last . . .'

Dickens's Dictionary of London, 1888

Chapter Three

Seven Dials in the Parish of St Giles was, perhaps, the poorest area in west London, for it was said that nearly three thousand people were crammed into little over a hundred dwellings. Named for the seven lanes which converged together below Oxford Street, each court and alleyway leading off these contained slums and rookeries. Decrepit lodging houses, shops and stinking taverns leaned this way and that, shored up with old planks and rusty sheets, their broken windows boarded over, and tarpaulin nailed over holes in the masonry in an effort to stop the rain coming through. Those living in the houses were poor, but not quite destitute. None had an income that could be relied on, however, and thus they lived hand to mouth, hoping that each day would bring forth enough money to feed them and their families for the next twenty-four hours. They were costermongers with stalls in the marketplaces, street sellers of matches and pickled whelks, crossing sweepers, laundresses, sewer cleaners and boys who contrived to earn a living by holding a gentleman's horse or turning somersaults in order to amuse. Below that level, in the very worst hovels, lived packs of scoundrels and ne'er-do-wells, thieves and beggars.

The stalls and shops around them sold all manner of things for, though some could manage without shoes, even the very poorest needed food and something to wear. The clothes for sale in Seven Dials were never new, but second-, third- or fourth-hand: old dresses, hats, shoes, stockings, crumpled petticoats, fraying jackets and tattered shawls. A large number of the shops were for bird fanciers and almost every variety of pigeon, fowl and hen could be found there, together with thrushes, finches and other songbirds. At the southern end of Seven Dials, one could find shops selling cheap household goods: brooms, dustpans, dusters, washing bowls, wiping cloths and rags, for even the poorest woman knew that cleanliness was next to Godliness, and strove to keep up her standards.

Mrs Macready's boarding house in Brick Place, Seven Dials, was four storeys high with two rooms on each floor, and a basement which was green and mouldy with damp. Mrs Macready lived on the ground floor, keeping a watch over the comings and goings and a tally of rents paid, and presiding over a kitchen which the lodgers were allowed to use for a ha'penny or two. There was a makeshift privy in the backyard and also a well, but owing to the proximity of one to the other, the water from the well was polluted and undrinkable – so much so that, some years before, several of Mrs Macready's lodgers and those from the next-door house had died of cholera. Since then, everyone had queued to get their water in pails, kettles and bowls from the standpipe in the street.

Mrs Macready was a stout and cheery landlady who took up and wore whatever raggedy items her lodgers left behind when they moved on, hardly differentiating between men's and women's clothes. Thus she would wear torn lace blouses with old suit jackets or crumpled skirts with threadbare shawls and waistcoats, and top the lot off with a bonnet decorated with artificial flowers. Out of the kindness of her heart, she kept strictly to her maxim of having only one family to a room and charged them well below the going rate. She charged so little, in fact, that she couldn't maintain the property, which was in a state of hopeless disrepair. When, she was fond of saying, the house finally fell down about her ears, she was going to live with her well-to-do son in Connaught Gardens.

As Grace journeyed on the Necropolis Railway to Brookwood Cemetery, her sister Lily looked out of a grimy window in the smallest room on the second floor of Mrs Macready's, impatient for her return and sighing continually. Grace was being an *awfully* long time, what on earth could she be doing? Did it take that long to have a baby? Why, she'd been gone a whole day and a night now – or was it two?

She knew that Grace would be coming back with a child, for Grace had explained in very simple terms that there was a little baby inside her and she had to go and find someone who would help bring it out. In the meantime, Lily had been instructed to go to the market to buy watercresses (she knew how to do this, for she'd accompanied Grace to bargain with the market traders many times), then bunch them and sell them in the streets as usual. The day before, she'd carried out these instructions faithfully, but owing to her indecision in selecting what cresses to buy, she'd missed selling to the labourers on their way to work. All day it had rained, so there had hardly been a housewife to be seen on the streets, and though Lily had stayed out until after six o'clock, she'd not sold nearly enough bunches of watercress to cover what she'd laid out. She'd bought a boiled meat pudding for her supper, for Grace had said she could, but on her way home with the money she had left, she'd met a sharp who'd promised to double the coins in her pocket if she could guess what cup a bean was under. She'd been quite sure she could do this – he made it look so easy, and wouldn't Grace be pleased with her? – but the bean was never under the one she chose.

Waking the next morning, Lily realised with horror

that there was no money, not a penny, to go to market and buy the fresh bundles of watercress to sell that day. This was not the first time this had happened to them, however, and lying in bed, Lily had been thinking hard about what she should do. The answer came at last: of course, she would pawn something! This was what Grace always did when they'd not made enough money to buy stock.

She looked around the room for likely objects but apart from the bed (which belonged to Mrs Macready anyway), it contained very little: a straw-stuffed mattress, two pillows, three thin blankets and several wooden crates. Some of these crates held their spare clothes and possessions, and two were empty and had been upturned to use as seats. Grace had already been thinking – as far as she'd planned anything – that she might use one of the crates as a cradle for the baby.

Lily frowned, looking about. She knew Grace wouldn't want to sell the blankets, for they'd need these when the weather turned cold. They'd had five blankets when they started living at Mrs Macready's, and four pillows too. Before that, when they'd started living in the orphanage, they'd had soft bleached-linen sheets, an eiderdown containing ducks' feathers and a coverlet Mama had sewn, together with the framed mottoes Mama had embroidered as a girl: *Home Sweet Home*, *Bless This House* and *Walk in Love*. Some of these things had been stolen over the years, though, and the rest had been sold or pawned, along with most of their winter clothing. Lily had borne losing the clothes well, for she hardly cared what she looked like, but very much missed her doll, Primrose, who'd been as big as a life-size baby, with real hair and a pretty rosebud mouth set in a porcelain face. She was hoping that the baby Grace brought home would be like Primrose, a pretty thing they could play with and who could be tied up in a bundle and put on their backs when they went selling cresses. She thought that customers would stop to pet and admire the child – and maybe give a little more money for its own pretty sake.

Lily began to look through the possessions in the crates. One crate contained what they called 'Mama's treasures': a fragile teapot and one cup and saucer hand-painted with birds, an empty ring box, a shell made of china but painted pearly pink and looking real, the bonnet which Mama had been married in and a length of lace which had been her veil. Lily unwrapped and admired each of these in turn, then, breathless with the effort of having to be so careful with such delicate items, placed them all back in the crate. There were a few items of clothing, but not, unfortunately, any of that most valuable commodity – shoes – for each girl was wearing her only pair. Lily fingered a shawl, wondering if she should sell that rather than a blanket. Would Grace be cross with her if she did, or commend her for being sensible? If she took the shawl to a rag fair, how much should she ask (for it was very thin and worn in parts) and would Grace approve of this amount? Would it be enough to buy stock with? Should she buy watercress with the proceeds, or purchase a potato pie she could put in Mrs Macready's oven to have for their supper that evening? But suppose Grace didn't come home in time to eat it and it went to waste?

The questions spun in her head and Lily let out a little cry, confused and worried about all the choices. Supposing Grace didn't come home at all? She'd heard people talking about having babies, saying that the process of getting them was fraught and dangerous. Suppose Grace died and was put into the ground, like Mama had been? This notion was so bewildering and frightening that a wave of terror washed over Lily, causing her legs to tremble so much that she had to sit down on the bed. What would she do without Grace?

It took some time before she stopped shaking and was able to get moving again. By then, however, it was too late to go to the wholesale market and buy watercress. Besides, she still didn't have any money. She looked through the things again and gave a sudden gasp. What about clothes for the baby Grace was going to bring home? What would it wear? How could they take it out when it had no shawl?

The baby must be dressed! Realising this, she went to the first crate and took out Mama's teapot. Pawning this would bring in the most money; enough, surely, for several days' cresses, food to eat that night (of course Grace would come home!) and a layette for the baby. She would go out and buy all the clothes herself and Grace would be so pleased that she wouldn't ask what had been sold in order to provide them. She'd buy sleeping robes of brushed cotton, pretty lace bonnets and the softest white shawl. It would be like having Primrose again.

Lily took the teapot from its newspaper and stroked it. It was of fine china which rang out when you tapped it gently with your fingernail, and covered all over with little painted birds – bluebirds of happiness, Mama had called them. She had named them individually and told the girls on what sort of flowers they feasted, but Lily couldn't remember all those details now. The teapot was very pretty, she thought, but it might as well be sold because they had no further use for it, tea being much too expensive a drink.

She rewrapped it carefully in the newspaper. She knew this was *The Times*, but she couldn't read even the date on it. Grace could read. Sometimes she found a page or two of a newspaper blowing in the street, brought it home and read the advertisements on the front page. '*Mr Lucas seeks a bay gelding,*' she'd declare. '*A governess seeks a position with an aristocratic family. Five pound note lost in Bishopsgate Street. Madame Oliver sings tonight at Tremorne Gardens. Help wanted for destitute crippled boys.*' Sometimes Grace would make up stories about the people they read about – a governess

25

had a bay gelding for sale, and she answered Mr Lucas's advertisement and they fell in love. One of the destitute crippled boys found a five pound note and didn't know whether to hand it in and claim the reward, or to buy meat pies for himself every day for a year. Madame Oliver had been going to sing at Tremorne Gardens, but instead had passed the time riding on a bay gelding.

Many a happy hour was spent in this way, for Grace excelled in making up stories and, if Lily became anxious about anything, she'd tell her about castles and princesses in order to soothe her to sleep. She told the stories so well that, when Lily thought about them the following day, sometimes she couldn't recall whether they were made up or had truly happened.

Relieved that she had at last decided what to do, Lily set off for a pawnbroker they'd used before, a kindly man known – as were others of his breed – as Uncle. She found his door closed, however, the blind down, and a notice written on a piece of paper stuck on the window.

Asking a passer-by, a man selling candle stubs, what it said, she was told: '*Shut because of Death*'.

'Shut because of Death,' Lily repeated, struggling to understand what this could possibly mean.

'It means it's closed because someone's died,' said the man. 'The owner of the shop, most like.' He then looked at Lily with interest. 'You 'ad something to sell at Uncle's, then, did you?'

Lily nodded and held up the package. 'A teapot.'

'Not much call for them,' said the man, almost before she'd got the word out of her mouth. 'Tell you who'll give the best price for that, though – old Morrell down Parsnip Hill. Tell 'im Ernie sent you.'

Lily thanked him and went on her way. Meanwhile, Ernie slipped down a side alley, ran across two lanes, went over someone's back wall and arrived at Morrell's Pawnshop two minutes before Lily. He looked up and down the lane and nipped in.

Morrell specialised in buying, selling and pawning china and glass objects, and his grimy windows held any number of dulled crystal vases, chipped ornaments, gaudy fairground animals and glass drinking mugs. Having such a teapot would, to him, be like owning the crown jewels.

'I just sent you a pigeon,' Ernie puffed to Morrell, a man with a paunch so large it prevented him from getting too close to his counter. 'Young girl, bit simple. Teapot. Do a switch and we'll go 'alves on it.'

Morrell nodded, grinned and, as Ernie left, reached for a small cardboard box which he secreted on a shelf just under the counter.

Lily reached the shop, said that Ernie had sent her and that she had a teapot to pawn. On the way there, she'd had some worries about taking it in, but reassured herself that it was only going to be pawned, not sold. If Grace was really cross with her, then they'd be able to go and buy it back later, when they got rich. They always got rich in the stories that Grace told.

Morrell's eyes brightened when he saw the teapot. Meissen, he thought. Quite old, hand-painted by craftsmen and worth a fair bit. However, he shook his head regretfully.

'What a pity,' he said. 'Thought you 'ad something good there, but it's just a scrap orf a market stall. Got a chip in it, too,' he lied.

Lily, though crestfallen, nevertheless regarded him trustingly. 'But it must be worth something,' she said. 'It was part of a set that my mama had.'

'Pass it over, then,' said Mr Morrell. 'Let's take it to the window an' give it a proper butcher's.'

Lily passed the teapot, still partly in its newspaper wrapping, across the counter. As Morrell took it from her and turned towards the window, somehow it slipped from the paper.

'Ooops!' said Morrell as something crashed on to the brick floor.

'Oh!' cried Lily, aghast.

'Lordie! You let go of it too soon, girl.'

Lily pressed her hand to her lips and her face paled. 'Is it . . . is it quite broken?'

'A nundred pieces!' cried Morrell.

'Might it be repaired?'

'Never! Just you look.'

Lily peeped fearfully around the end of the counter. Sure enough, shards of china lay scattered right across the stone floor.

'Pity,' said Mr Morrell. 'Still, it weren't going to be

worth more than a few pennies anyways.'

Lily's bottom lip trembled. 'Is there nothing that can . . . be . . . done?'

'Got any more like it at 'ome?' asked Morrell cheerfully.

Lily shook her head. How had that happened? Perhaps she hadn't been careful enough; Grace sometimes said she was clumsy. Now the teapot, their mother's precious teapot, was gone for ever. And soon Grace would be home and there would be nothing to eat and no clothes for the baby either.

Lily turned away and trudged home, too traumatised to cry, while Mr Morrell and Ernie the candlestub seller admired the Meissen teapot, safe on the secret shelf below the pawnbroker's counter.

As through the fields he walked alone
By chance he met grim Death
Who with his dart did strike his heart
And robbed him of his breath

Epitaph on a tombstone

Chapter Four

'*The great garden of sleep,*' Grace murmured to herself, reading the notice on the station platform. Then she added, 'My baby will be safe with Miss Susannah Solent in the great garden of sleep.' Said like that, it was almost bearable. As if those who'd died were merely resting themselves in the ground until a spring when they would all rise up again, which Grace knew she was supposed to believe but could not quite manage to.

The train drew into the station amid billows of steam and, as it came to a standstill, the top-hatted representatives of the funeral companies disembarked and made ready, with many obsequious bows, to guide the bereaved families to the allotted burial places of their loved ones. As the mourners grouped and regrouped themselves ready for the final stage of their journeys, Grace drew a little closer to the van which held the coffins. Out of public view, these were now being nailed down (this little ceremony being left as late as possible to guard against anyone being buried before they had breathed their last), following which the van's doors were opened and the coffins removed. Most of the first-grade funerals had their own individual hearses waiting, with a priest or black-clad mute to lead the way, while the pauper burials made use of a handcart and the willing labour of any friends and family who could afford the train ticket out of London. The poor were glad to give their custom to Brookwood because its many acres ensured that, although the pauper funeral service would be a communal one, there was space enough for everyone to have individual burial plots; the bodies would not be tumbled together in a pit as they would have been in London.

When the coffins were moved out of the hearse van, Grace, viewing it from some way off, knew exactly which one was Susannah Solent's – the pale oak casket in the final section. She watched it being taken out and placed on to the shoulders of the undertakers' men, then slid gently into the waiting glass-topped hearse, where it lay shrouded in white flowers. Keeping at a safe distance, she followed the black-plumed horses on their slow journey through the trees and shrubs, wanting to know exactly where it was to be buried so that later, if she ever was in possession of enough money for the journey, she could come and pay her respects.

There were about twenty mourners walking behind the cortège for Miss Solent, and of these only one was a woman, and she was so wrapped and shrouded in veils and black crêpe that very little about her could be discerned. Was it Miss Solent's mother? Her sister, her aunt, a great friend? There was no way of telling.

The procession halted. Miss Solent's grave was to be in a cleared space behind a row of newly planted cedars – so newly planted, in fact, that until the arrival of that morning's train the gardeners had still been digging there. On hearing the train arrive, they had moved off quickly so as not to compromise the privacy of the mourners but had left a heavy fork in the ground. Grace tripped on this, hurt her ankle and couldn't help crying out, but only one of the nearby mourners heard her, the rest being intent on the priest's words and their own sorrow.

Mr James Solent, standing at the back of the group of people around his sister's grave, thought the noise must have been made by a woodland animal caught in a trap, and it was only when he turned and looked through the undergrowth that he saw a girl slowly getting to her feet. He couldn't see her face, but she appeared very young, with loose curly hair (for her shawl had slipped off her head) the colour of the crisp beech leaves underfoot. He hesitated a moment, then silently removed himself from the funeral service to see if he could do anything to help. His sister, he knew, would not have minded him doing such a thing and would certainly have done the same if their positions had been reversed.

Grace saw him coming towards her and thought of running away, but then realised she lacked both the spirit and energy. Besides, she told herself, no one knew why she was at the cemetery or what she'd done; she'd paid her fare and had as much right to be there as all the other mourners.

'Can I help? Are you injured?' James spoke to her as gently as possible, thinking that she might take fright and bolt if he were too direct or too loud. She looked to be about thirteen, he thought, and was pale with a tragic and beautiful face. Her clothes, although deeply unfashionable, looked as if they'd once been of good quality, but he could see they were darned, patched and almost worn through in parts.

Grace sat down on a mossy bank, feeling as weak as a kitten. 'It's nothing, sir, I thank you. I merely tripped on that fork.'

'But you're hurt!' James protested.

Grace shook her head, covering her ankle carefully. 'The injury is slight. It was my own fault.'

'I say it was the fault of the Brookwood gardeners!' James said. 'But show me your ankle.'

'It hardly hurts at all,' Grace protested, tucking her skirts so that they went right over her feet and hid her shabby shoes from him. 'I . . . I just want to sit here a little while and recover myself.'

'Then may I sit beside you?' James asked. 'For I've

heard enough today about the vale of death, the wrath of God and the land of everlasting sleep, and 'twas not at all what my sister was about. Besides, I do not want to be there the moment when her coffin is lowered into the ground.'

'No.' Grace shook her head, for she'd not wanted to see those last moments either. 'It's your sister being buried today?' she asked timidly.

James nodded and sat down beside her. 'Susannah.' He sighed. 'She was a merry girl, always laughing – that's how I want to remember her. But look at all this!' He indicated the gloomy scene of black-cloaked mutes and top-hatted mourners before them. 'All these plumes and pall-bearers, feathermen and coachmen! All the talk of hearses and horses and how long we should wear mourning clothes – that is not Susannah! My father seeks to build an Egyptian mausoleum over her body and have an eternal flame burning, but none of that will bring her back.'

They were both silent for a while, then James said, 'But I do beg your pardon. Are you here for a funeral, too?'

Grace shook her head. 'I merely came to tend my . . . my mother's grave.'

'That's sad. But 'tis a beautiful place for her to be at rest. The statuary is very fine.'

Grace nodded in agreement, for already she'd seen tombs with wonderful marble angels and cherubs, stone anchors for old sailing men, a fine riderless

34

horse for a dead jockey and even a grand piano on the tomb of a musician.

'My father intends to have himself and my mother interred in the Egyptian tomb in due course, and then myself and my brothers.' He paused. 'But if it doesn't grieve you too much to speak of it, tell me when your mother passed away.'

'A long while back – near ten years,' Grace said, speaking truthfully now.

'But you still have a father to care for you?'

Grace shook her head. 'Our father died some years before Mama,' she said, for this was what she believed, although Lily still thought what Mama had always told them: that Papa had gone off to seek his fortune and would return one day.

'So you are an orphan?'

'Yes, sir.' Grace felt rather shy speaking to him, for although she had conversed with young gentlemen before, it had only ever been to ask them to buy cresses from her. 'I live with my sister and we survive quite well,' she went on, not wanting him to think she was destitute.

'But how did you manage after your mother died? You must have been scarce more than babes in arms.'

'I was about five and my sister was six,' Grace said. 'We were taken into an orphanage which was run by a kindly woman and we were quite happy there.'

'And then . . . ?'

'Then when I was fourteen we were taken to a training establishment, where I was to learn to be a teacher.'

He looked at her closely. 'I can see by your face that you didn't care for it there.'

Grace felt a fluttering of panic, but tried to speak calmly. 'I did not, sir. And so we decided to leave.'

'When was this?'

'We left near a year ago. And since then we have been fending for ourselves and . . . and doing quite well. We sell watercresses on the streets.'

He nodded. 'And as your sister is older than you, at least she is able to provide you with some of a mother's attentions.'

Grace inclined her head. There was no reason to tell him that Lily was, in fact, only older than her if you counted the years; that actually it was the other way round, Lily would need *her* care and attention for the rest of her life and could never manage on her own.

As the nearby funeral service neared its conclusion and the group at Miss Solent's graveside gave their responses to the priest, James got to his feet, saying he must join them. He reached into the inside pocket of his coat as he bade her farewell and Grace froze with shame, thinking he was going to offer her money, but he did not.

'I'm a lawyer's clerk at Lincoln's Inn,' he said, handing over a business card. 'If at any time I can assist you, do please call into the office and ask for me.'

Grace could not think of any possible circumstances where she might need his guidance, but she took the card, which read:

'I can see by your face that you wouldn't ever presume upon me, but if I can help you at all, please allow me to do it for my sister's sake.' He smiled a little sadly. 'Susannah was a great girl for helping young ladies in distress, you know. Who's to say that she didn't somehow contrive that we should meet here at her funeral?'

Grace smiled. 'It's a pretty thought,' she said. She got to her feet, tested her ankle and found it quite pain-free. 'Thank you for your attentions,' she said, 'and may I wish you as good a day as possible.'

'Until we meet again,' said James, giving a slight bow.

The Necropolis train did not leave Brookwood until after three o'clock in the afternoon, so Grace went into the small chapel and, making herself as inconspicuous as possible in the back row, thought of all that had happened to her over the last few days, endeavouring to make sense of it. Occasionally – for she was extremely weary – she found herself drifting off to sleep, but when she did she had a frightening recurring dream that the baby was still inside her and she was running hither and thither looking for somewhere safe to give birth to it.

When half past two struck (and her life made no more sense to her than it previously had), she decided to join the train ready for the return journey. Reaching the little station and discovering that the engine was not yet in position, however, she waited with the mourners as they spilled out from the refreshment rooms on to the platform.

From a young age Grace had studied people, and this had come in useful since going into the watercress-selling business, for she'd quickly learned who might be best approached in order to achieve a sale, and who would be a waste of time. Looking at the top-hatted funeral directors shepherding their flocks of mourners, she could not help noticing that one set of undertakers seemed more assertive than the others. They were more voluble in their condolences to the bereaved; more solicitous in their care; ever ready with an extra shawl or black-edged handkerchief; patting, comforting, cosseting and mopping tears; speaking to the bereaved families of a 'good death' and 'the solace of a fine funeral'.

This was Grace's first encounter with the Unwins.

Mr George Unwin owned the largest firm of undertakers in London and was willing – one might even say eager – to supply bereaved families with their every funereal need. At the Unwin Undertaking Establishment one could choose from twenty-nine different coffins, all with interchangeable silk interiors and a choice of brass or silver coffin furniture. They could provide glass carriages pulled by black-plumed horses, velvet palls, mourning bands, streamers, staves, funeral wreaths and mutes wearing any amount of black crêpe. The only thing they could not provide was mourning wear, but fortunately every variety of this nature of garment, plus veils, bags, gloves, stoles and all the other trappings of the first, second and third bereavement periods, could be purchased at the largest mourning warehouse in Oxford Street, the Unwin Mourning Emporium, owned by Mr George Unwin's cousin, Mr Sylvester Unwin.

Mrs Emmeline Unwin, wife of George, saw Grace standing still and silent on the station platform with, apparently, no family to support her. Mrs Unwin was an unusual but inspired addition to a modern undertaker's business, for her sole purpose at a funeral was to comfort those of the female sex who were overtaken by their emotions. She was tall and thin, with a sallow face, small eyes and a smile which showed as much gum as teeth. She nearly always wore black in order to empathise more fully with her clients, and had a score or more fashionable outfits complete with matching hats and veiling. It was her mission to persuade the bereaved that wearing the latest in mourning wear was not so much an expense as a tribute to the departed, and now, wearing the most fashionable crinoline-skirted gown supported by a cage that rocked from side to side, she glided smoothly towards Grace.

'My dearest girl, are you all right?' she asked softly, laying a hand on her arm. At close contact, however, she noticed the shabbiness of Grace's garments and, realising that there was no money to be earned by recommending a marble monument to soothe her saddest hour, immediately saw a different sort of opportunity. 'Dear child, you appear utterly devastated!'

Grace, even though weary, dropped a small curtsey. 'I thank you, but I am bearing up quite well.'

'You have such a soulful face!' Mrs Unwin lowered her voice. 'Have you ever thought of going into the undertaking business as a mute?'

Grace looked at her, startled. She wanted to shake off the woman's hand, but knew that to do so would be very rude.

'You may think it indelicate of me to speak of such a thing, but I must tell you that I believe you would be perfect for a position as a professional mourner.'

Grace still didn't reply, so surprised was she.

'You're young, yet look as if you have witnessed all the sadnesses of the world. You would make the most marvellous mute!' Grace not denying this, the woman went on, 'The funeral business is expanding, dear. We always need faces such as yours. You could come and live with us, become part of the Unwin family.'

Grace shook her head. 'I'm sorry, but . . .'

'You'd be paid five shillings per funeral, and when you weren't working as a mute you could help the girls in the sewing room with the coffin interiors. With a tragic face like yours, you'd be *very* much in demand at high-class funerals.'

Grace shuddered a little at the thought. 'I'm sorry,' she said again. 'I live with my sister and couldn't think of leaving her on her own. And I think I would find being a funeral mute too miserable a life.'

'But 'tis a wonderful thing to bring solace to others!' Mrs Unwin cried. 'If we can, it is our Christian duty to do it.'

Grace shook her head once more. 'I could not, but thank you for thinking of me.'

'As you wish,' Mrs Unwin said. She pulled a card from her black velvet muff. 'But if you ever change your mind ...'

Grace took the card and curtseyed her thanks, thinking how strange it was that she had never even held a business card in her hand before, but had now been given two in one day. This one was black-edged, like a mourning card, and upon it were engraved the following words:

The Unwin Undertaking Establishment

Maple Mews, Marble Arch, London.

Let a Good Death be followed by a Good Funeral.

Discretion is our Byword.

The blue and black train appeared out of its siding at last and, steaming copiously, drew level with the platform. Mrs Unwin glided off, veils ashake, while Grace climbed into one of the third-class carriages, sat down and forgot her immediately.

The train shunted forward and fell into a rhythm. Sighing with relief that everything had gone just as the midwife had instructed, Grace closed her eyes, willing the train onward so she could get home to Lily. Oh, she hoped her sister had been managing all right without her...

Chapter Five

The lodgers at Mrs Macready's house were a disparate bunch. The top floor comprised a fairly large area divided by a thin board wall, with a married couple on each side of it. Both the men were costermongers with street stalls; their wives worked alongside them. One couple sold cheap fish – herrings, sprats and whelks – the other specialised in apples or potatoes according to season. If they ever had rotting or substandard stock on their hands then they'd share it amongst Mrs Macready's lodgers, all of whom were always more than happy to take it.

One flight down from the costers, on the third floor, lived Mr Galbraith, who came and went at strange times in the night, usually in full evening dress, while in the room next to his were the Cartwrights, an Irish family with a brood of seven or eight noisy children. The Cartwrights worked as match sellers, pickers-up of cigar ends, errand runners, and the youngest, a boy aged two, as a decoy. He would attract attention by 'getting lost' while his older sister picked the pockets of those sympathetic souls who stopped to help him. Grace and Lily were on the second floor in a small room next to a frail old couple, Mr and Mrs Beale, who were both nearly blind and went out selling bootlaces in order to keep from being parted in a work-house. They suffered dreadfully from living just underneath the noisy Cartwrights, who were in and out at all hours.

In the first-floor rooms, next to each other and all the more convenient for fighting, were two families, the Wilsons and the Popes. The Wilsons – mother, father and three children – worked as crossing sweep-ers and had the best pitches in Seven Dials under their control. Next door, the Popes had four children still at home who took whatever work they could get: rag gath-ering, collecting horse dung, tumbling to amuse people or, if times were hard, begging or outright thieving. Mr Pope also had a good line in bird-duffing and many a pale finch had entered the Popes' room only to emerge as a newly painted, multicoloured bird of paradise. ('Most rare, madam. Brought over to this country by a seaman cousin of mine.')

After the trauma of the teapot, Lily returned to their room, feeling dreadfully gloomy. She turned to her treasures – a polished oyster shell, a foreign coin and some other near-worthless possessions she kept in an old cigar box – but even these failed to comfort her. Almost another day gone by and still no Grace. Whatever was she going to do? Should she tell Mrs Macready? Her old fear returned: suppose Grace didn't come back *ever*? She'd have to go to the Parish and tell them. She'd have to go to the beadle, that big, frightening man, and say that she didn't have any money to pay the rent, then he'd make her go into the workhouse – and once she was in there she'd never get out. She'd be locked up for ever, her head shorn, living on turnips and wearing smocks made out of sacking which itched her to death. If Papa came back, he'd never find her. *Someone* would find her, though, she thought with a shiver: that man who'd come in the dead of night and got into bed beside her. Why hadn't she screamed? Why hadn't she told Grace about it? Thinking about him now, she worked herself up into a fright and began crying lavishly and uncontrollably.

Grace, hearing sobs as she was coming through the front door, ran up the stairs as fast as her skirts and delicate condition permitted.

'Lily! Whatever is it?' she cried in alarm. She took her sister into her arms. 'What are you crying about? I'm home now . . . I'm here. Hush! Tell me what's happened.'

Lily sniffed and sobbed, enjoying being comforted. The one-handed man was in the past now and she didn't want to talk about him, but of course there were other, more recent things to cry about. As sometimes

45

happened with Lily, the distinction between truth and stories became somewhat blurred.

'I was crying because . . . because a horrible man came in and stole Mama's teapot!' she said, bursting into another passion of crying.

'The teapot!' Grace felt tears spring to her own eyes, for they had precious few things left to remind them of Mama. 'Hush,' she said again. 'It doesn't matter as long as you're all right. As long as whoever it was didn't hurt *you*.'

Lily settled a little. It was as she'd thought; the teapot had gone but that didn't matter compared to other, more important things. She suddenly remembered one of them. 'Where's the baby?' she asked, looking over Grace's shoulder and around the room. 'Didn't you bring it home with you?'

Grace sighed deeply. 'There isn't a baby.'

'It wasn't in your tummy after all?' Lily asked, blushing as she spoke, for she could still remember Mama telling them that they were never to mention bodily parts.

'It was there, but it wasn't strong enough to be born safely,' Grace said carefully. 'It has died and has gone to Heaven.'

'Oh.' This was very sad, Lily thought, because the baby would have been a good plaything.

'I took him to be buried today, Lily, in a wonderful cemetery in the country. That's why I've been away so long.'

Lily pondered this. 'Can we visit him and take flowers?'

'One day, yes,' Grace said, remembering the day when a kind person from the orphanage had taken them to see Mama's grave and, left for a moment to her own devices, Lily had collected up flowers from nearby graves and redistributed them to those that didn't have any. Now she set Lily away from her and looked at her steadily. 'But how have you been managing? Did you buy cresses yesterday? And when did this thief come in and steal the teapot? Did you see him? Did he take anything else?'

Lily frowned as she thought about this. Inventing stories was quite difficult and she usually got muddled; there was always some little detail or other that sounded odd and which Grace would pick up on.

'Someone took it,' Lily said vaguely. 'I don't know who. Someone came in and smashed it all up.'

Grace looked at her. She knew her sister was lying, for she was chewing her nails, anxiety writ all over her face. She couldn't pursue the matter now, though; she felt too exhausted. The truth would come out in time. With Lily it always did.

Later that afternoon, Grace took the bluebird cup and saucer to a pawnshop – not Morrell's, but to an establishment owned by a younger and more honest Uncle who gave her a silver sixpence for them. Grace knew that this would keep them going for a day or two, but had started to wonder what would happen when every scrap from their former life had been pawned to raise money and every trinket, blanket and spare garment had gone. How would they eat, keep warm and buy candles to light the dark? Whatever would happen to them? She shuddered – not the workhouse! No, never, never, never.

She held on to the sixpenny piece tightly all the way home, as if it were a talisman. Surely something good must happen before it came to that; maybe their father would return and find them, or the market for watercress would increase and they'd be able to sell ten bunches for every one sold now, or maybe she'd find a banknote blowing along the road in a gust of wind, for people always seemed to be losing them in the newspaper. Maybe – she smiled wryly to herself – maybe a fairy would come along and wave a magic wand to transform her and Lily into one of those fine young ladies they saw being driven around in gaily painted barouches, for *that* was just as likely as any of those other stories.

As she went past the kitchen on the way upstairs, Mrs Macready called out a greeting. Grace hadn't said anything to her about the coming child, in part because she feared the landlady might have said she wasn't allowed to bring it back with her, and in part because she thought it might just go away if she didn't acknowledge it. Hoping Mrs Macready might not have noticed her thickening figure under her voluminous skirts, she called 'Hello', and said that she had to hurry because Lily was waiting.

'Oh, do come in and speak to me, dear!' Mrs Macready persisted.

Grace flounced out her skirts slightly so that it was impossible to see the outline of her figure and went into the kitchen, where Mrs Macready was sitting with one of the costermongers, enjoying a glass of stout.

'I haven't seen you for a few days, dear,' she said. 'Are you all right?'

'I'm very well, thank you,' Grace replied, thinking that Mrs Macready would probably have made an excellent confidante, but there seemed to be little point in telling her now.

'Are you quite sure of that?' Mrs Macready said, giving her a meaningful look.

'Perfectly, thank you,' Grace said, her smile fixed. She did not feel perfectly all right, in fact she was glad now that the costermonger was there, for if he had not been, she might have thrown herself on the floor by Mrs Macready's chair, told her everything and wept until she could weep no more.

'And how's the trade in cresses?' asked the costermonger.

'Fair to middling,' Grace said.

'Slow everywhere at this time of the year,' he grunted.

'It is,' Grace said. 'But if you'll excuse me, Lily's waiting for me.'

'Ah,' said Mrs Macready. 'You're a saint with your sister, indeed you are.'

The next morning before light, when the only people about were milkmaids and drovers taking sheep to Smithfield, Grace and Lily set off to buy watercress at Farringdon Market. It was mostly the very old and very young who gathered to buy the cresses, for the stock money needed was no more than a few pennies and the goods were easy to carry. The people were of the very poorest, however, and Grace and Lily were among the few who were wearing shoes. Cresses were always sold along the railings at the entrance and gaslights burned brightly above here, enabling the buyers to see more clearly the quality of the goods being offered. A coffee seller had set up his stall by the entrance and lit a charcoal fire, causing the earliest customers to crowd about him trying to gain a little warmth from his brazier.

As it turned five o'clock, the country sellers opened their hampers and baskets and began to display their goods. The buyers – clutching bags, shawls, trays or fraying baskets of their own to collect their green stuffs – began to go up and down, looking carefully into the hampers, asking prices, inspecting the stock for its colour, sniffing it and holding it towards a light to judge its freshness. Grace and Lily's own purchases eventually made – six large bunches for a penny each –

the girls took the cresses over to a water pump to freshen them and discard any discoloured leaves. They then sat down on the stone pavement to break each large bunch into three or four smaller ones and tie them with a rush. Lily suffered with cold hands and had neither the patience nor the deftness to tie the fiddly little bundles, but Grace had become quite neat and quick at it and was fast enough to do four bunches to Lily's one.

The bunches prepared, they set off to sell them, Lily with half of them in her spare shawl and Grace with the others displayed on an ancient tea tray carried in the crook of her arm. Grace's cry was, 'Fine, fresh watercress!' and Lily's, 'Cresses, fresh and green!'

How discomforted they'd been, Grace reminded Lily that morning, when they'd first gone out shouting their wares; how humbly they'd called – whispered, almost – as if apologising for having anything to say at all. They had grown braver over the months, for if they hadn't they would have starved.

It was a busy morning, fine and bright, and the two girls managed to sell several bunches of watercress to labourers going to work and, a little later, to housewives looking for something sharp and tasty to have with their bread-and-cheese dinner. It proved a good day for them, because by eleven o'clock Grace had sold all her stock, her pretty face and solemn demeanour provoking sympathy from gentlemen and ladies alike and often drawing over the asking price of a ha'penny a bunch. Once Grace's tray was empty, the sisters walked together, calling in harmony, and by midday they had more than tripled the money laid out that morning. Grace was tempted, then, to redeem Mama's cup and saucer, but knew there would be a premium to pay on it which, together with that week's rent, would not leave them enough to buy both stock and food the next day. She therefore decided it must be left at Uncle's.

How normal everything felt, she reflected as they walked home that day; as if the baby had not happened at all, as if the ordeal in Berkeley House had been nothing but a nightmare. Apart from the knowing look Mrs Macready had given her, none of their neighbours had referred to the matter of her pregnancy, and Grace suspected that this was either because they genuinely hadn't noticed, or hadn't wished to become involved. If Grace *had* wanted to speak of her ordeal, if she had wished to unburden herself and tell of the visit to Brookwood and her conversations with Mr James Solent and Mrs Emmeline Unwin, there was no opportunity. Lily, sadly, did not make a satisfactory confidante.

Beside her now, Lily hummed a popular ballad as she walked along, happy because they'd sold all their cresses and because Grace was home safely – and, well, perhaps it was better that there was no baby, because babies had to be fed and some days they had no money for food. She loved babies, but they probably took a lot of looking after and . . . Suddenly, as they were passing

Morrell's Pawnshop, Lily stopped thinking anything because there, on a glass shelf of its own, all the better to show its beauty, was Mama's teapot.

She stopped, gasped and pointed, for it seemed to her that a miracle had happened – the teapot they knew and loved had somehow come back to life.

'It's Mama's!' exclaimed Grace, seeing it at the same moment. 'Or one very like.' She looked first at the teapot and then at her sister. '*Is* it ours? Lily! Did you take it to be pawned?'

Lily couldn't speak, so bewildered was she. How had this happened?

'You *did* take it, didn't you?' Grace looked at Lily, crestfallen. 'How could you, Lily? How could you tell me such a terrible lie about someone coming in to steal it?'

Lily began crying. 'I . . . I only went to pawn it because I didn't sell all my cresses and there wasn't enough money for stock. And I thought the . . . the baby would need clothes.'

Grace gasped. 'How much did they give you? What have you done with all that money?'

'They didn't give me anything! The teapot broke. It broke just as I was giving it to the man.'

'*What?*'

'I was handing it over the counter and the man dropped it. Well,' she went on meekly, 'he said I dropped it, though I don't think I did.'

'Did you see it smashed?'

She nodded. 'It was on the floor. A hundred pieces.'

'But there it is now,' Grace said, pointing at the teapot.

'Is it . . . is it magic?' Lily asked fearfully.

'No, it's not magic,' said Grace, 'but it's a trick, certainly.' She was quiet, thinking, while they carried on walking to the end of the lane. 'I'm going to wait here while you run home as fast as you can,' she said to Lily then. 'On the mantelpiece in our room you'll see two little white cards, which I want you to bring to me.'

Lily, anxious to make amends, did as she was told and returned with the cards within minutes. Grace told her to wait, then straightened her shawl, pulled herself up to her full height and went in to Morrell's.

Morrell was not pleased to be interrupted, for it was Saturday and he was hunched over a racing paper making his selection of horses.

'Yes, missy?' he asked, chewing a stub of pencil between his lips. 'What is it?'

'That teapot in the window . . .'

'The one with the bluebirds?' He looked up. 'That is a *very* nice, quality piece. We don't often have things of that hexcellence here. You're a very astute young gel.'

'It's very similar to a teapot my sister brought in yesterday,' said Grace.

'Hoh yes?' Morrell asked, his lips coloured purple from the indelible lead.

'Yes,' Grace said firmly.

'And are you going to tell me that I didn't give her a

54

fair price for it?'

'You didn't give her *any* price!' Grace said. 'You dropped the teapot as she was giving it to you.'

'Breakages are not the responsibility of the management,' Morrell muttered automatically.

'But it wasn't broken at all,' said Grace, 'for it's there in your window on a shelf.'

'That's a different one!' Morrell blustered.

'I've been warned about people like you, who make a pretence that something is broken when it isn't.'

'I tell you that that there pot in the window is another one,' said Morrell. 'A different one. That one's quality, that is.'

'That is our mother's teapot in your window,' Grace said sternly. 'And my brother, who is a lawyer's clerk,' she brandished the card belonging to Mr James Solent, 'says that if you do not return it to us immediately then he will begin a court enquiry into the matter.'

Morrell looked at the card and his jaw dropped so that the pencil fell out of his mouth. 'Oh, hoity toity,' he said. 'No need for that. Court enquiries indeed.'

'Then I demand that you give it back right now!' said Grace.

Ten minutes later, Grace and Lily were home and Grace was putting the teapot carefully into the crate. Her hands were shaking a little as she did so, for standing up to Morrell had taken more out of her than she had thought.

She'd removed a couple of sheets of newspaper from Morrell's counter to wrap the teapot and now smoothed out one of these. To amuse Lily and show that all was well between them (for indeed, Grace did feel that a teapot lost and found was nothing compared to other things), she began to read some of the advertisements.

'*For the best treat of the Season, visit Madame Tussaud's Historical Gallery with a full-length model of the Murderer James Mullins, with a replica of the awful brown paper parcel, the discovery of which led to his capture.*'

'Should you like to go to see that?' Lily asked her fearfully.

'No, I should not,' said Grace. 'But I should like to see this: *Captain Green's silk balloon shown daily at the Crystal Palace. See the balloon which has made ascents from all the major cities in Europe. Captain Green will be on hand to answer questions and receive your approbations.*'

'A silk balloon?' Lily questioned. 'How big would that be?'

'I believe it's big enough to have a basket below it which can hold people.'

'People who go up in the air with it?'

Grace nodded.

'Like birds!'

'Yes, like birds,' Grace said. 'Oh, there are several advertisements for dogs here: *Sociable, first rate and handsome toy terriers. A fine companion for a lady.* I should like a nice dog. Wouldn't you, Lily?'

'But dogs would need to be fed every single day,' Lily reminded her.

'Of course,' Grace said. 'We won't have one, then.' She glanced down the page. 'A considerable number of ladies are looking for situations as governesses – oh, and under *Missing Friends* there is someone looking for a Miss Caroline Thomas *regarding a matter both delicate and urgent.* I wonder what that can be?'

As she paused to think a little longer, her fingers traced the outline of a small, neat oblong which had been cut from the bottom of the page. 'Look,' she said wonderingly, 'someone has cut out one of these advertisements. Perhaps they mean to answer it. I wonder what it said?'

Lily shook her head impatiently. 'Never mind that. Read me some more, do! Make me up a story about a toy terrier going up in a balloon!'

The Mercury

Chapter Six

The discreet announcement, a neat oblong, had come from the front page of *The Mercury*. The man holding it, wearing his usual Saturday garments of a loud tweed jacket and yellow cravat, had cut it out before taking several items wrapped in newspaper to sell at Morrell's, who never asked questions about an item's provenance.

This man and one other were in Barker's, a gentlemen's club in London's St James's, and were occupying the largest leather seats in the smoking room. They had paid considerably over the odds to secure their membership to the club, for being 'trade' rather than 'society', by rights they shouldn't have been there at all.

The man with the yellow cravat passed the announcement over to his companion, who was much more formally dressed in an immaculate dark suit with handmade boots and the softest of leather gloves. This man was puffing on a cigar, trying to blow smoke rings. This was the only point of levity about him, for his heavy face, bulbous nose and arrogant expression pointed to him having an altogether different character. He stared at the ceiling and a smoke ring rose into the air.

'You read it to me.'

'Well, I won't bother with the details, but basically it says they're looking for two pigeons and are offering a reward for their finding.'

'Two pigeons, you say?'

'Mother and daughter,' said Yellow Cravat, glancing up at a fine oil painting of Her Majesty Queen Victoria over the fireplace and saluting her with his glass of port.

'And you reckon there's a chance of finding them, do you?'

'I should say it's worth looking,' said the first, dodging a cloud of smoke. 'My nark at the law courts says there's a small fortune waiting around in unclaimed inheritances. He mentioned the case concerning these two, as a matter of fact. The person who locates them will take ten per cent of a tidy sum.'

The second blew out another perfect circle. 'Worth a try, then. Mother and daughter, you say?'

'The girl's seventeen so the mother's probably . . . what? Thirty something?'

'I'll use my contacts.'

'We'll go halves, eh?' Yellow Cravat said.

'We've got to find them first,' said the other. Above his head, the smoke circle bloomed and dissolved. 'Anything else to report?'

The first shook his head. 'Just the usual: several substitutions of painted chipboard for oak. Oh, and I got a couple of nice wedding rings this week. The family said they wanted 'em buried with the corpse.'

'More fool them! Bet that raised a cheer.'

'It did,' said Yellow Cravat, 'but only after they'd left the premises.'

Dickens's Dictionary of London, 1888

Chapter Seven

For the next four or five weeks, matters went quite well for Grace and Lily. At the beginning of July, the watercress which came into London from the outlying farms was at its most abundant, meaning that a large bunch could be purchased for a ha'penny, doubling all their profits. After two weeks of this, therefore, they had their rent money put aside for a whole month, and a little later Grace redeemed her mama's cup and saucer and also bought two straw baskets in which to carry the watercress around and display the bunches to their best advantage. The other thing she'd managed to do was to put aside two shillings for her train fare to Brookwood, so she could go sometime and pay her respects to her dead child.

At the end of August, however, things changed again, this time for the worst, when the free-flowing brook used by one of the largest watercress farmers in Hampshire dried up, the authorities having diverted the brook to bring fresh water to a nearby village. This event caused such a shortage of watercress that the Farringdon Market sellers were able to double and double again the price of a wholesale bunch. It also rained every day for near three weeks so that there were few buyers on the streets, with the result that by the end of September their fortunes had turned again, and Grace and Lily were as poor as they'd ever been. The shillings Grace had saved for the Necropolis Railway had been used for food and Mama's cup and saucer had been pawned again, together with the teapot and the baskets. Besides this, they had no money to put aside for that week's rent.

'We've just six pennies left, so tomorrow we'll buy three large bunches,' Grace said, laying out the money along the top of one of the crates. 'If we're very careful, if we make four bunches from each bunch we buy and sell them for a penny, then we will have . . .' She counted on her fingers. 'Twelve pennies.' She sighed. 'And then we must lay out six for stock the next day, and two towards our rent and two for some potatoes – oh, and a penny to use Mrs Macready's oven to cook them. Even if we have them dry, it is barely enough.'

'We could put an advertisement in the paper!' Lily said. She was sitting on a crate with Grace kneeling beside her. 'We could say we need money, being gentle-women in trying circumstances . . .' Grace had read out such an advertisement a few days before and, although

Lily hadn't known exactly what the words meant, she'd been fascinated by them.

'And how much do you think such an advertisement in *The Times* would cost us?'

Lily shook her head in doubt.

'Certainly ten shillings.'

'Ten shillings! So the gentlewomen couldn't have been in *very* trying circumstances at all,' said Lily. She frowned deeply, thinking. 'One of us could do something else to obtain money, get some different work . . .'

'Perhaps,' Grace echoed, thinking that now they were selling fewer bunches, there was certainly no need to have both of them out with cresses.

'I could sweep the roadway!' Lily went on. 'I could buy a broom, look for ladies coming along and offer to make a passageway for them. That's what the Wilson children do. Or I could hold horses for gentlemen.'

'All the good crossings are taken,' Grace said. 'And it's only boys who have the strength to hold horses.'

'Well then, I could wait outside shops and carry parcels for ladies. Or pick up things in the streets. Patrick Cartwright told me that he once found two silk handkerchiefs.'

'What he means is, he found them in someone's pocket,' said Grace.

'Or I could go down to the river to look for things in the mud.'

'No!' said Grace. 'Not that. You and I will never do that. I would rather go to . . .'

Lily looked at her and then burst into tears. 'I'm not going back to that last place!'

Grace moved closer to put an arm around her sister. 'No, Lily. Never. We shall never do that.'

'You promised that we wouldn't go back there. You said that whatever happened we never would!' Once she'd started crying, Lily always found it difficult to stop. 'You said that even if we had no shoes and were starving to death, we wouldn't! You *said*!'

'I meant every word,' Grace said, smoothing her sister's hair. 'I promised you then and promise you now: we will never go into a workhouse or go back to the training house.' She looked at her sister carefully. 'But why was that place so very awful for you?'

'That man might come for me again!'

Grace felt the blood drain from her face. 'What do you mean?'

'That wicked man. Oh!' She looked at Grace in horror. 'I said I'd never tell anyone. He said he'd kill me if I did.'

Grace was silent for a while, controlling her feelings, then she said, 'We're away from there now and we'll never go back, so he couldn't possibly know that you've told me.'

Lily gave a shuddering sob.

'Tell me what you remember,' Grace prompted gently.

'He came at night-time. You weren't there . . . one of the little children had called out for you and you'd gone into another room, so when he got into my bed, I thought at first it was you coming back.'

'And then . . .'

'Then he did something . . .' Lily looked away, deeply ashamed. 'He was improper with me.'

'And did he say anything?'

'Hardly anything, and he spoke very low, in a growl. He said that I should be a woman soon and it was as well that I found out what was in store for me.'

Grace nodded sadly. It had been the same for her. 'Did you see his face at all?'

Lily shook her head. 'You'd taken the candle and there was no moon that night. Besides, I was so frightened that I kept my eyes tightly shut the whole time – until he was getting out of the bed. And then I looked and saw the back of him, and when he pushed away the bedclothes . . .' She shuddered again. 'I saw that he only had one hand. Where the other should have been, there was just a stump.'

Grace nodded and swallowed the bile which had risen in her throat.

'He told me that he visited all the girls once. He said he was a very important man and it was his special, secret treat for them.' She suddenly realised the implications of what she'd said and gasped. 'Did he come to you, too, Grace?'

Grace managed to control herself before replying, 'Yes.'

'Did he say the same things?'

Grace nodded.

'And do . . . do the same?'

'Yes, the very same. But because of that . . .' She hesitated, but thought it was as well that Lily should know the facts of life.

'Yes?' Lily stared at her, somehow knowing that something even more serious was coming.

'It was the baby, Lily. When a man and a woman do that, it can lead to the woman having a baby. And that's what happened to me.'

'And will it happen to me, too?'

Grace managed to smile. 'No, dearest. If it was going to happen, it would have been before now. You're perfectly safe, and so am I.'

'Suppose he finds us?'

'He doesn't know where we are – or who we are – because when he visited us it was darkest night. I don't believe he saw any more of us than we did of him.'

'And besides, he has the other girls in the home if . . . if he wants . . .'

Grace sighed. 'Yes, I'm afraid he does. But if we ever see a man with one hand, we will know him.'

'And then?' Lily prompted. '*Then?*'

Then she would kill him, Grace thought dispassionately.

Between them, the girls decided that perhaps the best way of earning a little money would be for Lily to wait outside shops and offer to carry parcels for lady shoppers. Early the following morning, therefore, after going to market with Grace, Lily set off for Burlington Arcade in Piccadilly, which was known to have the classiest, most opulent shops and, as a consequence, the richest lady shoppers. Unfortunately, this was such a well-known fact that, even by seven o'clock in the morning, a parade of tattered children had already assembled waiting for the arcade gates to be opened so they could take their places outside their chosen shop. Most of them were girls and were all very poor. Only a few of them had shoes, but all had made some attempt at gentility. The boys had battered top hats, while the girls had some form of head-covering, even if it was just an out-of-shape and fraying straw bonnet, or ragged scarf wound around their hair.

Lily approached the wrought-iron gates of the arcade and stared through. Beyond she could see curved, glittering glass windows filled with all manner of delightful things: soft leather purses and handbags, fur tippets, exquisite porcelain, jewellery, perfumes, soaps and lotions. Mama had had a real fur coat, she remembered, and lovely clothes, but all those things had gone years ago.

At half past seven the arcade gates were opened by two uniformed men who tried to scare off the would-be errand-runners by shouting that a couple of burly peelers were on their way and would arrest the lot of them for begging. This made the nervous ones, including Lily, hang back a little, but the threatened policemen never arrived and, after a few moments, she followed the braver ones into the arching passageway. Here she discovered that the arcade had two ends, and that a similar number of children had been waiting at the far one, so that there were already two children waiting outside most doors – three, in the case of the larger shops.

Lily walked through the arcade, pretending to look at the things in the windows, but actually trying to find a shop with a single person outside it. She found one, The Gentlemen's Shaving Emporium, but standing sentry outside was a hefty boy of about seventeen, with an aggressive stare and large hands already curled into fists. Lily, too scared to speak to him, went on, reached the end of the arcade and walked back again, discovering as she did so that if she slowed down in any way, those already outside shop doors would hiss at her, or tell her in no uncertain terms to move on.

She thought it might be better when the ladies actually arrived and began shopping, but then she remembered that ladies of quality hardly rose before eleven o'clock, then spent the morning putting on their clothes and having their hair dressed before venturing forth in the afternoon to do a little light shopping and make their social calls. And they usually went with companions or ladies' maids, so wouldn't *they* carry the purchases? Lily made one attempt to speak to a little girl of about eight, asking if she might stand with her and take a chance, but the girl turned on her like an angry cat, saying that she'd fought for this place and it was hers and she would kill anyone who said otherwise, so Lily retreated.

Leaving Piccadilly, she went towards the Strand, intending to wait outside what was billed as the largest drapers' store in London, but found a similar system there run by a team of boys who made it clear to Lily that she would never get any parcel-carrying work while one of them stood upright on two feet. And so it went on at every store or shop Lily approached, ensuring that she went back to Seven Dials that evening with precisely what she'd started with: nothing.

'How did you fare?' Grace asked anxiously. She, too, had had a bad day. Watercress had long been a favourite garnish for a bread-and-cheese dinner, but under the present circumstances most Londoners thought it was too expensive, and chose to go without.

Lily shook her head sadly. 'But tomorrow I could try picking up cigar ends in the street, for I heard someone say that it's a really good and profitable job.'

'No!' Grace said. 'You can't do that. Watercress-selling is one thing – and even carrying parcels for ladies is not too disgraceful – but we must never hunt along the gutter like tramps or wade in river mud. Mama would dislike it very much.'

'But Mama's not here to see us!' Lily, tired and hungry, burst into tears, and Grace could offer her little comfort.

We are looking for several beneficiaries to wills, including, most urgently, information on the whereabouts of Mrs Letitia Parkes and her daughter Lily. If these ladies, or anyone who might know their whereabouts, would contact the offices of Binge & Gently in the Strand, London, WC, it will be to their considerable advantage.

The Mercury

Chapter Eight

At Barker's in St James's, the same two men were reading the newspapers, occasionally putting them to one side to discuss some aspect or other of the past week's business. One man was sporting his usual tweed jacket and yellow cravat, the other – the one with the arrogant expression – was dressed as formally as before, and had just put out his cigar.

'Unfortunately, not so many dead this week,' said Yellow Cravat, who was, in fact, Mr George Unwin, the well-known funeral director. He gave a guffaw of a laugh, then looked about them quickly to make sure no one else had heard. 'I know how that must sound to outsiders,' he said, holding up his hand in mock protest, 'but business is business!'

'Quite, quite. And without the funeral, we are

without the mourning. Not a good situation to be in at all,' said his companion and cousin, Mr Sylvester Unwin.

'Luckily for us, everyone dies sooner or later.'

'And even more luckily, we have some secondary earners until they do, eh?'

'Talking of which, I see the two pigeons haven't been traced yet.' George Unwin stabbed a finger at the advertisement.

'I've got my employees on the lookout.'

'And my usual squealers have been primed.' George folded the paper so that the advertisement was uppermost. 'I've got a feeling about this one, you know.'

'What sort of a feeling?'

'A feeling we're going to find Mrs . . .' He consulted the paper again. '. . . Mrs Parkes and dear little Lily.'

'Be nice if you're right, George. Be *very* nice,' said Sylvester Unwin.

'Indeed it would,' said George complacently.

Lost, stolen or strayed: small beagle
answering to the name of Scout lost
in the Seven Dials area. Please apply
with live dog to 7 Beauchamp Place,
London, SW, where a substantial
reward awaits.

The Mercury

Chapter Nine

When Grace answered a tap at the door, she opened it to find old Mrs Beale there, anxiously threading a handkerchief through her fingers and looking as if a strong wind might blow her away.

'I've come to say goodbye, dear,' she said. 'Mr Beale and I are leaving Mrs Macready's.'

Grace ushered her into their bare little room, knowing that however low one sank down the social scale, manners were still important. 'I'm sorry to hear that,' she said. 'Where are you going?'

'We're going to a . . . to a . . . well, to a *workhouse*.' As the old woman managed to say the last word, it seemed to stick in her throat and nearly choke her.

Grace, trying not to show her dismay, took Mrs Beale's hand. 'Well, who could blame you for seeking shelter elsewhere?' she said. 'This coming winter promises to be a harsh one.'

Mrs Beale's handkerchief became even more twisted. 'We've tried to manage on our own, but last week Mr Beale was knocked down and all his shoelaces were stolen, and yesterday he fell in the middle of the street and only just missed being run over by an omnibus. Now we're three weeks late with our rent and though Mrs Macready is the best of women, we can't abide being in debt to anyone.'

Grace squeezed the old woman's hand.

'Is it so very terrible in these homes?' Mrs Beale asked. 'You hear such tales. You were in a home, were you not?'

Grace nodded. 'I think they're all very different,' she said diplomatically. 'At the first place we went, the orphanage, they were very kind to us. We were allowed to take our own possessions, and there was always enough to eat.'

'Then may I ask, dear, why did you leave?'

'From there, we were sent to a training establishment for young women, and it was this place that . . .' Grace swallowed, feeling nauseous. '. . . that we didn't like.'

'Might I ask why?' Mrs Beale replied.

Grace shivered and seemed to feel again the weight of the man as he knelt on her, pinning her down. She took a deep breath. 'There . . . there was a man who made himself objectionable to me,' she said at last, her voice little above a whisper.

'Oh!' Mrs Beale's tissue-paper cheeks went pink and

she hurried to change the subject. 'Forgive me, my dear, but how long ago did your poor mother die?'

'Near ten years back,' Grace answered.

'Were there no other relatives who would take you in? What about your father?'

Grace shook her head. 'I've never known much about my father or his family,' she said. 'When Mama and he were married neither family approved of the match, and two years after that, when Lily was a year old and before Mama even knew she was expecting me, Papa went off to the Americas to seek his fortune.'

'Your poor mother! To be left without a protector!'

Grace nodded. 'She brought us up on a little inheritance she'd had from her grandparents and taught me to read and write quite early, hoping that one day I'd make a good marriage and be able to keep Lily as my companion.' She smiled wryly as she spoke, knowing that good marriages were not made in Seven Dials, and that the most a girl here might hope for would be to marry a coster with his own barrow. 'I started my training as a teacher and Lily was to learn about domestic duties, but then we had to leave . . .' Here Grace stopped and found it impossible to continue.

'And when was this?'

'Some . . . some nine months ago.'

'Nine months,' Mrs Beale repeated, and if she made the obvious connection was refined enough not to say anything about it. 'And you never heard from your father again?'

'Never.' Grace shook her head again. 'Mama always used to say that sea travel was dangerous and that he might have perished, but perhaps he just didn't love Mama enough to come back to her.'

Mrs Beale squeezed her hand now. 'My dear girl, I'm sure some other occurrence prevented his return from overseas.'

'Perhaps.' It was Grace's turn to change the subject. 'But I'm sorry you have to go into a workhouse.'

'Neither of us want to, but another winter like the last one would kill Mr Beale. Life gets harder as you get older, you see.'

Grace nodded and, as she wished Mrs Beale all the very best, mused that her and Lily's lives seemed to be growing harder already, for the market in watercress hadn't improved, especially since a rumour had spread that some of the big watercress rivers were unclean and might harbour cholera. She always came home with unsold cresses now, and sometimes struggled all day to sell even six bunches. Lily had tried her hand at selling combs and then matches, but whereas people often bought things from Grace because of her shy beauty, Lily had no such appeal. She had their mother's dark auburn curls but had, unfortunately, inherited their father's looks – his square jaw and deeply set eyes. (Their mother had painted a little portrait of their father which once, years ago, had stood beside her bed, and she had often remarked on Lily's likeness to him.) Grace had now pawned Mama's wedding bonnet and veil, and following this had taken a pillow and two blankets to a dolly shop – one of the unofficial pawn-brokers that had sprung up in the poverty-stricken locality.

'We can manage perfectly well with one blanket,' she'd said to Lily. 'And by the time it's really cold, things may have improved for us.'

'And then we can buy some new blankets!' Lily had said happily. 'Or perhaps Papa will come back.'

Grace didn't reply, for she didn't think it was right to encourage Lily in such thoughts and *she'd* stopped believing in Papa long ago. Besides, even with what she'd pawned she hadn't managed to put aside their rent money for the following week and was more concerned about that than about a man whose very existence was in doubt.

When Mrs Beale had gone, Grace looked around the room. What else could she pawn to keep them from starving? Could they manage without shoes? She sighed. *Some* folk did – the youngest Cartwright boy, a lad of about six, seemed to have neither shoes nor clothes of his own, since he only appeared outside when one of his brothers was indoors. Once, sent by his mother to beg a slice of bread from Grace, he'd appeared at their door wearing no more than a shabby shawl tied around his waist. After some thought, Grace decided that their petticoats and the last pillow could be pawned if absolutely necessary, but not their shoes.

She glanced at the two small white cards still

standing on the shelf above the fireplace. She loathed the thought of asking for charity, but she would if she had to. Anything to help prevent them from being taken to a workhouse. And she knew there were even worse fates than that: recently she hadn't been able to prevent herself from looking with awful fascination at the sad young women who plied the oldest of trades in the slum that was Monmouth Street . . . those girls with matted hair, sores, bruises and utterly wretched expressions. Oh, pray that God hadn't deserted her and Lily entirely and that *that* didn't become their fate.

While Grace was speaking to Mrs Beale, Lily was standing with Alfie Pope watching a conjurer perform in a paved square off Oxford Street. The square held a good amount of people, for it contained several popular shops, two best-quality fruit stalls and a small swing-boat of the type you might get at a fair. Just then it also contained the Magnificent Marvo, and it was in front of him that most of the crowd, including a dog and a man, were gathered.

'Look, see that dog?' Alfie hissed. 'The beagle dog?' He took Lily's arm and pointed to the small brown and white hound waiting patiently beside its owner in the cobbled square. 'It's lost, see. All you gotta do is pick it up and take it to that fence over the back where my brother Billy is. He'll take the doggie off you and see it gets to its rightful 'ome.'

Lily frowned. She was tired and, after a day looking

for bottles on the streets and earning only a penny, was anxious to get back to Grace. 'Are you sure it's lost?' she said to Alfie. 'That man's got it on a lead.'

'That's not its real owner,' Alfie said, running a grubby hand through his shock of black hair. 'It's been nicked. See, its real owner wants it back and is off'ring a reward. A big reward.'

Lily's eyes gleamed. 'Did it say so in the newspaper?'

'Exactly,' Alfie said.

'So why don't *you* take it?' Lily asked.

"Cos the cove's going to be on the lookout for anyone gettin' too close to his nice new doggie,' Alfie explained diligently. 'He'd be suspicious of me, but he won't 'spect an helegant young gel like you.'

Lily beamed at him.

'You can easily cut the doggie's lead an' —'

'Cut the lead?'

'Yup. I got a sharp knife here,' said Alfie. 'Cut the lead, pick up the doggie and you'll be orf before he knows it. Then you just goes to that fence over the back there and gives him to Billy and he'll give you a shillin'.'

'A shilling!' Lily's eyes gleamed.

'Sure! Easiest money you'll ever earn. 'Ere's the knife.' He pressed a small penknife into her hand. 'Off you go now. Look smart.'

Lily didn't hesitate, for in all her life she had never before had the opportunity of earning a shilling. She concealed the penknife in her hand, slipped around the corner into the square and went to stand beside the dog in the heart of the crowd. Everyone was intent on watching the magician who was bringing out innumerable silk handkerchiefs from the sleeve of his jacket, colour upon colour, larger and larger, until the last emerged, as big as a flag. This achieved, he rolled all the flags into a bundle and threw them in the air, whereupon, to cheers and applause, they turned into a white rabbit. Lily could scarcely believe her eyes. A real rabbit! She looked towards Alfie, gasping and pointing, but he merely shook his head at her and urged her on. She immediately bent over, cut the dog's lead, picked him up and ran out of the square with him.

Amid the throng, it was some moments before the owner of the dog realised that he was holding half a lead with no dog on the end of it, and by this time Lily had the dog grabbed out of her hands by Billy, the second Pope boy.

'Give 'im 'ere!' he said urgently. He grabbed the beagle and turned in order to drop him over the fence, where a third brother was concealed.

'Where's my money?' Lily asked.

Billy pressed a coin into her hand and Lily scrutinised it. 'Is this a shilling?' she asked, for she didn't think she'd ever seen one before.

''Course it is!' Billy held the dog high above the fence and the obliging 'Scout' was dropped over with a yelp to George, the third brother. As George fled with the dog under his arm, Billy turned back to Lily, smiling genially, for all the world as if they were there just to enjoy the show. 'It's one of the new shillings,' he said.

'Oh,' said Lily.

'They changed, see. When did you last see one?'

Lily shook her head. 'Don't know.'

'There you are, then. That's a shillin' all right!'

Suddenly, from the area in front of the magician there was a cry of 'My dog! Someone's taken my dog!' and half of the crowd left the Magnificent Marvo (for anyway, he was about to pass his hat round) to seek out the lost dog.

Had they glanced towards the fence they would have just seen Billy Pope leaning on it, quietly whittling a stick with the penknife he'd got back from Lily, and Lily herself, looking slightly disconcerted, walking home clutching the 'shilling'.

'This is not a shilling!' Grace said. 'Whoever told you that?'

'It's one of the new ones,' said Lily. 'He said it was one of the new ones.'

'Who did? You said you found it in the street.'

Lily coloured. 'Billy Pope said.'

Grace looked at her sister sadly. She felt infinitely weary, having been out since five that morning with the cresses and only taking a few pence. The money she'd earned was going to be put towards the rent, and then she had to decide whether to buy stock the following day or something to eat that evening. 'Why was Billy Pope giving you money?'

Lily did what she normally did when things got too much: she burst into tears.

'Lily! I hope it was nothing wicked.'

'No, it wasn't – it wasn't at all. There was a dog, you see, and a man had taken it who shouldn't have, and the Pope boys were going to return it to the proper owner and get a reward.'

'But what did *you* do?'

'I just took the dog off the man who'd stolen it!' Lily sniffed. 'I cut its lead and –'

'You stole it!'

'Yes, but –'

'Lily, I've told you this before. There are many wicked thieves about – they steal a dog in the street and wait until the owner advertises a reward for finding it.'

'Then what?' said Lily sullenly.

'Then they take it back and pretend they've found it running loose. The owner is usually so pleased to have it that he doesn't ask too many questions.' She went to the window, all the better to look at the coin. 'Anyway, this is a ha'penny painted silver – and not painted all that well, either. Is this what they gave you?'

Lily nodded.

'I shall go and speak to the Popes. If anyone had seen you and caught you, you could have been arrested by the police and taken away from me, don't you realise that?'

Lily hung her head, looking suitably ashamed, but

nevertheless feeling better. It wasn't her fault; it was all to do with those Pope boys. Grace wasn't really cross with *her*.

Grace wrapped her shawl about her, brushed down her skirts and left the room, feeling agitated. Before she'd gone more than five steps down the passageway, however, she'd started to change her mind: there was only one of her against six Popes and she was bound to come off the worst. She sank down on to the bottom stair. Perhaps it was her own fault; Lily was easy prey for anyone and shouldn't really have been allowed to go off on her own collecting bottles. Mama had impressed upon Grace – even when very small – that she must look upon herself as the older sister, rather than the younger. 'I fear that Lily will always be a child,' she'd said more than once, 'and it will fall to you, Grace, to prevent people from taking advantage of her.'

Thinking on all this, Grace began weeping. She'd let Mama down, she'd let Lily down, the watercress season was over, there was hardly anything left to pawn and winter was coming. What was to become of them?

Any number of puppies, kittens, chicks and other small animals can be supplied for home menageries and to complete your family groups.

Docile and comatose animals a speciality.

Apply to Wilton's Hardware Emporium, Seven Dials, Holborn.

Chapter Ten

Before the Beales left Mrs Macready's the following morning, Mrs Beale gave Grace her tattered shawl and apron, for they'd been told that they wouldn't be allowed to enter the workhouse with any possessions of their own. Even the clothes they were wearing would be taken away and, after being hosed down, they'd have to wear crude workhouse garments made of sacking, with a number on their backs.

Despite the threadbare condition of these two items of Mrs Beale's, Grace was able to get a penny for them at a rag fair and, with this and the painted ha'penny, to buy a large bunch of watercress (rather yellowing, hence the price) which she split into five. After managing to sell these bunches for a penny each, the two girls began making their way back to Mrs Macready's, Grace hurrying because she had a job to do. Winter was fast advancing, and because one of the two small windows in their room was broken it was very draughty. She planned to beg a few old crates from a stall in Neal's Yard, and a hammer and nails from one of the costermongers upstairs, and try and nail boards across the gaps. It would make it even darker in their little room, for the houses opposite were so close that little light penetrated anyway, but to be dark seemed better than being cold. Cold they surely would be, however, at some time in the coming months, for – now that everything they had of any value had been pawned – this winter there would be no money to buy firewood or coals.

Coming close to the lane where they lived, with Mrs Macready's house already in view, Grace was struck by the unusual number of people milling about – not only the normal stray children, hawkers, tinkers, peddlers and housewives going to and from market – but workmen in blue serge, and two or three men with top hats and dark suits. She turned to mention this to Lily, but her sister had wandered off, having seen a hawker with a kitten and puppy together in a cage, one of the 'happy families' – kittens with mice or ducklings, or cats and dogs together – that had recently become popular begging accessories. On Lily showing some interest in these, however, the cloth which covered the cage had been replaced, and the showman refused to let her see the animals unless she produced a ha'penny.

Lily ran back to Grace. 'Just a ha'penny!' she pleaded.

'Only a ha'penny to see the dearest kitten and puppy playing together.'

Grace shook her head, intent on discovering why there were so many extra people in the area. She craned her head to see along Brick Place. What was happening?

'And *you* can see them, too, at the same time!' Lily persisted.

'And pet them, miss, for just a small extra charge!' called the showman, a gaunt individual, his coat tied up with string.

'I'm sorry, I cannot. Lily, please come along!' Grace waved the showman out of the way, but tried to do it in a civil manner, for she knew that he was only doing what everyone else in London was doing: trying to earn enough money to survive.

Lily reluctantly left the animals and joined her sister, staring where she was staring. 'What's happening? Why has our house got wood over the windows?'

They went closer. Mrs Macready's house was the second along in a small terrace of four, all of which were in similar states of shabby disrepair – two were without chimney pots, several had glass gone from their windows or their frames broken, and one had the front door missing entirely. Mrs Macready's house also had a vast crack which ran across the brickwork in a diagonal line from the top to the bottom. These four decrepit dwellings were now in the process of being boarded up, with solid wooden planks criss-crossed over all the window apertures and doorways to prevent occupation.

'What are they doing?' Lily asked. 'How will we get in?' Thinking about the few worthless little things she kept in her cigar box, she began to cry. 'I want my treasures!'

'Wait here,' Grace said to her firmly. 'Don't move!' She approached who seemed to be the foreman; the man bearing the most paperwork, with the tallest hat. 'We live here, my sister and I –' she began.

'Not any more you don't,' said the man, not even glancing up.

Grace felt shock gust through her. 'But what's happening? We've paid our rent, we don't owe anything, we haven't been in trouble –'

The man flattened his papers against his chest and looked at Grace for the first time, surprised at both her voice and her manner (for most of the other tenants of the houses had screamed, threatened and blasphemed). 'Government orders,' he said in a more conciliatory manner. 'Slum clearance, see. Orders of Prince Albert. They're going to build better homes here. They don't want you to live twenty to a room and eighty to a privy any more.'

'You mean, these houses are being improved?'

'Not exactly, miss. They're being pulled down. They're going to build places with inside privies and water on tap, and when they're all finished, you'll be asked if you want to live here again. Always supposing you can afford the rent,' he couldn't resist adding.

'But where shall we go in the meantime?'

The man shrugged his shoulders. 'Haven't you got any family who'd take you in?'

Grace didn't even bother to reply to this. 'But where are all the others gone? The Popes and the Cartwrights and everyone?'

'Blessed if I know,' the man said. 'They were all here earlier, running around like a family of dung beetles. Why, someone had a zoo in their room – dogs, cats, squirrels, birds – a regular menagerie!' He looked about him, then pointed to the steps of the end house, where three ragged shapes were bent over, weeping. 'There are some of them.'

Grace looked, but didn't see anyone she recognised. 'But what of Mrs Macready?'

'Gone to her son's house in Connaught Gardens. We just do what we're told, you understand,' he said, so she would know he had nothing against her sort personally. 'The bigwigs are very keen on slum clearance. They want all the stinking, rotten places pulled down. They breed disease, see.'

Grace was silent for a moment, trying to think clearly and not just begin weeping. 'What about our things?' she asked after a moment. 'Can my sister and I go in to collect them?'

'Too late, miss. You should have asked this morning.'

'But no one told us!' Grace thought of their few remaining trinkets and clothes, the crates, the sparse bedclothes and Lily's treasures. 'Oh, please,' she said to the man earnestly. 'It would break my sister's heart to lose what few things we have.'

'I thought all the stuffs was out of the place,' said the man. He gave an exaggerated sigh. 'Look, I'll let you in for two minutes, all right? Go in, get what you want and come straight out. And don't tell anyone I let you in!'

Grace thanked him profusely, called to Lily and, while the man shouted to a workman to prise a plank of wood from the front door to allow them access, tried to explain to her what was happening.

Lily didn't understand. Of course not; Grace didn't understand either. But it would be all right, she tried to reassure her sister as they clattered upstairs, they would be sure to find some other accommodation – even if they had to share a room with another family for a time. She had heard of a soup kitchen where you could get meals . . . and perhaps there was help from the Parish for those who were made homeless through no fault of their own. She would go to James Solent, she decided there and then, and ask where they stood in regards to the law of the land. He'd said that if ever she needed help she could call on him, and though it might be embarrassing to ask for help from such a fine and handsome young man, she would do it if she had to.

Inside Mrs Macready's house it was dim, dusty and as silent as the grave, as if it had already given up on life. Lily was crying before they even got to their room, and when Grace pushed open the door she began crying, too, for the room was completely bare: bed, blanket, pillow and the crates containing the little items that the girls had still owned all gone. The room was absolutely empty apart from the two small white business cards on the mantelpiece, standing out brightly in the darkness.

'Where shall we go now, then?' Lily asked, looking trustingly at Grace as they walked along the Strand. Lily's tears had dried, she had been reassured (*promised*, for it was the only way that Grace could stop her from crying) that things would soon come right again.

'We are going to a young gentleman I know, Mr James Solent,' said Grace. 'He's a very clever legal man who will help us.'

James Solent, Susannah Solent . . . Grace, making the connection, felt her heart ache within her. My baby lies safely with Susannah Solent, she thought. But this did not console her; instead it made her want to weep and sob and tear at her clothes. Everything about her life was wretched.

Reaching the beginning of Fleet Street, with the elegant spires and pinnacles of the Royal Courts of Justice coming into view, Grace looked again at the card she held in her hand and then nervously approached a doorman to ask if he knew the way to Moriarty Chambers. He directed them across the road and under an archway, where another uniformed man asked what they wanted. Grace showed him the business card at the same moment that a hansom cab clattered up, however, and he waved them on without even looking at what was written on it.

Through the arch, a cobbled lane opened out to a different, much more genteel world: a spacious park-like area with grass and trees, and beyond that the grey streak of the Thames. Legal men in white collars and black gowns, some with curling grey wigs, walked busily to and fro. Some had files under their arms, some pulled boxes on wheels which were full of papers, and none spared a moment to glance at either of the girls.

Lily gazed about them, enjoying the unusual scene and peaceful atmosphere. 'Is Mr Solent one of those funny men in a wig?' she asked.

'I'm not sure,' Grace replied. Was he? More importantly, would he help them? Would he even remember his promise to her?

Spaced all around the park-like area were handsome buildings and, walking closer to these, Grace saw that they all had names painted above their arched door-ways. She found Moriarty Chambers to be the last one in a terrace of six, its long windows overlooking the river.

'Do you think it was the Pope boys who took our things?' Lily chattered as Grace tried to compose herself to knock at the door. 'I bet it *was* them, for once when I let Matthew into our room he kept looking at my shell and saying that he liked it.'

Grace didn't remind Lily that she'd always told her to stay away from the Popes and that she should never have let him in the room in the first place, because none of that really mattered now. What mattered was that their lives were unravelling, and if James Solent couldn't help them then she had no idea what she was going to do next.

She climbed the stone steps to the front door of the big house and rang the bell.

Nothing happened.

'Ring again!' Lily called up from street level. 'Can I ring it this time?'

Grace ignored her and, after a polite interval, rang the bell again. Twice. It was eventually opened by an elderly man in a pinstriped suit.

'Yes?' he asked, frowning at Grace. It was not usual for women to enter the hallowed land belonging to the Inns of Court, and recently two prostitutes had come in through the gate as bold as anything, dressed scantily and flaunting the names of several most respectable barristers. How they'd come to be in possession of such information had not been discovered, but, as a consequence, security was supposed to have been stepped up.

Grace showed the business card. 'I'm looking for Mr James Solent.'

'Mr Solent is not available,' said the grey-suited man disdainfully. 'At least, not to such as you.'

'But he said I could call upon him. Please can you

tell me where to find him?'

'Certainly not. Haven't you heard of the confidentiality of the courts?' He looked over Grace's shoulder and saw Lily. 'Be gone, both of you,' he said. 'We don't allow the likes of you in here.'

Grace flushed. 'Could I just –' She wanted to ask if she could leave a message for Mr Solent, but the man was looking at her with such disgust that, knowing what he was thinking, her voice trailed away.

The door was shut in her face, the man gestured for her to clear off and stood glaring through the glass to make sure she did so.

Slowly, Grace went back down the steps.

'Was that the man who was going to help us?' Lily asked.

'No! No, of course it wasn't.'

'Isn't he here?'

Grace shook her head wordlessly. *Had* he been there? She'd seen several pairs of eyes looking out of the windows. Had he seen her and told the pinstriped man to send her away? Was he ashamed that he'd offered to help her?

'What shall we do now?'

'Well . . .' Grace fought to control herself. It would do no good at all to start crying, for then Lily would start and there would be no stopping her. 'We'll try and find the place where they give people soup, then . . . and then . . .' Then, perhaps, something else might occur to her. She fingered the other card in her pocket, thinking of Mrs Unwin's offer of work and lodging. She hadn't liked the woman, but if it came to it, she would have to go and seek her out.

Finding the soup kitchen at long last (for it was far away over the river in Southwark), they discovered that they were not allowed to have any actual soup, for all persons applying were required to bring with them a letter from their home Parish explaining why they were in need of such charity.

By this time, however, they were so hungry that Grace decided they should use two of their precious pennies to buy a hot potato each. They began eating these in the relative comfort of a pew in Southwark Cathedral, but after being moved on by a verger, ended up sitting on the stone steps that ran from the top to the bottom of London Bridge. It was not the most comfortable venue, for despite it being well past the end of the working day there were still a great deal of people around, and many purveyors of ham sandwiches and beers, so that with every mouthful they took they were jostled and hassled to buy this and that, and accidentally kicked more than once. Grace wondered very much at the enormous number of people there, but was not to know that a few years previously Mr Charles Dickens had set a gruesome murder scene from his most popular and famous book on these very steps, and the site now attracted the literary, the ghoulish and the plain curious in equal measure.

Darkness had fallen by the time they'd finished eating and Grace, knowing prices were cheaper on the Southwark side of the river, set herself the task of finding somewhere for them to stay for the night. After asking in a tavern (and turning down the offer of a shared room at four pence as being too expensive), she was directed to an old warehouse standing just by the Thames. The tattered, peeling advertising hoardings in the streets, the broken bottles and rubbish underfoot, and the ravens and seagulls squawking overhead made the area even more uninviting and dismal than Seven Dials, but Grace resolved to go on, for they had to sleep somewhere. The warehouse, when found, was a rickety building constructed of rusty corrugated iron. On the ground floor during the day animal bones were boiled to make glue and the nauseating smell permeated the first floor, which was divided by thin curtains into small, separate units at a charge of tuppence per night.

On being shown to their 'room', Grace asked the woman in charge if she knew of any casual work nearby.

The woman shook her head and gave a bitter laugh. 'Don't you think I'd be doing it if there was?'

'Is there really nothing at all? My sister and I are very hard workers,' Grace went on. 'Is there ever any packing work to be had in the warehouses?'

'None for the likes of us,' the woman said. 'If there is work, then it goes to the men, for they have families to keep. The only job for women round here is the usual one.'

'What's that?' Lily asked eagerly, but the woman merely laughed and made a vulgar gesture with her hand.

Many of the sleeping units were already taken up by regulars, watermen mostly, and the girls' neighbours were a married couple with two young children on one side, and on the other, three burly dockers. When night fell and the dockers went out to the nearest tavern, both girls, exhausted, fell asleep straight away. After midnight the men returned much the worse for wear, singing, shouting and falling all over the place, and woke not only the married couple and their children, but all the other residents. The married man fought the dockers, the children cried, his wife screamed, and on their own side of the curtain Grace and Lily sat huddled together, too scared to move.

By one o'clock in the morning most of the people in the warehouse seemed to be involved in the fight in some way or other, and at two o'clock someone went for a peeler. Order was soon restored, for the dockers had passed out by this time, and Grace and Lily fell into an uneasy sleep. When they were woken at six o'clock by the lighting of the boilers below them and the shouting of the workers, it was to discover that the last penny had gone from Grace's pocket and their shoes had been stolen off their feet.

Chapter Eleven

'Well, this morning we shall have to have a
Seven Dials breakfast,' Grace said to her
sister as they sat on the riverbank a little
later. The river was packed with smoking boats and
there was a stink in the air of hot oil, boiled animal
carcasses and something even more unsavoury, for
there was a tannery nearby which relied on the use of
fresh dung to treat the hides.

'A Seven Dials breakfast? What's that?' asked Lily
with interest.

'It's a joke,' Grace said. 'It's nothing. Nothing at all.'

'But how can it be a *breakfast*, then? I don't
understand.'

Grace squeezed her sister's hand. 'It's just a saying,

Lily. It's supposed to be droll.'

'I'd rather it was breakfast.'

Grace sighed, looking at the chugging, wheezing boats on the river and the engine smoke drifting across the water. She fingered the black-edged card in her pocket, the card bearing the address of the Unwin Undertaking Establishment, knowing this was their last hope. The weather was quite clement now, but she knew they would never survive on the streets of London in snow, fog and freezing rain. She was wondering how she was going to explain this job to Lily and – now that they were without shoes – if she looked respectable enough to call on Mrs Unwin about such a matter anyway.

Lily, the traces of tears still on her face, was counting the number of boats that went by. Every time she got to twenty she would start again, for that was as high as she could go. At last she tired of this and asked what they were going to do next.

'I've been thinking about a woman I met recently,' Grace said cautiously. 'Her family have an undertakers' establishment, and she once said I might be able to go to work for them as a mute.'

'What's that?'

'Someone who attends funerals dressed all in black, and looks sad.'

'Can I be a mute as well?'

'Yes. Perhaps,' Grace said. It couldn't be too difficult for someone to stand around looking mournful? Surely even Lily would be able to do that? She took the small card from her pocket. 'We'll go and find out, shall we?'

The undertaker's was at the far end of Oxford Street, off the Edgware Road and about half a mile from the great Marble Arch, which had recently been moved from its site in front of Buckingham Palace. The traffic here went round and round the arch in both directions, a horrendous swirling mess of noise and mayhem, with omnibuses fighting for space alongside horsemen, hackney coaches, broughams, heavy eight-wheeled wagons and sedate private carriages, and all accompanied by a tremendous hooting, shouting, neighing and cracking of whips.

The building bore a small, tactful notice:

The Unwin Undertaking Establishment
(Proprietor: Mr George Unwin)
Discretion is our Byword

The substantial two-storey red-brick house with decorative plaster and fancy brickwork had been built for a wealthy industrialist some forty years earlier. When the Unwins had purchased it with an inheritance from Mrs Unwin's parents a dozen years past, they'd changed the house from a family dwelling into a commercial concern. As the undertaking business became more successful, they had bought up the large mews area behind it, which included several stables, and over time had built a carpentry workshop, a stonemason's yard and garaging for hearses, together with various workrooms. Following this, the attic rooms in the house were made into makeshift bedrooms for those females who worked for the Unwins and needed accommodation, while the blacksmith, stable boys and carpenter's lads bunked in the hayloft above the stables.

The front two reception rooms of the house were where relatives of the departed were taken to choose what sort of farewell they intended to give their loved ones. One room had an entire wall made up of squares of different coffin wood, plus examples of brass and silver nameplates, while the other, larger room (painted a deep and soothing red) was where they decided more delicate matters, such as what type of mattress, pillow and interlining was wanted for the coffin interior. An alcove in this room served as a study and contained a substantial mahogany desk with various brochures from which the bereaved could choose funeral flowers, marble memorials, the type of procession and number of horses, what mutes and plumes and palls to use and other essential items. Behind these two reception areas were the various workrooms, a private parlour and a kitchen. A comforting fire burned in the red room summer and winter, and this perhaps calmed the mourners and lessened the shock of finding out how much the funeral was going to cost.

Everything the newly bereaved family might require could be supplied here – apart from clothing, so when a family came to arrange a funeral they were warmly recommended to visit Mr Sylvester Unwin's Oxford Street warehouse for their mourning garments. Mr Sylvester Unwin, of course, returned this compliment, and the substantial profits from the two businesses were shared.

Grace did not know the extent of the vast empire fronted by the shiny, black door, or she may have felt more nervous than she did about knocking on it. She made an effort to brush Lily's skirts clean of dust, then straightened her shawl around her head and pushed the more unruly of her curls out of view. If she kept her hands clasped in front of her it would hide the muddy streak at the front of her gown, she thought, and if she did not sit down, then perhaps the fact that she didn't have shoes would escape notice.

'Do I look passable?' she asked Lily.

'Of course.' Lily hardly glanced at her, for she was staring at a nearby pie shop and sniffing the air like a dog. 'If they let us be mutes, will they give us some food?'

'I don't know,' said Grace, distracted. What if she were turned away; what if *this* business card proved as useless as the other? She tapped at the door, but so quietly that the noise was swallowed by the sound of the traffic and she had to tap again before a housemaid opened it. She had been about to bob a curtsey, but she stopped at the sight of Grace and Lily, for they were not at all the sort of persons who normally called at the

Unwins and their appearance didn't seem to merit this courtesy.

'I'm afraid we don't do pauper funerals,' said the maid, whose name was Rose. She spoke kindly enough, thinking that by the look of the two girls they didn't seem to be vulgar people.

Grace bobbed her own curtsey, and nudged Lily to do the same. 'Good morning,' she said. 'We aren't here to arrange a funeral, but to see Mrs Unwin.'

'You won't get nothing from her,' said the maid. 'You'd be best going round the back and trying to beg something from the blacksmith. He looks fierce but he's known to be a soft touch. He's sure to find a crust or two for you.'

At the mention of food, Lily turned her attention to the maid. 'I was hoping for a pie.'

The maid hid a smile. Oh, Lord, she thought, but one of them is simple-minded.

Grace felt herself flush. 'We're not here to beg,' she said. She held out the Unwins' business card. 'Mrs Unwin asked me to call on her.'

'Oh!' The maid's eyes widened. 'Sorry, miss.'

Leading Grace and Lily into one of the reception rooms, she planned what she'd say to the other girls: *'Poor as church mice – you should have seen them! No shoes* (for of course she had noticed this straight away), *and one of them simple! And with the mistress's business card, if you please.'* She indicated a plush sofa. 'If you'd like to sit down, miss.'

'No, we'll stand, thank you,' said Grace, although Lily had already taken a seat and was looking around her in awe, gently bouncing up and down and showing grimy feet with each movement of her skirts. Grace knew she should have begged her to show some decorum, but somehow couldn't summon the energy. She looked around as well: the windows were hung with silk drapes in a soothing shade of grey and the walls were plain, all the better to display examples of the statuary available to order from the Unwin memorial workshop. One could have a cherub, angel, broken column, obelisk, flaming torch, covered urn, or even, if you were very rich, a magnificent depiction of Hope weeping upon a rock.

Mrs Unwin was some time coming, being busy in a workroom devising a new moneymaking innovation she'd seen in a foreign graveyard: immortelles – little arrangements of everlasting flowers under glass domes. She was reluctant to put this trial product aside, but when she did so and entered the waiting room, she almost reared back in disgust, for she prided herself on having a nose for the lower orders.

She tried to breathe as shallowly as possible. 'Yes?' she asked faintly.

'Mrs Unwin, thank you for seeing us.'

It was the girl standing by the window who'd spoken and, really, Mrs Unwin thought, now that one was looking at her, one could tell from her tone and accent that she was not as coarse as her appearance at first suggested. Her face had a certain purity, a gravity of expression – and hadn't she seen her before, somewhere?

'What is it you want?' asked Mrs Unwin.

'Excuse my temerity in calling, but I met you some weeks ago at Brookwood,' Grace said. 'You were kind enough to say that if I ever needed employment, you would take me on as a mute.'

'Ah.' Mrs Unwin hesitated. The girl had just the right sort of tragic face to complement a grieving family, and she was, in fact, always looking for young women who were discreet and sensible enough to work in the funeral trade (for most had an instinctive horror of the business, believing that it was bad luck to work among the dead). She did not, however, want this girl to feel she actually needed her, for then she might ask for more than the paltry few shillings a week she was willing to pay. 'Things have changed a little since then,' said Mrs Unwin, shaking her head as if to dismiss her. 'The funeral business is not a thriving one, and we have several good mutes already.'

'I can also sew and embroider,' Grace said. 'I'm a very hard worker.'

Mrs Unwin tried to look unconvinced, although someone who could be a mute *and* embroiderer would be extremely useful to her.

'I'm excellent with my needle,' said Grace fervently, seeing Mrs Unwin waver. 'I can assure you of my utmost dedication to the job. My sister, too, would serve you well.'

Mrs Unwin turned her attention to the girl sitting on the sofa and saw a lanky girl, heavy-jawed and plain, scratching along her arms as if troubled by fleas. *This* one did not have the qualities of her sister. Mrs Unwin shook her head. 'I'm afraid that even if I could find you a position, I couldn't take on your sister. She would never make a mute.'

'But I couldn't come here without her!' Grace looked at Mrs Unwin with some desperation. 'We've always lived together.'

'Then I'm sorry.' Mrs Unwin turned away, shaking her head again. She was certainly not in the business of charity, to take on two girls in the place of one.

This might have been the end of the matter, except that Mr George Unwin happened to be passing the red room on his way to check on something with one of the stonemasons. Hearing his wife speaking to someone (and hoping that it was a wealthy customer), he waited to hear more.

Grace tried – and failed – to maintain her calm. 'Please,' she said to Mrs Unwin, 'you are my last hope. We have no father, and due to circumstances beyond our control Lily and I have lost our lodgings. Our money has been stolen and with winter coming on . . .' She stopped here, put her hand to her mouth and bit her fingers to prevent herself from crying.

Mr Unwin heard the words '*We have no father*' and the name *Lily*, and stood, suddenly rapt. It was a long shot, he thought with mounting excitement, but the missing Parkes had to be somewhere.

'I'm sorry,' said Mrs Unwin briskly, 'but there are many in London who are in dire circumstances. I can't take them all on! I suggest you apply to one of the charities. Or the workhouse.'

Realising that they were being rejected, Lily burst into noisy sobs just as Mr Unwin swept into the room.

'Forgive me, my dear! Forgive me!' he said to his wife. 'I was passing and couldn't help overhearing your conversation.'

Mrs Unwin frowned. The hiring and firing of staff was always left to her.

'This is a very sad tale I've just heard,' he said to the two girls. 'Your father dead, you say, and you've lost your lodgings? And is your mother dead, too?'

Grace nodded, startled by this sudden intrusion.

'Our papa sailed away to make his fortune,' Lily blurted out, wiping her nose on her sleeve. 'He might come back one day, mightn't he?' she appealed to Grace.

'Perhaps,' Grace said in a low voice.

'And what have you been doing since your mother died?'

'We . . . went into an orphanage,' Grace said, and glanced at Lily warningly not to say any more.

'And how old are you both now?' George Unwin asked.

'I think I am seventeen.' Lily looked at her sister for confirmation.

Grace nodded. 'I am almost sixteen.'

'And how long has your poor father been gone, Miss . . . ?'

'Parkes. We are Grace and Lily Parkes,' Grace said, and, looking at Lily to try and stop her bouncing on the sofa, missed the flash of utter joy which passed over the face of Mr Unwin. 'Father has been gone over fifteen years,' she added.

As Mr Unwin said to his wife later, he had never heard anything so marvellous in his entire life. 'Sad, exceedingly sad,' he said, endeavouring to stop himself whooping with glee. 'Don't you think so, my dear?' he said to Mrs Unwin.

His wife stared at him, wondering if he had gone mad.

'Can we not afford to offer these two well-born young ladies a little charity?'

'*Charity?*' The very word was abhorrent to Mrs Unwin, reeking as it did of fusty clothes, workhouses and fleas.

He pointed at Grace. 'This young lady, with training, would make an excellent mute, surely?'

'Yes, I had already –'

'And this one . . .' He hesitated for a moment, then said, 'This one could be trained, too, I'm sure.'

'What on earth as?' said his wife.

'A maid!' he announced. 'And Miss Charlotte needs a maid!'

Mrs Unwin looked at her husband as if he had

106

completely lost his wits. It was true, their daughter was sixteen and would soon need a maid of her own, but certainly not this gawky, dim-looking girl. Mr Unwin returned a look to his wife. This said that she was to go along with him for now, *only for now*, and he would explain everything later.

Grace pressed her lips together nervously. What Mrs Unwin said next would determine their fate.

'Well,' said Mrs Unwin, 'I suppose we could take your sister on at our home in Kensington.' She looked at Lily doubtfully. 'Would she be all right there, without you?'

Grace nodded, putting aside the reservations she felt. 'We are used to working together, of course, but as long as I know she's in good hands, and we could see each other sometimes . . .' She touched Lily's shoulder, praying that she wouldn't say or do anything untoward. 'How would you like to learn to be a maid-servant, Lily?'

Lily looked from her sister to the Unwins and back again. She didn't want to live apart from Grace, but it seemed that staying together wasn't an option. And anything would be better than spending another night in that warehouse.

'We couldn't pay you much,' said Mrs Unwin quickly. 'As neither of you are trained, it would be like an apprenticeship for you both. You'd have board and lodging, of course, and perhaps one shilling a week each.'

Grace smiled, deeply relieved and grateful to the Unwins. She thought that at Brookwood the woman had mentioned the sum of five shillings just to appear as a mute at one funeral, but really she would be pleased enough just to be off the streets, sheltered and fed. And to think that Lily was going to be sheltered, fed *and* trained as a maid – it was more than she'd ever hoped for.

'If you bid your goodbyes to each other now, I'll have Rose walk your sister across the park to Kensington,' said Mrs Unwin. She looked around the room. 'Where are your things?'

'We'll send for them later,' Grace said. Lily looked at her in surprise, seemed about to say something and then thought better of it.

As Mr and Mrs Unwin disappeared into one of the other rooms, Grace took Lily's hands in her own. 'You have a real chance now to learn to be a maidservant,' she said. 'Do everything that you're directed to do, work as hard as you can and always be willing and polite. It won't be for ever. We must both save as much as we can and hope to be together again one day soon.'

Lily rather excitedly kissed her sister on both cheeks and promised to be good. Grace, for a change, was the one who wept.

Chapter Twelve

Mr George Unwin, needing to speak to his cousin urgently, sent a message asking to meet him for a quick snifter at Barker's that afternoon. By the time his drinking companion arrived, the undertaker had already drunk a double scotch.

'What's all this?' said his cousin, waving his cigar at the empty glass. 'Got something to celebrate, have we?'

'We have!' said George Unwin. 'Oh, most certainly we have.'

'What is it, then? New wave of cholera hit London? Massed funerals all round?'

'Even better!' He looked ridiculously pleased with himself. 'I've landed 'em!'

'Landed what?'

'Two plump pigeons!'

His cousin began to cut his cigar. 'Didn't know you

were a shooting man. And where do you shoot around here?'

'Not *literally*, old chap. I've caught the heiress!'

'What?' He stopped fiddling with the cigar immediately. 'The legendary Mrs Parkes and her daughter?'

'Almost,' said George Unwin. 'The mother is underground in a box, and it appears that there's another child that the father didn't know about – born after he left.'

'Damned if there is!' said the other in astonishment.

'What's more, at least one of them is simple-minded.'

'Better and better. And where are they now? Got them under lock and key, have you?'

'I certainly have. They're right under our noses, working for the Unwin family. Discretion is our byword, eh?'

'It most definitely is!' Smiling to himself, the second man restarted the ceremony of cutting and tapping the end of his cigar on the marble-topped table. 'Capital,' he murmured, 'capital. And by way of a coincidence, I found out something this week on that very subject.'

George Unwin looked at his cousin expectantly. He never ceased to wonder at this man who, as well as managing the mourning warehouse, had fingers in so many pies: this manufacturer, that charity, fine wines, import, export, offal into dog meat, toadying to the rich, feeding the poor and taking as much as he could from both. People said he would be Lord Mayor of London one day.

'The father – the Parkes man – died abroad.'

'Good, good . . . makes things easier.'

'Died where his extremely large fortune had been made, in the Americas, by all accounts.' He began drawing hard on the cigar to get it going. 'And what I'm thinking now that you've got her in the bag is that the ten per cent being offered for finding her may not be quite enough. I mean, there are *two* of us.'

'You think we should get more?'

'More?' Sylvester Unwin asked. 'I think we should get the lot. I think you should make the girl part of the Unwin family circle – adopt her if you have to – and then gently acquire the money on her behalf.' He paused for thought. 'Yes, you may need to adopt her, but you must be canny about it.'

'How d'you mean?'

'You don't want it to look as if you only adopted her when you found out she was an heiress, do you?'

'Certainly not!'

'So we'll have to have the adoption papers forged and backdated ten years.'

'And what will the girl have to say about that?'

'Nothing much! You say that she's simple?'

George Unwin nodded.

'Then it should be easy – with a little persuasion – to convince her that she's been living with you for ten years or more.'

George Unwin nodded again. 'Should be . . . should be. And what about the other girl? The sister?'

'No one knows about her, and she doesn't know about the inheritance. We'll keep it that way. Maybe we can send her away on a nice long journey with no return ticket.'

George Unwin clapped his cousin on the back. 'An excellent idea,' he said. 'Excellent! By heck, no wonder they call you Sly!'

> HYDE PARK – 'the park' par excellence – is the great fashionable promenade of London. For two or three hours every afternoon, the particular section of the drive which happens that year to be 'the fashion' is densely thronged with carriages moving round and round at little more than a walking pace, and every now and then coming to a dead-lock.

Dickens's Dictionary of London, 1888

Chapter Thirteen

'Come *on*, can't you? Hurry! I've got to take you right across the park and then go back again.'

Rose, the housemaid who'd opened the Unwins' door, pulled at Lily's hand in an effort to get her to move along, but having passed the park's carriage drive – which, as always, had been over-full of the fashionable – they had reached Rotten Row and Lily was staring, entranced, at the immaculately dressed horsewomen in their tailored riding habits and shiny top hats. As their horses clip-clopped past, each rider wished the other the compliments of the day in formal manner, lifting their silver- or gold-tipped cane as they did so. Occasionally a gentleman rider came along, all polished leather boots and jangling stirrups, calling greetings and raising his top hat to every attractive lady.

'Why are they all out and riding their horses now – in the middle of the day?' Lily asked Rose.

'Why?' Rose answered. 'Because they want to, that's why.'

'Haven't they any work to do?'

Rose gave a snort of laughter. 'Not they!'

'Are they all very rich?'

'I should say so.'

A lady and gentleman trotted by together under the golden-leaved, fast-falling trees, each horse lifting its hooves in perfect unison with the other. Rose looked at them searchingly, for she knew that sometimes Queen Victoria and Prince Albert took a little riding exercise together in the park and, having seen them once, she very much hoped to see them again. Especially Albert, whom she'd thought a *very* handsome gentleman.

'They're so rich that they don't need to work,' she reiterated, pulling at Lily's hand again. 'Not like me. Or you.' She stared at her companion. Whatever must the master and mistress be thinking of to take on a girl like this, shoe-less and dunder-headed? The other girl seemed decent enough and could possibly act the mute and attain the high funereal standards expected by the Unwins, but really, there was no hope at all for this baggage. A maid for Miss Charlotte? Oh, Lord, she was glad she didn't have to tell her!

By threatening and persuading in equal measure, Rose managed to get Lily away from the horse riders, across Hyde Park and into Kensington Gardens, where they were then delayed by Lily wanting to have a closer look at the nannies rounding the pond with their perambulators.

'Oh, may we go and look at the babies?' she asked. 'Just for a moment.'

Rose was about to say no, but gave in, for she very much liked looking at the babies herself. What was more, she knew that lace-trimmed royal babies were sometimes to be seen taking the air there. On reaching the pond, however, Rose rather wished she hadn't permitted such a thing, for Lily would keep staring hard under the pram hoods and then shaking her head dismissively. What she was actually doing, although Rose couldn't have known it, was comparing the prettiness of the babies to that of Primrose, her late doll, and finding the babies sadly lacking.

'We must go now,' Rose said, after half a dozen babies had been approached and rejected. 'Madam knows exactly how long it takes to walk across the park to Hardwood House, and if I'm late back I'll be for it.'

'I like babies,' Lily said, at last allowing herself to be led away.

'Mmm,' came the reply.

'My sister had one once.'

Rose looked at her, startled. Surely she couldn't be talking about that quiet and anxious girl she'd arrived with? 'Are you sure?'

Lily nodded, frowning deeply. 'I *think* so.'

Rose didn't take the questioning any further. The girl was just spinning a tale.

Hardwood House was in quite the smartest road at the country end of Kensington, looking out on to a flourishing, tree-lined square to which only its residents had keys. Each house was tall and of noble proportions, with steps running up to the front door which were whitened every other day by scullery maids. The front doors were painted in gloss paint, and the brass doorknockers and letter boxes polished to a mirror shine every day of the week bar Sundays.

Lily stared at the house: four storeys up and one down. When they'd been with Mama she could remember that they'd had a whole house to themselves, but that had just been two rooms down and two up. *This* house looked as if it might contain twenty rooms – or even more if she knew what number came next.

'It's a very big house. Who else lives here?' she asked Rose.

'Who else? No one, just Mr and Mrs Unwin and Miss Charlotte. Oh, and the servants, of course. But they hardly count,' she added.

'All these floors and windows, just for them?' Lily stood on tiptoe to see in the front parlour and took away a jumbled impression of plump sofas and chairs, lavish fabrics, patterned wallpaper and occasional tables on which objets d'art fought for space.

'Yes, just for them. Now, round the back quickly!' Rose said, for Lily had been about to go up the front steps. 'Servants don't use this entrance. Not *ever*.'

Lily had peered into the Unwins' front parlour, not knowing that she'd seen a room at the very pinnacle of fashion: walls newly papered with Mr William Morris's wallpaper, cluttered with armchairs, tables, stuffed birds in glass boxes and sideboards on which stood china elephants, cupids, depictions of Victoria and Albert, amusing items from abroad and glazed jardinières containing copious amounts of fernery. All rooms above stairs were furnished to this height of opulence, but as soon as one opened the door which led downwards, different standards prevailed, for the domestic offices were in a dark, stone-flagged space and the cooking appliances, sinks and fireplaces were horribly work intensive. There was no hot water, the sinks were of lead and, in order to be able to see what you were doing, candles had to be kept burning on the brightest of days. The vast kitchen range contained two coal grates, a bread and a pastry oven and several rings for pans, but the fires needed constant care: raddling, coaxing and feeding from before dawn to dusk and beyond if they were not to go out in the middle of preparations for a meal.

It was in the kitchen that Rose now introduced Lily to the other domestic staff: to Mrs Beaman the cook-housekeeper, Blossom and Lizzie the parlourmaids, and Ella the kitchen-maid.

The servants, as one, reacted to the newcomer with dismay and some amusement, gasping at her grimy feet, sniffing conspicuously when she wriggled out of her shawl and visibly shuddering when they saw the flea bites (gained after the overnight stay in the warehouse) on her arms. The only person a little pleased about Lily's arrival was Ella, who realised that she was no longer going to be the lowliest member of the household.

Rose, who was actually quite warm-hearted, became embarrassed at how Lily was being regarded by the others and told the girl to go outside and take a little walk around the garden.

'The state of her!' said Blossom the moment the back door closed.

'Who knows what germs she might be harbouring – why, she doesn't look as if she's ever been on the receiving end of a bar of soap!' said Lizzie.

Mrs Beaman heaved her bosom. 'Master wants to take her on as a lady's maid?' she asked no one in partic-ular. 'Master must have gone mad.'

'Mistress did look quite stunned when she told me to bring her over,' Rose volunteered.

'Anyway, apart from what she looks like, does she know what a servant's duties are?' Lizzie went on, with a superior smile. 'Has she been in service before? Can she iron a pleated petticoat? Can she dress hair?'

'Can she, my arse!' said Mrs Beaman, and the others dissolved into shocked giggles. 'Did he give instructions as to her dress?' she asked. She looked down at herself. She and the rest of the house servants were wearing white linen pinafores over deep-blue cotton dresses. 'Is she to wear our livery? She hasn't even got any shoes!'

'Where did she come from?' Blossom demanded.

Rose shrugged. 'All I know is that she has a sister who's been taken on by the Unwins as a mute. I think they had to take both girls, or the first one wouldn't have come. Mr Unwin will probably tell you more tonight,' she added, for the family came back to their Kensington home in the evenings.

'The Unwins – taking on charity cases? There's a first!' said Mrs Beaman, as she and the others stood in a line at the back window, shaking their heads and watching as Lily walked around the garden, smelling flowers, squeezing pungent herbs between her fingers and admiring the abundance of vegetables growing in the walled garden.

It was sad that she and Grace had to live separately, she was thinking, but she'd been promised that it wouldn't be for ever. And just look at all the things to eat here: the shiny, red tomatoes, the marrows and onions and fat, white cauliflowers – not to mention the chickens pecking in the gravel. She was willing to bet that no one ever went hungry here! Used to taking food where she could get it, she reached up, picked several ripe blackberries and popped them into her mouth. When Mrs Beaman rapped hard on the window in order to admonish her, she merely looked back, waved and smiled.

'The cheek of it! *That* one will never make a lady's maid,' said Mrs Beaman.

'Or any sort of a maid!' said Blossom.

'Certainly not until she's had a bath,' said Lizzie, sniffing the air where Lily had left a faint, foul smell of boiled animal bones behind her.

Rose looked at Mrs Beaman, knowing that the very latest in all-enveloping hot-water showers had recently been installed in the house. 'Do you think perhaps –'

'No, she certainly could *not* use the bathroom,' snapped Mrs Beaman. 'The very idea!'

Rose bade her goodbyes and walked back across the park to the Unwin Undertaking Establishment while the debate about the new servant continued. After Blossom had declared it an impossibility to be in the room with anyone smelling as bad as Lily did, Mrs Beaman decided that she should, under the care of Ella, be given a penny and taken to the public baths in Hammersmith to be scrubbed and disinfected to the standard expected of a maidservant in a gentleman's house. Before they set off, Mrs Beaman found several items of clothing which had been discarded by Miss Charlotte as being too awfully unfashionable, and a pair of shoes, soles worn as thin as paper, which she had thrown out herself. In this way, Mrs Beaman hoped to improve and enhance the new maid before introducing her to the daughter of the house.

'Now she's cleaned up, let her take in afternoon tea!' Blossom urged Mrs Beaman much later that afternoon.

'Oh yes, do!' Lizzie said, winking at Blossom. 'Let's see what Miss Charlotte has to say about her.'

'I'm not sure,' said Mrs Beaman. She gazed doubtfully at Lily, who, although clean and freshly dressed, still did not look quite right for a gentleman's house.

There was something ungainly about her: her feet stuck out at angles, like a duck's, her aimless expression and her dark auburn hair – despite being washed three times and having had a comb dragged through it – still a mess of strands and knots. The colour of Miss Charlotte's cast-off gown did not suit her, either, its pastel green seeming to emphasise the shining hue of Lily's face, which – due to the strong carbolic soap used at the baths – had unfortunately come up the colour of a pillar box. Nevertheless, on the ringing of the drawing-room bell for tea, Mrs Beaman equipped her with a white apron and a tray of silver tea things and led the way into the drawing room to introduce her to Miss Charlotte Unwin.

Miss Charlotte was sixteen years old and, having always lived a life of luxury, comfort and plenty, had the glowing skin, bright eyes and abundance of thick golden hair to prove it. She also had a personal dressmaker, a wardrobe of the very latest gowns and every little frou-frou novelty to which a fashionable young lady in the year of 1861 might be entitled. She was very much looking forward to the following year when she would 'come out' in society and be presented to Queen Victoria, for then would follow a whole season of dances, hunt balls and lavish dinners at which (she felt sure) she would be the glittering centre of attention. Her mother had promised her a lady's maid of her own for this period and she was happily anticipating some smart young woman who would not only be capable of dressing her hair in ringlets and repairing a lace collar, but also know which tiara should be worn on which occasion.

Sadly, Lily was not that young woman.

'Miss Charlotte,' said Mrs Beaman, not without a little well-concealed delight, 'may I present Lily?'

She indicated to Lily that she was to put the tea things down on the nearest table, but Lily was staring about with her mouth agape, her eyes swivelling around the room as she took in the windows, the walls, the floor and the furniture with gasps of pleasure and amazement. On the mantelpiece, she suddenly spotted a jug painted with the familiar bluebirds, and crashing the tea things down on the table, she hobbled painfully (Mrs Beaman's shoes were too small) towards it.

'This is like the teapot Mama had!' she said. She excitedly scratched the flea bites along her arms. 'Did you get it from Uncle's?'

Miss Charlotte stared at her with astonishment. It was as if, Mrs Beaman was to report later, she had witnessed a unicorn entering the drawing room to serve cucumber sandwiches.

'Grace had to pawn *our* teapot – she got a shilling for it,' Lily said, beaming at Miss Charlotte. She picked up the jug and, moving swiftly to prevent a possible catastrophe, Mrs Beaman rounded the sofa and took it from her. 'Do you go to Uncle's often?' she asked Miss Charlotte.

'Mrs Beaman, who is this person?' Charlotte asked faintly.

Mrs Beaman couldn't reply for a while, for she was dodging around and about behind Lily, taking from her whatever she picked up and trying to move between her and the most delicate items. Finally, as Lily stopped and stroked the heavy velvet curtains as if they were the pelt of an animal, she managed to say, 'Lily is new to the household, miss. She's just been taken on by your father and mother.'

'I can hardly believe it. What as?'

'As, I believe, a lady's maid.'

'Who on earth for?'

Mrs Beaman coughed delicately. 'For yourself, Miss Charlotte.'

Charlotte Unwin let out a little scream of horror which was heard by her mother and father, who had just arrived home. Striding into the parlour and quickly sizing up the situation, Mr Unwin told Lily to go back into the kitchen immediately. She did so, giving him a beaming smile and taking a spiced biscuit from the tray.

Mr Unwin gestured for the cook to stay and, while

Mrs Unwin was soothing Charlotte, reached into his inside pocket to pull out a ten-shilling note. 'Mrs Beaman, I thank you in advance for doing your best in a difficult situation,' he began.

Mrs Beaman bobbed a curtsey, trying not to look at the value of the note but hoping for a pound.

'The fact is, the new young person in question . . .'

'Lily?' Mrs Beaman asked. The note was the wrong colour for five pounds, she couldn't help thinking.

'Lily,' Mr Unwin confirmed, 'has been taken on by Mrs Unwin and myself as a charity case. Her sister will be working as a mute for us, and was anxious that Lily should be looked after, too, because she is rather . . . rather . . .' At a loss how best to put it, he made a wavy motion with both hands about his head.

'Quite, sir,' said Mrs Beaman. Obvious, that was.

'I'm afraid I assured her sister that Lily could be taught to be a maid, but you and I know, of course, that she would not make a very satisfactory one. She could, perhaps, clean boots or somesuch?'

'Perhaps, sir,' came the doubtful reply.

'I'm sure you will do your best with her,' Mr Unwin went on, unfolding the note, 'and thank you for your understanding. There's just one other thing: Mrs Unwin and I are very interested – in a charitable way – about this young person.'

Mrs Beaman raised her eyebrows slightly. 'Yes, sir.'

'We are anxious to know how it can happen that girls from good families fall on hard times. So that it might be prevented in future, you see.' He waited for Mrs Beaman to nod and continued, 'Perhaps if she mentions anything about her background, you wouldn't mind passing it on to us.'

Mrs Beaman tried to hide her surprise. 'If you wish, sir.'

'Thank you. And of course this matter must remain completely confidential between ourselves.'

'Of course, sir.'

The banknote was pressed into her palm at last and Mrs Beaman bobbed another curtsey and went back to the kitchen, frowning a little at its value. Only ten shillings! Well, as long as he kept them coming . . .

A whispered consultation between the three Unwins followed in the parlour. Mrs Unwin had been told the whole story and the likely amount of the inheritance (and was already planning to buy a seaside villa in newly fashionable Brighton), and now Charlotte was informed of the situation. Both were then told of the new plan to 'adopt' Lily.

Mr Unwin had been rather fearful of Charlotte's reaction, but she – eagerly anticipating the Season – readily undertook to try and persuade Lily that she'd been adopted some years previously, in return for a smartly painted gig. With this, and a competent lady's maid of her own, she was quite sure that she would take London society by storm . . .

Chapter Fourteen

The following day, by the round pond in Kensington Gardens, an extremely elegant woman, holding a small child by the hand, stopped to admire a baby in a smart new bassinette.

'What a beautiful baby!' she said. 'A little cherub!'

Mrs Robinson paused and smiled. 'He *is*, isn't he?' she said. 'I know one shouldn't really praise one's own, but really, my husband and I think he's absolutely adorable.'

The woman looked once more at the baby, and then at Mrs Robinson, as if comparing them. 'Lovely features. And I think he has your eyes!'

The new mother went slightly pink with pleasure. 'Yes, they do say that.'

The other woman picked up her own small child and held him aloft so that he could see into the

126

bassinette. 'See the baby, George! Such a pretty thing!' Young George seemed more impressed with the boats on the pond, however, and the woman put him down again. 'You have no nanny, I see.'

Mrs Robinson shook her head. 'Never! I wouldn't let anyone else look after Baby. Baby is precious!'

'Quite. I have three children – quite well spaced out in age – and I nursed each one myself.' She smiled slightly. 'To tell you the truth, I mostly did it because I was worried that they might come to prefer Nanny to me!'

Mrs Robinson laughed.

'And where does he get his colouring from?' The woman looked once more into the bassinette. 'I can see curls under that bonnet! Your husband has the auburn hair, does he?'

Mrs Robinson started, as if she'd been asked an impertinent question. 'Yes. Yes, he does!' she said quite defiantly.

The woman looked at her, wondering at what she'd said, and nodded very formally. 'Then may I wish you good morning.'

'Good morning,' said Mrs Robinson. She was already regretting the tone she'd used with the woman, but people went on so much about appearances and whether Baby looked like her or Stanley, and really, it was none of their business. She knew what Stanley would say – that they didn't mean anything and were only being friendly. She really must try to remember that and not get upset . . .

Epitaph on a tombstone

Chapter Fifteen

F our weeks later, Grace, standing outside an imposing church in central London, shivered in her black crêpe gown and cloak. The weather was growing colder now and crêpe, although the most fashionable fabric for both the bereaved and the funeral mute, was not comfortable to wear, for it didn't keep out the wind and, at the faintest hint of damp in the air, would attach itself clammily to one's limbs.

Grace and the girl she was partnered with, Jane, were positioned each side of the church porch, twin harbingers of doom in their black hoods and veiling, holding staffs with trailing ribbons. They had been booked by the bereaved family to stand in front of the door maintaining expressions of poignant and awful grief for six hours, until the main funeral party arrived and the interment commenced, so had been there since seven o'clock that morning.

It was to be a grand and lavish funeral. The family of Cedric Welland-Scropes, the dead man, owned a large mausoleum in the church grounds where up to twenty family members could be entombed, so there would be two ceremonies: one in the church and one at the corpse's final resting place on the far side of the churchyard. A feather-bearer was to lead the procession of mourners from the deceased's home to the church, the horses would have newly-dyed black plumes, a richly fringed velvet pall would cover the oak coffin in its glass carriage and there would be at least twelve funeral carriages behind this. For all those attending there would be gifts of black silk scarves, hatbands and gloves.

Grace had tried several times to begin a conversation with her matching mute in order to make the time go more quickly, but Jane had lived and worked at the funeral parlour for ten years now, since a child of nine, and took her role extremely seriously. She had no difficulty in maintaining a tragic face at all times and sometimes actually managed to shed tears by convincing herself that she, personally, had suffered a death. Anxious and apologetic, she spoke little when off duty, and not at all when on, for Mrs Unwin had impressed upon her that a mute should be just that – mute – and she believed that what Mrs Unwin said was law. Grace, therefore, after trying to persuade her to speak, fell to silence and passed the time watching preparations for a pauper burial not thirty feet from where they were standing.

St Jude's was one of the few old churches in London to still have space for new bodies and here, in an unkempt and uncared-for part of the churchyard, two gravediggers were breaking up the earth in a rough space about ten feet across. As they dug, they came across a selection of human remains which had been lurking near the surface from previous burials: here a femur, there a collar bone and once an entire skull pulled from a great clod of earth. Unmoved by their macabre finds, they whistled as they dug, swore merrily at each other and exchanged witticisms. They could work as they pleased that morning, for, it being paupers from the workhouse to be buried, there were no relatives or friends of the deceased to be considered and no need for any attempt at piety.

To one side of the pit stood a donkey and cart. This held three ragged, clumsily rolled bundles, for none of the paupers had been afforded even the most basic of coffins, but were carelessly wrapped in mean pieces of cloth provided by the Parish. A hank of human hair and an unwrapped leg protruded from one of these bundles, and Grace, noticing these, shuddered. At least, she thought, Mama had been spared the awful fate of a pauper's grave, for there had been money enough when she'd died to give her a proper funeral and private burial space. Kindly neighbours had arranged this, although she could barely remember it. Grace silently thanked Mrs Smith the midwife for her guidance, too, for without this and the fare to

Brookwood, her own baby would have gone into a mass grave such as the one before her.

At midday the gravediggers stopped to eat their newspaper-wrapped hunks of bread and cheese and, with no one to consider, didn't hesitate to throw the paper, discarded rind and apple cores into the burial pit after. ('Did you see that?' Grace asked her companion, shocked, but Jane remained silent, staring dutifully ahead.) Their rough dinner finished, one of the men disappeared to the nearby tavern, The Fox and Grapes, and came back with a jug of ale which he balanced on top of the dug-up skull, causing the other man a great deal of merriment. The jug being emptied, work resumed and, having dug deeply enough, the pauper bodies were thrown in the pit, covered with earth and a light sprinkling of lime, and the gravediggers went back to the tavern to drink their wages.

Grace and Jane carried on waiting. Waiting, Grace thought, was not altogether agreeable, for it afforded too much time for worrying about her plight and, more especially, that of Lily. Her sister had always been protected, first by Mama and then by Grace; she'd had allowances made for her simplicity and been sheltered from the harsh truths of life. Who was looking after her welfare now? Was she being treated kindly at the Unwins'? Grace had asked Mrs Unwin several times how her sister was faring, but had only been told 'The girl is doing as well as one might expect' and 'You can't make a silk purse out of a sow's ear' – statements which did nothing to allay her concerns. Grace knew that she'd feel easier in her mind if she could visit Lily and see for herself, but so far she'd been unable to get to the Kensington house. The Unwins allowed their servants to have Sundays reasonably free, but on this day they were expected to go to the public baths, do their personal washing, darn their stockings, make repairs to clothes, press and brush down their mourning clothes and attend church morning and evening. However, Grace had calculated that it would take about an hour to walk to Kensington, and decided that she would get up very early the following Sunday, complete all her chores before the church service at noon and set off for Kensington straight after.

In the weeks that she'd been working for the Unwin family she'd learned a lot. The first few days had been deeply miserable while she tried to come to terms with all that had happened and endeavoured to accept that, from now on, this was how her life was going to be: she'd be separated from Lily; working long, hard hours (for when not attending funerals she was busy making shrouds, sewing coffin linings or embroidering mourning souvenirs); sharing a tiny room with Jane and having neither privacy nor a life of her own. But at least she had no concerns about the rent, she kept telling herself, or where the next crust was coming from, or about dying of cold on the London streets. Life at the Unwins' wasn't hard in the way it had been hard before, with starvation, destitution and the workhouse always at her shoulder, but hard in that she worked fourteen hours a day in miserable conditions and had no one she could call a friend.

She had a feeling, too, of something like home-sickness. This didn't make sense when her last home had been a bare and awful room and she and Lily had near starved to death in it, but that was the only word that came close to her feeling of being lonely and dispossessed.

All of it was that man's fault, she knew that for certain; the man with one hand who'd come in the night and destroyed everything. If *that* hadn't happened then she wouldn't have run away; she would have stayed at the training establishment with Lily, learned to be a teacher and in time, perhaps, made a good marriage. Now that decent and ordinary life had slipped from her grasp, and what lay ahead seemed dark. She was a fallen woman, and would remain so.

Cold and weary from standing for such a long time, Grace wriggled her feet in her cheap black boots to try and warm them.

'Aren't you freezing?' she asked Jane, still motion-less beside her. 'Don't you long to be sitting in front of a good coal fire?'

Jane stared ahead.

'Or placed under a parasol in the sun?' Grace said recklessly. 'Or in a boat on a lake, being rowed along, with a picnic basket beside you? Oh, do answer me, *do*!'

By way of reply, Jane altered her expression very

slightly and gave a nod towards the street, where the slow roll of carriage wheels on gravel and the sound of drumbeats heralded the arrival of the funeral procession. Following the feather-bearer and just ahead of the mourners on horseback, Mr George Unwin led the dead man's riderless stallion, his leather boots reversed in the stirrups to illustrate his demise. This was followed by several empty carriages owned by important families who, being out of London, had sent their landaus as a mark of respect.

As the coffin carriage passed them and went into the church, Grace noticed a neatly folded Union Jack lying on the expensively fringed pall, together with the great man's feathered tricorne hat, which had been part of his official uniform when he was Lord Mayor of London some years previously. The family had requested that this hat, together with the flag, should be buried with the corpse, but Grace had spent enough time with the undertakers now to know that these would miraculously escape the grave and, come the next grand funeral, rise again and be charged for, as both items were worth a considerable amount.

None of these underhand goings-on surprised her. The Unwins were crooked, but no more or less than any of the card sharps, pawnbrokers, bird duffers or child kidnappers who populated the city of London. So what if they showed the client top-quality mahogany for their coffin but actually used cheap board? Who cared if they used tin nameplates instead of the promised silver? What did it matter if they stripped a corpse naked and took his gold watch instead of burying him, as his nearest and dearest had requested, dressed for an evening on the town? None of it was her concern. She couldn't afford to worry about rich people who had money enough to spend on fancy funerals. Not if she wanted to keep her job.

Grace kept her eyes down as, following the coffin, the bereaved's family, friends and acquaintances entered the church. A great number of those who considered themselves important members of society were there, for, since leaving the army, the dead man had been a shining example of a good citizen; maintaining charities, opening homes for unfortunates, even putting himself at risk by going about the London alleyways at night handing out blankets. He'd had a special interest in homeless and fallen women and worked tirelessly to try and reform them, sometimes even taking them into his own home to train them for domestic service.

Grace watched from under lowered lids as, two by two, the mourners went into the church: the ladies who were able to overcome their grief sufficiently to attend the funeral wearing the very latest in Parisian-style mourning gowns (full bishop sleeves, vast wide skirts over boned crinolines, impenetrable black veils falling from head to floor). The men were no less fashionable in their own way, for stockists of mourning wear put it about as certain truth that it was unlucky to keep mourning clothes in the house; they should be purchased afresh with each death. Thus, as George Unwin was fond of saying, the dark clouds of bereavement had silver linings.

It was when nearly all the mourners had entered the church that Grace experienced a strange and unpleasant frisson. Thinking about it after, she couldn't determine which of her senses had caused the unease; had she sensed a faint aroma, an icy finger down her spine, a sudden dizziness, or merely that shiver which is usually described as someone walking over your grave? Whatever it was, the person who'd been walking past her at the precise moment she'd felt it went straight into the body of the church and sat down in the last pew. Knowing that the mourners were inside now and it was safe to move her head, Grace looked in his direction and saw the back view of a man in late middle age, immaculate in full mourning clothes, holding a hymn book in one black-leather-clad hand and carrying his top hat in the other. She didn't know him, and there was nothing at all to distinguish him from any of the other gentlemen mourners.

Perhaps, she thought as the great doors closed, she had imagined it . . .

On Sunday, as she'd planned, Grace made the walk across the park to Kensington and knocked at the back door of the Unwins' home. She had spent some time wondering about her outfit, for although she'd been issued with new black boots and clothing suitable for a mute (the cost, of course, to be deducted from her wages), people might have stared to see her dressed in veils and mourning bonnet in the street. However, Rose had kindly given her an old brown velvet jacket and bonnet and these, worn with a dark bodice and black crêpe skirt, did not look too funereal.

'The mistress doesn't allow visitors below stairs,' Mrs Beaman said, standing four-square across the tradesmen's entrance, arms folded. 'Not without permission.'

'But please could you ask?' Grace pleaded.

'I can't do that. All the family are out visiting.'

'But I'm Lily's sister.' Grace looked at Mrs Beaman beseechingly, the way she'd once looked when starving and trying to sell watercress. 'Please may I come in for just one moment to reassure myself that she's all right? She and I have never been parted before and I'd be so grateful to you.'

Mrs Beaman looked at Grace's solemnly beautiful face ('Like one of them angels on a monument,' she told Blossom later) and relented. 'Just for ten minutes, then,' she said, moving away from the doorway to allow her inside.

Grace was not really surprised to be shown into a freezing cold scullery instead of the servants' parlour, where a lady's maid might normally have been found on a Sunday afternoon. Here she found Lily cleaning knives, rubbing their blades with abrasive paper and emery powder rather fiercely, for she'd already done them twice, and twice they'd been rejected by Mrs Beaman.

On seeing Grace, Lily ran to her, clasped her around the neck and began to cry so heartily that Grace feared her ten minutes would be up before they'd even exchanged a word.

'Sshhh . . . sshh . . . Is it really so bad?' Grace asked, brushing emery powder from her shoulders. 'Do tell me that you're all right.'

Lily choked out several more big sobs and then fell to sniffing. 'I am all right.' She heaved a great sigh. 'But I do miss you!'

'What's it like here? Are you being trained?'

Lily nodded. 'I'm allowed to clean boots and do the knives. Although Mrs Beaman usually says they're not good enough.'

Grace looked down at Lily's hands, which were red and raw. It was just as she'd known really, deep down: Lily was not the sort of girl to make a lady's maid and Mr Unwin had only pretended she was in order to help the situation. How curious the world was! To think that someone like Mr Unwin – penny-pinching, seemingly cold-hearted and insensitive – had not only been kind enough to employ Lily, but had been especially thoughtful about the way he'd done it.

She asked, 'But are they good to you?'

'They feed me well enough,' Lily said, wiping her face on her sleeve. 'We have meat every day.'

'And have the other servants made you welcome?' her sister continued, for this point had been particularly troubling her: that Lily might be an outcast. 'Do they include you in their conversations and so on?'

'Oh, the servants don't!' said Lily. 'Blossom and Lizzie are too high and mighty for that. But Ella speaks to me sometimes – and the young lady of the house is very kind.'

'Miss Charlotte?' Grace asked, most surprised. She hadn't met the young lady, but rumour had it that she was a selfish and spoilt flibbertigibbet.

'Yes, Miss Charlotte. *She* likes me,' Lily said with some pride. She gave a gasp. 'You should see the parlour and the drawing room! They have a jug with bluebirds on it!'

'Do they really?' Grace said, stroking Lily's work-worn hands. 'But when is it that Miss Charlotte finds time to speak to you?'

'Oh, she sometimes comes into the garden when I'm out there on my own, or talks to me in the kitchen when the others are busy upstairs.'

'Really?' Grace asked. Stranger and stranger. 'And what do you talk about?'

'Oh, funny things. Sometimes she makes up stories – like you used to.'

'Does she? How kind of her,' Grace said. Perhaps the tales she'd heard of Miss Charlotte were not true, then. 'What are the stories about?'

'Oh, about Mama and so on,' Lily said vaguely. 'All

sorts of things. She's really interested in me.'

Grace thought to herself how kind it was of Miss Charlotte to bother to make conversation with the lowest of their servants. 'Then she must be a true lady,' she said to Lily.

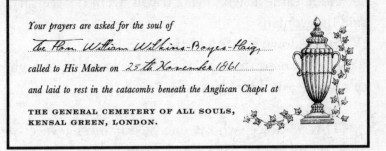

Chapter Sixteen

'I'm sure you want the best, so I suggest nothing less than highest-quality swansdown for your dear mother's coffin mattress,' said George Unwin.

'Oh,' said the bereaved woman. 'We were thinking of wadded wool.'

'Never!' said Mrs Unwin.

Grace, hands in a mute-like position of prayer and eyes lowered, gave no indication that she'd heard a word, or even that she was a living, breathing person. It was a week after she'd gone to Kensington to see Lily, and she'd been summoned into the red room as an indication of the type of mute available for a high-cost funeral.

'Swansdown *is* expensive, but reassuringly so,' chimed in Mrs Unwin, 'and of course one wants the very best for one's venerable parent, doesn't one?'

There came a sigh. 'Well, if you deem it necessary,' said the woman.

'Swansdown it is,' said Mr Unwin.

They paused in front of Grace. 'Have you thought of mutes?' asked Mrs Unwin.

'Well, no . . .'

'This is Grace, who is one of our most respectful and passive mutes. She can be supplied by the hour to stand, bereft and grieving, outside a door or by a graveside.'

'Surely that isn't . . .'

'Grace would be especially appropriate for an elderly lady's grave,' said Mrs Unwin. 'It would look *very* caring.'

'Well . . .'

'And to complement Grace, your mother would surely appreciate having a candle lantern kept alight on the grave for a whole month,' added Mr Unwin.

'But who would benefit from that?'

'Her *memory* would,' Mrs Unwin admonished gently. 'You must remember that old people don't like the dark.'

And so it went on, until, mutes, monuments and mourning flowers chosen, Grace returned to the small sewing room, took off her bonnet and veiling and set her stool beside the meagre fire.

How quickly we become used to things, she thought, picking up the piece of embroidery she'd been working on earlier. How soon she'd adjusted to a life without

Lily, to sharing a room with a stranger, to being confined within four walls and to measuring out her life in a series of shrouds sewn, funerals attended and embroideries completed. And, strangely, although she was living this life and growing accustomed to it, it didn't seem to be *her* life so much as that of someone whose identity she'd assumed by mistake. What would happen next? When would her new life start – the life she'd promised herself the day she'd gone to Brookwood?

She picked up her sewing. That day she was embroidering a tiny picture using human hair with a needle so fine that if she put it down on the workbench she knew she'd never find it again. The picture would show a tombstone under a weeping willow tree and would be put into a small gold frame and worn as a brooch. The customer had wanted her husband's name embroidered on the tombstone, but Mrs Unwin had said that this was impossible, for the man's name was William Wilkins-Boyes-Haig and even if anyone could have embroidered it, it would have been too small to read.

Before she began sewing, Grace paused for a moment and looked around her, marvelling anew at the size of the Unwin empire. Through the glazed door she could see the entrance to the coffin workshop where the carpenters worked around an engraver embellishing the brass or (highly recommended for the more discerning) *silver* coffin plates. To the right was a new workroom with a long bench where Mrs Unwin, having realised what a profit could be turned on everlasting flowers, was now teaching some of the girls how to make immortelles. Outside in the yard, the stonemasons could be heard chipping memorials, and beyond these was a smithy with a blacksmith and grooms in attendance. Close to hand, to the right of the space where Grace was sitting, was a flight of steps down to the enclosed and cool area known as God's waiting room, where – although it was more usual for a deceased loved one to remain at home – one or two bodies always lay awaiting burial. During Grace's first week at the Unwins', two of the seamstresses, jealously presuming from Grace's looks that she was going to become a favourite with the grooms, shut her in with two bodies overnight and hoped for hysterics. Grace, however, after acquainting herself with the cadavers and discovering nothing to be scared of in two old women who'd had a peaceful death, merely went to sleep on the floor. Besides, she'd not become a favourite of the grooms, for she didn't join in with any of their larks and rather kept herself to herself. She never forgot that she was fallen.

Now she carefully threaded the needle, positioned her stool in order to get the best light from the small window, and began feather-stitching, very neat and close, shaping the trunk of the willow tree. She would use tiny, tiny chain-stitches for its leaves and the slab monument would be outlined in back-stitch. Thank goodness Mrs Unwin had said no to the man's name! Besides, the bereaved woman already had two plaited wrist bracelets made from her husband's hair and an oil portrait painted after his death and surely, Grace thought, these reminders were enough for anyone.

It took the best part of a day, but by late afternoon Grace had finished the embroidery for the brooch and had been given a new task: that of stitching the man's initials on to what was to be his coffin pillow. Working white embroidery thread into white linen was not nearly as tiring as working in human hair, but WWBH were all quite large initials and, as dusk fell and the candle burned low, embroidering white on white became more and more tedious and Grace began to wish heartily that the corpse's names didn't begin with so many and such extravagant letters.

She finished this second task a little after eight o'clock. It was usually about this time that she went into the scullery to warm some soup, eat bread and cheese, or – if she were especially weary – merely went to the room she shared with Jane and, after washing and attending to any personal tasks, fell asleep. This particular evening, however, feeling a need to get out after being hunched up indoors for so long, she left the Unwin building intending to walk towards the Edgware Road, breathe in the dusky twilight and marvel at the traffic in all its noisy, hooting, shouting, neighing muddle.

While she stood watching, the swirling spider's web of roads that circled around the arch became jammed – a common occurrence – and all the vehicles came to a complete halt. A smart carriage reined in next to where

Grace was standing and its four horses stamped their feet, their breath making clouds of steam in the cold air. The carriage had purple-liveried footmen at front and rear, four brass lamps, and was such a glossy black that Grace could see her reflection in it. It also had some sort of shield on the door, and wondering what this might be, Grace bent to look a little closer. Seeing a shield with a lion and a unicorn on either side she realised, with a sudden pounding of the heart, that she was looking at the royal coat of arms.

Astonished, she straightened up and stared in the window, there to see the world's most famous royal couple, Queen Victoria and Prince Albert (she had no doubt it was them, for she'd been admiring daguerreotypes and paintings of them all her life), sitting on opposite sides of the brocade-lined carriage. Victoria appeared to be looking at something in her lap, but Prince Albert was gazing out of the window into the dark streets.

Grace's eyes locked with Prince Albert's and she immediately sank into a curtsey. On rising, she blushed scarlet to see that he was nodding in acknowledgement and smiling. Not knowing what else to do, she curtseyed again, and while her knee was still bent, the traffic eased and the royal carriage moved off.

Her heart began beating very fast. Such a handsome and noble face! No wonder the queen was said to be besotted by him.

*

A few days later, Grace found herself putting on her mute's black garb ready to attend the grand ceremonials of the minor aristocrat for whom she'd already done a considerable amount of work: the Honourable William Wilkins-Boyes-Haig.

The newly fashionable Kensal Green Cemetery, near Paddington, had been landscaped as carefully and beautifully as a park, with neat and elegant walkways along which, on summer Sundays, visitors would promenade to admire the fine statuary and visit their dead loved ones. Arriving with three other mutes by covered carriage ahead of the main funeral procession, Grace, alighting in the central drive, marvelled at the number of lavish private mausolea which had been erected, and the variety of sculpted objects. The corpse of the Honourable was not going into a mausoleum, however, but was to be interred in the catacombs beneath the great columned chapel, so the four mutes booked for the service were taken below by Mr Unwin and put into position at different points along the corridor to mark the passage of the coffin on its way to its final resting place. Grace was at the last position, beside the shelf on which the body would remain.

Waiting in the gloom, she tried not to become affected by her sombre surroundings, but this was difficult for, by the light of the tallow candles on the wall, all she could see were small square cells fronted with cobwebby iron grilles which contained coffins: coffins in pine, mahogany, elm, oak and rosewood, some with names on, some without, some studded with gold nails, some covered in velvet, some with long-dead wreaths of roses atop or bearing a single mouldering bloom. Several had a favourite possession of the dead person placed beside them: a toy, a vase, a mildewed cushion. So *many* dead, Grace thought in melancholy wonder, and realised, for perhaps the first time, that there were more dead people in the world than live ones.

She stood two hours in the almost darkness, unable to see another living soul and growing colder by the minute, until she felt that she might have turned into a marble statue herself. It was then that she heard, echoing along the stone corridors, a most strange and eerie sound: a mysterious soft whirring which sent shivers down her spine. She didn't find out until later that the sound was in no way supernatural, but merely the soft drone of the coffin as it travelled by hydraulic power down from the chapel at street level into the depths of the catacombs.

There was a silence, then came a murmur of voices and the shuffle of feet, and in a few moments a black-clad cleric came round the corner, followed by eight men carrying the huge coffin of the Honourable. They were almost buckling under the weight of this, for, having a great sense of his own importance, the Honourable had left instructions that he should be buried in no less than four coffins. The innermost was of pine, then came one of lead, then oak, and the final was of best-quality mahogany. All these were fitted their own locks and keys, for he had also had a fear of his body being taken by bodysnatchers. The Unwins, of course, had been only too pleased to comply with his expensive wishes, and were hoping that others might follow suit. Perhaps, Mrs Unwin had already suggested to her husband, it might become a fashion among the gentry to have four coffins, and they had agreed between themselves that they would mention it, in passing, to anyone planning a grand funeral.

Grace moved slightly to one side to allow the bearers access to remove the iron grille and slide the coffin on to its final resting place. Following this, the cleric gave a last blessing, the members of Wilkins-Boyes-Haig's family said their own private farewells and, slowly, ushered along by Mr George Unwin, the mourners moved off towards the steps and the upper world of the living.

Apart from one.

'Forgive me,' came a whisper, 'but didn't we meet at Brookwood?'

Grace, startled and rather alarmed, looked up to see Mr James Solent standing before her, his top hat beneath his arm. Feeling her face turning pink, she was glad that he wouldn't be able to see it for the veils.

'I mean, it's difficult for me to see you properly what with the darkness and the flummery,' he said, making a gesture to indicate Grace's veiling, 'but it is you, is it not? I fear I am at a disadvantage, as you never told me your name.'

Grace gathered herself and curtseyed. 'It *is* me. My name is Grace, sir.'

'Call me James, please. Are you well, Grace?'

'Thank you, yes.'

'I've often thought about you since that day at Brookwood, for you seemed so frail and vulnerable. I wondered how you were faring.'

'Thank you for your concern,' Grace said a little stiffly, thinking of how she'd gone to his chambers and been turned away. She pointed to her mourning clothes. 'But you see me now in circumstances which have improved somewhat.'

'Indeed,' he said, raising an eyebrow. 'You seem to have joined the death trade.'

Grace nodded, a little embarrassed, for he didn't sound as if he approved.

'May I ask how that came about?'

'It wasn't, perhaps, what I might have wished,' Grace said in a low voice, 'but my sister and I were turned out of our room and had nowhere to go. We would have been on the streets if the Unwin family hadn't taken us both in.'

James shook his head, rather surprised. 'Forgive my lawyer's curiosity, but what were the circumstances of your losing your home?' he asked. 'Did you fall into arrears with your rent?'

'No, indeed!' Grace said with some indignation. 'It

merely happened that one day we got back to the house and found it boarded up. I was told that the site is to be developed.'

James sighed. 'I fear that this is happening all over London: businessmen are buying up the land for railways, offices and industry. They promise to build new homes, but these don't always appear.'

''Tis not right!' Grace said. 'What about all those who find themselves homeless? Is there nothing that can be done?'

'Very little, I'm afraid. There are charities one can apply to; places where you might be taken in.'

'I could not have abided that,' Grace said immediately, for he seemed to be suggesting that they could have gone into a workhouse. 'When it happened – when we were made homeless – I came to ask your advice,' she said, suddenly deciding to confront him with how she'd been treated.

'Did you?'

Grace tried to judge whether he was surprised or already knew this, and decided it was impossible to tell. 'The man who came to the door of your chambers turned me away. He was very abrupt.'

'Then I can only apologise,' he said, 'and I shall tell Meakers that if you ever come again he must show you every courtesy. Believe me when I say that I –'

But before he could finish the sentence there came the sound of footsteps along the corridor and Mr George Unwin appeared out of the darkness. Grace, who had been booked to stand for another two hours beside the coffin, immediately returned to a mute-like silence, eyes lowered, head bowed, hands clasped. James Solent, who looked as if he might have had a lot more to say to Grace, merely nodded at Mr Unwin, replaced his top hat and walked away.

Chapter Seventeen

Four Conversations

Miss Charlotte Unwin had never entered a scullery before, and hoped that she'd never have to again. It wasn't just because it was icy cold that it was so uncongenial, but because it was also dark and cheerless, with a brick floor, ugly lead sink and splintered wooden worktops. A lady might never know such a place existed, and it was only the thought of the smart gig to be gained that made Miss Charlotte even think about entering.

'How deftly you work,' she said to Lily, watching as the girl tried to scrape burned and blackened fat from the fire irons. 'How beautiful and clean you are getting those . . . those *things*.'

'Yes, miss,' said Lily. She felt uneasy when Miss Charlotte came below stairs to speak to her, for she always looked very much out of place, with her lacy

153

trimmings and macassared curls. Today her crinoline skirts were so wide that they barely fitted through the scullery door.

'You have been with us some time now, have you not?' Miss Charlotte said, trying to affect interest. The combined smell of ammonia and carbolic was making her feel rather faint, however, and she hoped she wouldn't have to stay long.

'Yes, miss.'

'Some years . . .'

'*Years?*' Lily frowned and shook her head. Surely it couldn't be years? 'No, not years, miss. I think it's just a couple of months.'

'No, it's years,' Miss Charlotte insisted. 'I told you before. Your own dear mother died about ten years ago when you were just a little girl and my mama and papa took you in, and you've been living with us ever since. We are a similar age and I remember playing with you when I was quite small.'

Lily frowned and rubbed a streak of grease across her cheek. 'No, I don't think that's right,' she said. Miss Charlotte was making up stories again, the way that Grace used to make up stories for them from things she'd read in the newspapers.

'Yes, my mama and papa adopted you years ago,' said Miss Charlotte, smiling rigidly.

'Adopted . . .' Lily repeated wonderingly. 'I don't think so, miss.' She wasn't even sure what the word meant. 'I lived with Grace – she's my sister. We were in

Mrs . . .' She frowned, trying to remember. 'Mrs Macready's house, and then one day it was covered in wood and we couldn't get in.'

Miss Charlotte steadied herself (the gig would be painted a high-gloss red, she decided, with gold carriage lanterns at each side) and spoke again. 'Well, we won't worry about that now, Lily. Er, about your dear mother, didn't you say that when you lived with her, it was somewhere in Wimbledon?'

'That's right,' Lily said, then, 'Ow!' as she cut her thumb on a rough piece of iron.

'And can you remember the name of the house you lived in?'

'No, miss.' Drops of blood fell into the greasy sink and Lily gulped back a sob and put her thumb in her mouth to try and stop the flow. 'You've asked me that before. You keep asking me that.'

Miss Charlotte laughed gaily. 'Do I really? It's just that I do love hearing tales about your childhood in the country . . . although, of course, that was well before you came to live here some ten years ago.'

Lily thought for a moment – Miss Charlotte was doing it again. 'Not ten years, miss,' she said then. 'Only about a month or two. And before that me and my sister were selling cresses in the streets. We used to go to Farringdon Market in the morning and buy up what we –'

'Oh!' A look of irritation crossed Miss Charlotte's face that even the thought of having a pure white horse to pull the gig could not dispel. 'This is hopeless!'

'What is, miss?'

'Nothing!' she snapped. 'And anyway, don't just stand there bleeding all over those . . . those iron things. Go and get a piece of rag from the kitchen and clean yourself up.'

By the time Lily returned with her thumb circled round and round with rag so that it was as big as a turnip, Miss Charlotte had gone back upstairs.

'It's impossible!' Charlotte said to her mother. 'I talk to her, I tell her over and over again that she's been living with us for years, but she won't have it! It just doesn't go in her head.'

'Oh dear,' frowned Mrs Unwin, fingering a swatch of curtain material recently sent from the new Marshall and Snelgrove store. 'I really thought she was dull enough, *simple* enough, to believe anything she was told. I even promised to buy her a new bonnet if she'd play a game of Let's Pretend. She said she would, but one can't rely on her.'

'Perhaps she's being deliberately difficult,' Charlotte said. 'Maybe a couple of nights of being shut in the cellar would cure her.'

'I doubt it,' said Mrs Unwin. 'Nothing like that works with servants these days. Mrs Ormsby tried it and her maid just walked out as soon as she was released and began spreading dreadful tales about her.'

'Disgraceful!' Charlotte sat on the sofa and drummed her heels on the floor. She knew she was being childish but she was really quite desperate to have that gig. 'I've tried everything!'

Mrs Unwin carried the swatch to the window to look at it in a better light. 'Did you even find out the name of the house they lived in?'

'No, because she can't remember it,' Charlotte said petulantly. 'I know everything there is to know about watercress, though. I could *scream* at the amount I know about watercress!'

Mrs Unwin, unable to concentrate on colours, reluctantly put aside the fabric. 'Well,' she said, 'we must think of another way of persuading her. I'll speak to your father.'

Mr George Unwin was first at the usual meeting place in Barker's the following Saturday afternoon. Having been told of Lily's stubbornness but being unable to think of a solution, he greeted his cousin with a deep frown and a double whisky.

'We're in trouble, Sly,' he said as soon as the other sat down. 'The girl is being difficult.'

'What girl?'

'The pigeon!'

'I thought she was in the cage, learning her lines.'

'Oh, she's safe enough – but she's too simple to play the part we've allocated her. Or not simple enough,' he added as an afterthought.

'How d'you mean?'

'She won't play ball. We keep telling her we adopted her years ago but she just denies it. I tell you, the whole scheme is in jeopardy.'

'Hmmm.' Sylvester Unwin knocked back his whisky and sat for a moment, thinking deeply.

'You know, I think we ought to move this on as quickly as we can,' George Unwin continued. 'I wouldn't be surprised to hear that some other villains were planning the damn same thing.'

'Ah, but they wouldn't have the girl, would they?'

'For all the good she is,' said George Unwin in a dispirited voice.

'No, they wouldn't have the girl,' Sylvester Unwin murmured thoughtfully, 'so they'd have a stand-in.'

George Unwin looked at him.

'Someone to play her part,' Sylvester Unwin elaborated. 'And we could do the same. Why not?'

'But what would we do with the real one?'

'Lock her away somewhere.' He gave a guffaw of laughter. 'Tell you what, we'll put the two sisters together – we might get a cheap rate.'

'But we can hardly just go sending off people willy-nilly.'

'The simple one can go first – we'll put it about that she's run off. Servants do that all the time. And after a decent interval the other one can go, too.'

'Hmm,' said George Unwin thoughtfully. 'Might work. But where do we get our little impersonator from? We want someone the same age, a girl who is absolutely reliable.'

Sylvester Unwin grinned. 'My dear cousin, you need look no further than your own home.'

George Unwin gaped at him. 'You mean . . . ?'

'I do indeed. But we'll need as much information from Lily as possible: descriptions, dates, details of Ma and Pa – all that stuff.'

'On its way!' said George Unwin. As usual, his cousin had come up with the solution, although Charlotte would have to be bribed with something else, of course.

'So what else has been happening?' Sylvester Unwin wanted to know.

'I've got you a feathered tricorne!'

'Why ever should I need one of those?'

'As if you didn't know! As if you hadn't been told you'd be Lord Mayor of London within five years!'

'Lord Mayor of London! I don't know what you're talking about,' said Sylvester Unwin roguishly. 'Whatever have I done to be made mayor?'

'A leader in business, but with a caring and compassionate side,' said George Unwin, 'that's how you present yourself, isn't it?' He winked. 'And especially caring to fallen women, eh?'

The other ignored this. 'Anyway, I know whose feathered tricorne you've pinched. I was at old

Welland-Scropes's funeral and saw it going past on the bier.'

'*Were* you there? I didn't see you.'

'I was late – crept into the church and sat in the back pew. Didn't know the man personally, of course, but...'

'But it's the sort of funeral one wants to be seen at, eh?'

'Quite,' said Sylvester Unwin. 'And, yes, keep me the tricorne. Just in case.'

'Are you Mrs Macready?' asked the woman. She was thin and was clutching at her stomach as if it was paining her.

'Who's asking?'

'You don't know me, but I assure you that I mean no harm to you or to anyone else, madam.'

Mrs Macready relaxed slightly. She liked being called madam. 'Very well. Yes, I am she.'

'And did you keep a lodging house up in Seven Dials until recently?'

'I did. A very respectable and law-abiding establishment.' She sighed. 'They've pulled it down now.'

'Indeed. That's what I was told. Two young girls – sisters – had a room there.'

Mrs Macready nodded. 'I know who you mean: Grace and Lily. Lovely girls, they were. One was a little bit simple, but her sister used to look out for her.

Auburn curls, solemn face . . . a reg'lar beauty, she was.'

'It's that very girl who I'm seeking. Would you have any idea where she might be found?'

Mrs Macready shook her head. 'None at all, dear.' She thought for a moment. 'The two of them sold watercresses, you know. Have you tried looking for them at Farringdon Market of a morning?'

'I have.' The woman nodded. 'But no one's seen them for months.' A look of intense disappointment passed across her face. 'You were my last hope. Is there any chance that you might see her again, do you think?'

'Well, there's always a chance, I suppose,' said Mrs Macready in a voice which suggested the contrary.

'If you ever do, please would you tell her that Mrs Smith wants to see her urgently.'

'*Mrs Smith?*' said Mrs Macready, raising one eyebrow.

'That's who she knew me as. I live at Tamarind Cottage in Sydney Street with my daughter. Can you remember that?'

"Course I can.' Mrs Macready hesitated, then said, 'But you look all in, dearie. Do you want to come and rest for a while?'

Mrs Smith shook her head. 'I'll be all right. But I'd be obliged if you could write down the address I've told you, just in case.'

'Tamarind Cottage in Sydney Street. I'll get my son to make a note of it as soon as I go in,' said Mrs Macready, and she watched as the other woman walked slowly, nearly bent double, back down the street.

Hark from the Tomb a doleful sound
My ears attend the cry
Ye living Men come view the Ground
Where you must shortly ly

Epitaph on a tombstone

Chapter Eighteen

When the contingent of funeral workers from the Unwin Undertaking Establishment arrived at Waterloo Necropolis Station in the early morning, the train and its carriages were rimed with frost and its windows patterned with ice crystals, making it look ethereal and other-worldly; a ghost train, shining dully in the drear gas-lit station. Grace, going into the undertakers' carriage and positioning herself at a window, fancied how it might look as it passed through the countryside, snaking through the icy landscape, white and glittering with frost, cold as Death itself.

Reaching the suburbs of London and nearing a level crossing, it gave a long, low whistle – an especially mournful tone. Looking out of the window, Grace noticed that several farm labourers who'd been working in the fields had downed tools, doffed caps and were standing with lowered heads as it passed them. As the train slowed at the crossing there was a moment of almost silence, when the anguished sobbing of someone in third class could be heard, then the train went across, scalding steam hissing and bubbling and the wheels clattering noisily on the rails as it picked up speed once more.

Approaching Brookwood, a final deep cloud of steam appeared, and then, out of the mist, came tall evergreen trees, followed by a neat brick station. This was as plain and ordinary as any country halt, but had the distinction of bearing a line of funeral workers in black frock coats and top hats upon it, bowing from the waist as the train drew in. As it stopped with a squeal of brakes, the undertakers' workers put away their dice, cards and flasks of 'something warming', and jumped down from the carriage in order to get to their positions for the various ceremonials. Grace alighted also, adjusted her gown and put her veiling in place. The funeral she had to attend was likely to be particularly gruelling, for it was the burial of a young woman killed in a traffic accident the night before her wedding. She was to be buried in her wedding dress and veil, and her bride-cake was to be consumed in the refreshment room after the committal.

Waiting on the platform for Mr Unwin to give his final instructions, Grace took in the sights and sounds of Brookwood. When she'd been there before she'd been bowed down by grief, bewildered by what had happened to her, and had looked but hardly seen. Now she viewed clearly and sympathetically the dismal sight of a host of newly bereaved people, their expressions fraught, moving about the platform silently and awkwardly, like strange black insects.

She shivered. It was a freezing day, and though she was wearing a new pair of thick woollen stockings under her black skirts and petticoats, she was very much feeling the cold. When she'd bought them she'd also purchased a pair for Lily which she intended to take to her as soon as she possibly could. She hadn't seen her sister for three weeks now and had a lot to tell her, starting with the night she'd seen the handsome Prince Albert in his carriage.

As the first-class coffins were silently removed from the van, Mr Unwin signalled to Grace to go into position before the hearse. The night before, the dead girl's family had paid an extra guinea for Grace to keep a silent vigil by the open coffin at her home, while those women of the family whose sensibilities did not allow them to journey to Brookwood came to pay their last respects. Grace, therefore, had knelt by the coffin all night and was not only very cold and hungry now, but also very tired. (And she would not, besides, receive any share of the guinea, or even know that it had been paid.)

The white velvet-covered coffin was carefully placed on to the waiting horse-drawn hearse and, with head bowed and hands clasped together, Grace began to walk before it through the frost-touched glades. She was followed by the usual bag and baggage of the mourning industry: feather-bearers, stave-carriers and two child mutes who'd been taken off the streets for the occasion, followed in turn by the dead girl's would-be husband, family, friends and servants, all in deepest black, with mourning rings and black leather gloves supplied as funeral favours by her father.

The graveside service seemed interminable, for the two priests – one from the dead girl's local church, plus the old family friend who would have married her – seemed at loggerheads and could not decide who would have the last word on her life. As one droned a speech about death overcoming all, this was topped by the other giving a sermon on the frailty of life. When, eventually, the service was over and a great many tears had been shed, the mourners made their way to the first-class refreshment room for the cake and a nip of brandy, leaving Grace a little time on her own before the train went back to Waterloo.

She went straight to the resting place of Susannah Solent, and found there the mausoleum which James Solent had told her that his father was having constructed. It was a grand edifice, Egyptian style, with a pyramid roof, two sphinxes on guard each side of the doorway and shiny hammered-metal doors. Grace could not resist peering through the side window and there saw a picture of Queen Victoria and Prince Albert, a miniature altar with crucifix and two little tapestry-covered praying chairs such as one might find in a church. There were also marble shelves with spaces for eight coffins, although only the bottom one was filled.

Grace, seeing Susannah Solent's coffin and knowing what else it contained, began to weep, the force of her grief surprising her. She wept for her lost child, for the unhappiness of her life and because she was parted from Lily. She wept because she did not seem to have a future – or only one that was governed by the Unwins, and because they were not at all the sort of people to whom she wanted to be indebted. Mostly she cried because she didn't seem to be living the right sort of life, the life she'd always promised herself.

She stood there until she could get her tears under control, then said another sad and silent farewell to her child and began to make her way back to the path which led to the station. Reaching this, she found a well-dressed young lady waiting there and was immensely surprised when this person addressed her.

'Good morning,' said Miss Charlotte Unwin, 'and excuse me for asking such a thing, but did you know Miss Solent?'

Grace, unprepared for this question, thought it wisest not to lie in case the young lady was trying to catch her out. 'No, I didn't. Not personally,' she admitted.

'But – forgive me – I was watching you at her mausoleum and you were grieving very deeply.'

Grace felt a little alarmed at this and, playing for time, adjusted her veiling. 'She was not known to me personally, but . . . but her charity work was. They called her Princess of the Poor, did they not?' she said, recalling the engraved silver plate on Susannah's coffin.

'Oh. So you . . . ?'

'Yes, I benefitted from her aid,' Grace said. Which was true in a way, she thought. She looked at the girl standing before her, who was dressed in the very best and most fashionable shade of purple half-mourning, the gown expensively frilled and ruched, a white fur tippet at her neck.

'I'm sorry, I should have introduced myself, but I was just so surprised to see you there.' She smiled. 'I am Miss Charlotte Unwin.'

Grace, startled and wondering how long the girl had been watching her, was rather late in bobbing a curtsey.

'I came here with my mother today.' Charlotte Unwin hesitated, trying her hardest to look friendly and caring. 'She thinks I should learn about our business and wanted me to meet one of our best mutes.'

Feeling immediately that she was being spied upon, Grace did not know what to answer to this.

'There! Please don't go silent on me,' Charlotte Unwin said. 'I can assure you that I mean you no harm.'

Grace cleared her throat. 'I'm sure you do not. I didn't see you before, Miss Charlotte. Were you on the train?'

'No, Mama and I came down here by carriage, and now she is at the graveside looking after the poor dead bride's parents.' There was a pause. 'But your name is Grace, is it not? And how long have you been working for my family, Grace?'

'For several months now,' Grace replied. 'And I must thank you for taking such a kindly interest in my sister. She's told me of your attentions to her,' she added.

'Not at all,' Charlotte Unwin said. 'She's a hard worker and a . . . a great character, your sister.' She gave a light laugh. 'She hasn't only got *me* for a friend, though.'

Grace looked at her enquiringly. 'You mean – the other servants?'

'No, I mean she has a young male friend. A follower who works for one of our neighbours as a groom.'

'She has a *follower*?' Grace asked, astounded.

'Indeed she has! I do believe his intentions are serious.'

Grace shook her head. 'There must be some mistake, surely. My sister is . . . is . . .' She struggled for the right word to describe Lily's condition, but Charlotte Unwin seemed to know what she meant.

'Never fear! The young man in question is a simple country soul,' she said. 'I believe them to be well suited.'

Grace absorbed this information with some difficulty. Miss Charlotte must be mistaken. Lily couldn't possibly have a young man! She'd not said anything about it when Grace had been to the house and it was most unlikely – near impossible, in fact – that she could keep anything like that to herself.

'Please don't concern yourself about it,' Charlotte Unwin said. 'It's a decent match and I'm sure your family will approve.'

'We have no family,' Grace murmured, still stunned. 'There is only me and Lily.'

'Oh, of course!' Charlotte Unwin said. 'Do forgive me. Lily told me about your father going away and the death of your mama. You used to live in Wimbledon, I believe.'

Grace nodded.

'I have a very dear friend who lives in a lane just off the high street. Did you live anywhere near?'

'Quite close. Mama rented a cottage for us on the green – I can just remember it.'

'How delightful! Not the little white one which is smothered in flowers all summer?'

Grace shook her head. 'I don't think it was white. It had a mulberry tree in the front garden, and was named after that.'

'How lovely!' said Charlotte Unwin. It seemed, however, that she had got to know this particular Unwin employee quite well enough, for she abruptly bid Grace farewell and said she had to return to her mother.

To avoid walking back with her, Grace pretended she had something to do in the opposite direction and walked under the trees for a while, wondering about what Miss Unwin had said. Surely it couldn't be true about Lily having a follower?

To try and distance herself from this worrying information, she began to read the epitaphs on the stones, but they mostly seemed to indicate that your time on earth would not be long and that you would be gone before you knew it, which did not make for pleasant reading. After sighing over many young children dead before their time, Grace made her way to the third-class refreshment room in order to drink a bowl of hot soup, for she was feeling almost faint with hunger. She would have to stay out of sight of any Unwins, of course, for eating and drinking were against the rules. Mutes, Mrs Unwin maintained, should not eat or drink any more than they should converse, for they were supposed to be entirely dedicated, almost celestial figures, far above human wants and needs.

Throwing back her veil to drink her soup, Grace had the second spoonful to her mouth when she was tapped on the shoulder.

A woman said, 'Dear girl, is it really you?'

Looking round she found Mrs Macready standing there, dressed in black from head to toe, and consequently looking much smarter than she'd ever appeared in Seven Dials.

'Oh, my dear! Who has died?' Mrs Macready, continued, sitting down and taking in Grace's weeds. 'Not your sister?'

Grace assured her that Lily was perfectly well and working as a maid (which caused Mrs Macready to look rather surprised). 'And I'm only wearing mourning because I'm working for the Unwins as a mute,' she added in a low voice, 'and as such, am not supposed to speak with anyone.'

Mrs Macready gasped. 'Well, I never!'

As there were hardly any mourners left in the refreshment room by this time, Grace went on, 'But how are you, Mrs Macready? I trust no one too close to you has died?'

'Yes, well, I'm afraid it was old Mr and Mrs Beale,' that lady sighed.

Grace gave a little cry. 'How sad!'

'They went within a day of each other, God save their hearts, and the Blind Society paid for a third-class funeral here.' Her eyes gleamed. 'But bless me, what a place it is, and to come on the train and all! Such a treat to ride in a train with the gentry in the next carriage!' The old woman suddenly clapped her hand to her mouth. 'But I'm forgetting – someone came to my son's house asking for you!'

Grace looked at her in surprise. 'Really?'

'A woman . . . now, what was her name?' Mrs Macready scratched her head under her veil. 'She knew that you'd once lodged with me and said that if I ever saw you again I was to tell you to get in touch. Gave me her address . . . Her name was a very ordinary one: *Smith*,' Mrs Macready said triumphantly. 'Yes, she called herself Mrs Smith!'

Grace made a business of lowering her veil back into position, hoping that Mrs Macready wouldn't see that her hands were shaking. 'I don't think I know a Mrs Smith.' She tried to smile. 'It sounds very much like a false name.'

'I've got her address written down somewhere. I could let you have it if you like.'

Grace patted the woman's hand. 'I don't think I will, Mrs Macready, thank you. No reflection on you, but I've left that old life behind me now.'

'Of course, dear. You please yourself,' said Mrs Macready. 'She may have been on the make. You can never be too sure,' she added.

Grace nodded. That had been her first thought: that 'Mrs Smith' had found out that she'd got a regular job and was going to try and blackmail her about the baby.

'But I thank you for telling me, and hope that we meet again under happier circumstances,' Grace said, and she brushed her veiled cheek against the other woman's and went to board the train.

*

In the middle of that night – or at four in the morning, to be precise – Grace woke from a deep sleep to find Jane at the window of their room, looking out into the darkness.

'What's the matter?' she asked sleepily.

'Something . . . but I don't know what,' answered Jane in a nervous whisper. 'The bells have been tolling for an hour or more – can't you hear them? And I can see people in the street.'

Grace, realising that she too could hear bells, sat up in bed. It was a monotonous, heavy tolling, and not just from their local church, but also from what sounded like a score of others. 'Have you ever heard bells like this before?'

Jane shook her head. 'Perhaps it's war,' she said anxiously. 'Or a terrible fire.'

'Do go and ask someone!' Grace urged her. 'Find out who else is awake.'

But Jane was too scared, so Grace lit a candle, wrapped a blanket around herself against the bitter cold and went out on to the landing. She found two of the seamstresses there, talking excitedly to a mason down in the yard.

'What is it?' Grace asked. 'Why are all the bells ringing?'

'We don't know!' said one of the girls.

'We've sent Wilf into the street to find out,' said the other.

As they waited, from the direction of the reception rooms came the sudden clanging of another bell – the handbell that Mr or Mrs Unwin sometimes used to summon the servants for church, or to announce something noteworthy. Grace went back into her bedroom to tell Jane that she should make haste and come downstairs.

In a front reception room one gas light had been lit, its glimmer causing a tall marble angel to throw a soft, wavering shadow right across one wall. Mr George Unwin waited there, fully dressed and frowning, arrived from Kensington and eager to tell his workers the news.

After calling for silence, he said, 'No doubt you'll all be wondering what's happening.' There were voices of assent and he went on, 'It is my sad duty to tell you that the Prince Consort, the husband of our dear queen, died last night.'

There was a collective intake of breath from those in the room and one or two of the girls began crying. Grace thought of that handsome, ardent face she'd seen at the carriage window, and then about the epitaphs she'd read on the tombstones only the day before. They had spoken truly: Death was waiting in line for everyone, and was no respecter of one's station in life.

'I didn't know he was ill, sir!' someone called.

'What about the queen? It will kill her.'

Mr Unwin said, 'I need hardly tell you what a blow this is to the country. A national disaster.'

There came murmurs of agreement, several sobs.

'However . . .' Mr Unwin stopped, coughed. 'While this is doubtless a tragedy for all of us, some may, er . . .' He paused, wondering how to put it. 'Some may find it more of a tragedy than others. And some – though of course every bit as devastated as everyone else – may not be . . . quite . . .'

He gave up the effort of trying to tell them in the most decent way possible that he and Mrs Unwin had already discussed the matter and thought that Prince Albert's death would signal a renaissance in the mourning industry, for surely the whole nation would want to wear black.

'The thoughts of everyone are with our beloved queen,' he finished devoutly.

It was, Grace observed two days later, most extraordinary: the whole world seemed to have turned black overnight. Shops, omnibuses, hackney carriages, trains, trees, horses, restaurants and houses had all become draped in yards of bombazine or crêpe. Dogs wore black collars, cats had black bows and babies had their long white gowns trimmed with black grosgrain. It was as if people wanted to prove their loyalty to Queen Victoria and Prince Albert – or perhaps wished others to think they were part of the aristocracy and thus connected to the royals.

Ordinary funerals were hurried on or delayed until after Prince Albert's, which was fixed for the 23rd December, and Grace, desperate to call upon Lily in order to discover the truth about her mysterious suitor, soon realised that she was not going to be able to do this, for at six o'clock in the evening two days later, the funeral workers were again summoned into the red room by Mr Unwin. Mrs Unwin was there also, dressed in a very smart watered-silk mourning gown, a black fur bolero over her shoulders, a three-row black pearl necklace around her neck and looking, Grace heard one of the girls mutter, like Lady Muck.

'Staff and servants,' Mr Unwin began portentously, 'following the death of our queen's dearly beloved husband, a message has come from Buckingham Palace to say that the queen wishes everyone in the land to make a decent mourning.'

Some of the servants exchanged puzzled looks.

'A *decent* mourning,' Mrs Unwin repeated, adjusting her pearls in order to draw attention to them. She had been waiting for just such an event – a major and significant funeral – in order to give them an airing.

'In memory of our dear Prince Albert, the whole of Britain will be required to wear, at the very least, a black armband,' Mr Unwin explained. 'And those who have connections with Court will be required to be in full mourning for three months.'

Mrs Unwin gave a wise, sad nod at this. The Unwins had absolutely no connections with Court, but Mrs Unwin had decided that she and Charlotte would be in mourning for six months at the very least, would correspond only on black-edged paper and also have the family brougham relined in bombazine.

'Half-mourning will follow for another three

months after, and then quarter-mourning,' said Mr Unwin.

'Indeed.' Mrs Unwin dabbed her eyes with a black-edged handkerchief, planning her wardrobe of flattering lilacs and mauves.

While his wife was engaged in looking sorrowful, Mr Unwin went on, 'With regard to mourning wear, some of you will know that my cousin, Mr Sylvester Unwin, owns the Unwin Mourning Emporium in Oxford Street.'

The workers nodded. They all did know.

'He has asked for our help.' He paused momentarily for effect, then went on, 'The mourning store has been utterly inundated with shoppers, both personal and postal. They begin queuing outside at six o'clock in the morning, and are still arriving at six o'clock at night.'

'They have tried to order entry by timed ticket,' put in Mrs Unwin, 'but still can't cope with the vast number of people.'

'He can't take their money fast enough!' Mr Unwin shouted, becoming rather over-excited. His wife nudged him hard, and he continued in a more sober fashion, 'What all this means is that Mr Sylvester Unwin has asked for as many staff as we can spare to go to work temporarily at the store in Oxford Street. Everyone will be given brief training as to how an exclusive store works, and each of you will be partnered by an experienced person. We will only keep a skeleton staff here.' He paused. '*Skeleton* staff. Rather good, what?'

There was a little respectful laughter before he read out the names of those not expected to go to work in the store: the blacksmith and his boys, two country-born grooms and a few elderly seamstresses were clearly unsuitable for waiting upon gentry. All the young women, however, including Grace, were to go along first thing the following morning.

> ### The Unwin Mourning Emporium,
> ### Oxford Street, London.
> Garments in full-, half- and quarter-mourning.
> Your every stage of grief catered for.
> Patterns and samples dispatched immediately by post.
> As patronised by Members of English and Foreign
> Royal Families.

Chapter Nineteen

The Unwin Mourning Emporium was close to Oxford Circus in London's famous Oxford Street, and positioned quite close to Jay's Mourning Warehouse, the first and most famous of those large stores which sold nothing but mourning clothes, accessories and ephemera. A great deal of rivalry existed between them regarding who stocked the most garments – and the most *fashionable* garments – and who had the most aristocratic customers. Occasionally, a lord, lady or minor member of the royal family would contact one of the stores, causing the other no end of resentment.

Grace found she was looking forward to this temporary place of employ, for she was already tired of being a mute, of being permanently grief-stricken and of walking around half blind, peering at people through black veiling. Besides, department stores looked such enticing places. She had passed them often enough, but never been inside one, for stern uniformed men stood at the entrances and, if you looked poor or inadequate, refused to open the doors and tried to turn you away by hard looks or shouts of 'Be off!' Department stores were not – usually – for the likes of Grace.

The following morning, twelve workers from the Unwin Undertaking Establishment were walked in crocodile fashion by Mr George Unwin from Edgware Road to Oxford Circus. They arrived there at seven o'clock when, as predicted by Mr Unwin, there was already a queue of potential customers outside. A good number of these were ladies' maids or menservants with lists from their mistresses of garments required, or notes asking that a store dressmaker should call upon them personally.

As they passed in front of the store's vast gas-lit windows, those in the crocodile line admired the mannequins who, wearing the latest in mourning garments, stood distraught in a number of different situations. One model was shown gracefully descending a staircase, another was gazing mournfully out of an open window, a third was reading a 'last letter' before a fireplace. Each window scene, Grace thought admiringly, told a little story in its own right. Passing the store, the Unwin workers went along an alleyway and through the staff entrance at the far side. The rather shabby quarters here led through into the shop itself, where all gazed in awe at the soft furnishings, multiple gas lights, thick carpet, velvet curtains and general air of opulence. There was even a grand piano standing near the entrance in order to play contemplative music and soothe the shoppers' melancholy.

This was what it was like to be rich, Grace thought, looking around her. Not merely to have food and shelter, but to be able to live with luxurious trappings and an abundance of possessions, to own as many clothes as one wanted . . . to wander through stores like this, pointing at things and having your maid scurry to get them for you.

Mr Sylvester Unwin had been told by his cousin that Grace Parkes, sister of the more valuable Lily, would be coming to work temporarily in the store, but this had not caused him a moment's unrest. The swindle they were perpetrating against the Parkes was, to him, a thing apart. Besides, he reasoned, the Unwins were doing the sisters (both probably a little simple, he thought) a favour in taking them in and giving them shelter. What sort of a life would they have had otherwise? How would they have coped with such a fortune? Sooner or later someone would have taken it from them; this way they were spared even knowing they'd had it. And thus he reasoned his path to a clear conscience.

Before the store opened, Mr Sylvester Unwin stood halfway up the sweeping staircase which led to Footwear and Accessories, surveying both his old and new staff with some satisfaction. Those who had arrived from his cousin's business would not, of course, be allowed to actually serve customers, but would make themselves useful telling lady customers how extremely well a garment suited them, by tearing off lengths of brown paper for wrapping, tying up parcels with string, and coming and going with bills and receipts from the cash desks. The cash desks, he reflected complacently, rang from morning until night; they had never seen so much activity. Of course, it was terrible that Prince Albert had been cut down in his prime but, at least as far as the owner of London's premier mourning store and his cousin were concerned, it had its compensations.

Sylvester Unwin waited for complete silence from those standing below him on the shop floor, then bade a pompous good morning and said he had some very important things to say, especially to the newcomers.

'It is a grand and noble thing that in someone's hour of anguish and despair we may be able to soothe their troubled spirits,' he began. 'Prince Albert was a much loved member of our royal family, so by mourning him sincerely the country is showing its respects and helping our dear queen through her darkest hours. To this end, do not hesitate to offer your customer a little extra garnish to their mourning outfit in order to prove how much they care. If a gentleman seeks a black band for his top hat, suggest he has gloves or black spats, too. If a woman requires gloves, offer a veil, a jet mourning ring or a new black bonnet in addition.'

He cleared his throat. 'When mentioning the purchase of these items, remember to indicate to the customer that mourning clothes should not be kept in the house for any great length of time following the death, for custom dictates – and who are we to contradict? – that it is unlucky to keep them under one's roof for more than one passing.'

Grace heard this with some shock, knowing that half of London could barely afford to put food in their mouths, let alone purchase a new outfit each time a member of their family died. She gave her full attention to her new employer for the first time, seeing a man with a black tailcoat, shoes that were polished like dark glass, a shirt so snowy-white it could only have come freshly from the seamstress and black leather gloves soft as butter. Sylvester Unwin prided himself on his appearance.

'Of course,' he continued, 'not everyone who comes through our doors over the next few days will be here to honour the memory of Prince Albert. Some will be mourning a member of their own family. Here I ask you to recall that helping the bereaved into full and fashionable mourning helps focus their minds and ease their pain. In my charity work I'm often called upon to aid ladies who have been widowed, and I emphasise the fact that they owe it to their husbands' glorious memory to go into the very best mourning gowns they can afford.'

There was more of this ilk, but Grace found it difficult to concentrate on Mr Unwin's words. There was something about his appearance which jarred, something almost repugnant, but she could not work out what it was. She appraised his appearance yet again, but could see nothing amiss. On the surface, he was perfectly respectable. Was it something about his posture, then, or his face with its port-wine nose, or perhaps it was just his oily manner and the many faux-modest references to his charitable works that made him so objectionable to her?

Suddenly, mid-sentence, Mr Unwin smacked his hands together and pointed at Grace. 'You, there! What was I just saying?'

Grace went scarlet and shook her head to say that she didn't know, making Mr Unwin shake his own head mockingly in response. There was a ripple of laughter from the regular staff.

'Is that what you're going to do when my customers ask you something – shake your head at them?' said Mr Unwin. Playing to the crowd, he came down the steps and stood in front of her. 'Can you nod as well?'

At close quarters Grace found Mr Unwin's presence almost terrifying: the bulk of him, the strength, the faint aroma of something sweet and pungent.

'I said, can you nod?' he demanded again, putting his hand on her head and pushing it up and down.

Grace, frightened, nodded despite herself.

'Ah!' crowed Mr Unwin. 'She *can* nod!'

He turned around and went back to his position of superiority on the stairs. 'You see how you must all be alert to what the customer is saying! No matter if you are serving your first customer or your eighty-first, be alert and be aware. Never let an opportunity for a sale pass you by.'

Grace looked up at him, trying to hide both her fear and her loathing. That smell; that acrid, sugary smell . . . where had she smelt it before?

And then she remembered. It had been at the funeral of Cedric Welland-Scropes, when the last man to go into the church had passed her. And perhaps even before that, too, although she could not have said precisely where.

She was not able to ponder upon the matter longer, however, for the Unwin workers were divided up and she was assigned to a girl wearing a badge which named her as Miss Violet, who was several years older and quite pretty enough in her own right not to resent Grace's beauty. Miss Violet was one of five lady greeters and her job was to ascertain a customer's wishes as well as assess their status as soon as they entered the store, for Mr Unwin liked those who were at the top of the social scale to be served only by those similarly placed in the store's hierarchy.

Grace had not met a young woman like Miss Violet before. Educated and smart, with short hair in a mass of curls (and shiny lips which were not come by entirely naturally), she was one of the new breed of office and shop girls who, not content to sit at home waiting for a man to come along and propose marriage, went out into the world to begin carving a career for themselves. Grace liked her immediately.

'All you have to do,' Miss Violet explained, 'is accompany the customer to wherever I tell you to take them. I might say a department, or I might say a member of staff within that department. I might, on occasion, tell you to take a very important customer to be served by Mr Unwin himself.'

Grace nodded but, as the hated name was mentioned, could not stop a tremor of fear crossing her face.

Miss Violet patted her shoulder. 'Don't let him upset you,' she said. 'Sly is a bully who picks on someone every day – several people if he's being particularly horrid.'

'His name is Sly?'

'Sylvester, actually, but Sly by name and Sly by nature, eh?' Miss Violet smiled. 'I'll take you around the store now and show you where the different departments are.'

Grace found the amount of stock available in the store quite overwhelming, and as Miss Violet led the way through bodices, boas, bonnets, boots, skirts, shawls, capes, umbrellas, aprons and mantles, her head was spinning before they'd even reached the men's departments.

'So many garments; so much black!' Grace said, and

found it a welcome relief when they went into the half-mourning department where grey, lilac and pale mauve predominated.

'We have so much stock because Mr Unwin hates losing a sale,' Miss Violet said. 'I do believe a dart pierces his heart every time someone walks out of the shop without opening their purse.' She paused beside a discreetly curtained alcove. 'A new department,' she said in a low voice. 'Mourning undergarments.'

'Undergarments!' Grace repeated, terribly surprised.

Miss Violet smiled. 'Indeed. Ladies must show they are suffering right down to their most intimate attire.'

'And must all those garments be black, too?' Grace asked, trying to see round the curtain.

Miss Violet shook her head. 'No. They can be of white lawn trimmed with black lace, and white linen slotted with black ribbon,' she whispered.

They returned to the main entrance hall to stand beside the grand piano where Miss Violet was usually positioned, hoping to hand-pick the wealthiest-looking customers. Grace, relieved that Mr Unwin was no longer in sight, found she was enjoying herself – although if she could have had a wish it would have been that Lily had been there to see it all, too.

The day passed in a blur of faces and demands. It was mostly maids, menservants and the poorer sorts who came to the store early, but by midday the middle classes had begun stirring themselves to go out and spend conspicuous amounts on showing their affection for Prince Albert. By three o'clock another section of the population arrived as those of the upper classes who hadn't been quick enough to secure the services of a private dressmaker called at the store on their way to take afternoon tea with their friends and aunts. There were a great many of these upper-class ladies – so many, in fact, that the roadway outside became a seething mass of stamping, neighing horses, broughams and gigs, hackney carriages and traps, and this chaos was added to by a flock of sheep going towards Smithfield Market with two border collies and a farmer. The whole chaotic traffic jam caused a number of ladies to become marooned on the far side of Oxford Street, making it necessary for them to dispatch their maids into the morass of traffic with written instructions for the store and to proceed home without them.

While a number of dramas were unfolding outside, Grace became aware of a press of people outside the glass doors nearest to her and Miss Violet. Occasionally throughout the day the uniformed men had had to close the store until those customers already inside had been served and dispersed, and at first she thought they were doing this once again. She soon became aware, however, that there was a stately, bearded gentleman outside and that the uniformed men were endeavouring to pull him through the door.

Miss Violet, prompted by Grace, looked at the figure, said, 'O, Lord!' Then she went to greet him as he fell through the opening, hissing urgently as she did so, 'Forward, Miss Grace!'

Grace moved forward. The people outside, she noticed, seemed to have temporarily given up the struggle to get into the store and were now pressed against the doors and windows, their eyes following this new customer's every move.

'Good afternoon, sir!' said Miss Violet. She sank into a far deeper curtsey than any she had executed previously, and seeing this, Grace did likewise. 'May we conduct you to a department? What is it you wish to purchase, sir?'

'Damned mourning bands and a couple of black ties!' came the reply from the man as he pulled off his top hat. He had a deeply lined face, a greying beard and his hair was receding – but he also had very bright blue eyes, which seemed the youngest part of him. He waved his hand at the trappings of the store. 'Sorry to be blunt with you, but I don't hold with all this dealing in death!' He paused and seemed to recover himself slightly. 'But of course, my own feelings on the matter are not of your concern, and I apologise to you for my bad temper.'

'That's quite unnecessary, I assure you, sir,' Miss Violet murmured.

The man gave a slight smile. 'I was in the middle of a lecture tour in Liverpool when we heard, and I had to cancel six lectures and come back to London. Why this was, God only knows! The whole country seems to have gone mad with grief.'

'Indeed they have, sir,' said Miss Violet, gesturing to the great mob outside. 'But I'm sorry about your tour,' she went on. 'And may I be so bold as to say, Mr Dickens, how much my family and I are enjoying *Great Expectations*.'

Grace gasped slightly, but only to herself. She was glad that being a mute had imbued her with the skill of hiding her feelings or she might have stood there gawping.

'My mother and I are at loggerheads over who should be first to read each instalment as soon as the magazine comes through the door,' Miss Violet continued. 'And my brother has stopped his pocket watch at twenty minutes to nine in deference to the clocks at Miss Havisham's house. He says he'll not start it again until he's finished the book!'

'Capital! Capital! I'm pleased to hear it,' Charles Dickens said, smiling and quite placated, while Grace mentally added his name to the list of things she had to tell Lily.

190

Chapter Twenty

Mr and Mrs Stanley Robinson and their baby came into the Unwin Mourning Emporium quite late in the afternoon, when Miss Violet and Grace – and all the rest of the staff – were quite exhausted. Nevertheless, Miss Violet went forward to greet them, and after bidding them good afternoon, was unable to resist patting the head of the laughing, gurgling child that Mr Robinson carried.

'What a beautiful baby!' she said, beckoning Grace to come and see.

Mr and Mrs Robinson beamed at them both. 'One

is probably prejudiced, but he *is* beautiful, isn't he?' said the child's father.

'He is indeed,' Grace agreed, smiling and holding out a finger to the infant.

'And how might we at Unwin's be of assistance to you today, sir and madam?' asked Miss Violet.

'We want your advice, really,' said Mrs Robinson. 'Baby is being christened on Sunday. We left it until he was six months old, but now with the death of Prince Albert we are rather wishing that we hadn't. You see, a member of the aristocracy is attending the christening, a titled gentleman known to my husband's family, and we think he might be offended if we're not in full mourning.'

'And if *we* are, then should Baby be in black, too?' asked Mr Robinson. 'We have a christening gown which has been handed down from my great-grandmother, but wonder if it would be quite correct to let him wear it.'

'Well, sir and madam, for these matters I suggest you put yourselves in the hands of our baby depart-ment,' said Miss Violet. 'They know the correct protocol and will advise you.'

'And where would I find this department?'

'Miss Grace will escort you,' said Miss Violet, and Grace led the way through the crowds to the correct department, returning smile for smile with the baby along the way.

THE FUNERAL
OF HIS
LATE ROYAL HIGHNESS
THE
PRINCE CONSORT

———◆———

Yesterday, with little of the pomp
and pageantry of a State ceremonial,
but with every outward mark of
respect, and with all the solemnity
which befitted his high station and
his public virtues, the mortal remains
of the husband of our Queen were
interred in the last resting-place of
England's Sovereigns – the Chapel
Royal of St George's, Windsor.

The Times

Chapter Twenty-One

'I'm sorry, dearie, but she's not here.'

Grace, standing on the back doorstep of the Unwins' Kensington home, stared at Mrs Beaman, not understanding what she meant. 'You mean, my sister has gone on an errand somewhere?'

'No. I mean she's not here. She's gawn. Scarpered!'

'The Unwins have dismissed her?'

'No.' The cook spoke as if to an imbecile. 'No, I tell

you she's *gawn*. Run off.'

Grace swallowed and spoke hoarsely. 'When was this?'

'Oh, must be a good few days now. A week, maybe.'

'But where has she gone to?'

'Where? Who knows? She hasn't sent no calling card!' said Mrs Beaman.

'But she doesn't know anyone! Where would she go?'

'Gawd only knows!'

'But why? Please tell me what you know . . . I can't imagine why she would run off. Were the Unwins unkind to her?'

Mrs Beaman looked a little uneasy. 'Unkind? Not they! Treated her proper good, they did.'

'Then may I speak with the other servants – with Lizzie and Blossom? Perhaps they have some idea of where she might have –'

'We've got new servants here now,' the cook interrupted. 'A clean sweep of 'em, the mistress wanted. We've got Ethel and Maud and Charity. They don't know Lily; they were hardly here two minutes before she took off.'

Grace was silent for a moment. 'Mrs Beaman, have you any idea at all of where she may have gone? Did she say she was missing me? Might she have just gone off to find me?' As Grace spoke, she visualised her sister going to Edgware Road only to find that she was working in the Oxford Street store, and then not being brave enough to come through the mighty glass doors on her own.

The cook shook her head. 'I believe they did think she might have run off with one of the servant lads in the big house up yonder.'

'Which big house?'

Mrs Beaman waved in the general direction of the street, uncomfortable with Mr Unwin's request to put about this story. 'Don't ask me. That's just what I heard. Mrs Unwin said she caught her several times hanging out the back window talking to a groom.'

Grace felt tears start in her eyes. 'But why did no one say? Why didn't anyone tell me that she'd gone?'

'I suppose they didn't want to worry you,' Mrs Beaman said, beginning to shut the door. 'What with all the grief around at the moment, no one wanted to disturb you any further.'

'But she's my *sister*. I can't lose her. She's the only relative I have!'

'If I see her, I'll tell her to get in touch' were Mrs Beaman's parting words.

Grace's heartfelt plea had touched her deeply, though, and when the door was closed, she stood there for some moments composing herself before she carried on with her household duties.

It was the day of Prince Albert's funeral and a good proportion of the British Isles had come to a complete halt. Shop owners had been hoping that general trade, always slow in December and almost at a standstill since the death of the Prince, might have improved because of the festive season, but it seemed that Christmas had been cancelled that year and no one was inclined to be merry. In London, and in Windsor especially – where the funeral service was to be held in St George's Chapel – there was an aspect of the most profound gloom, with shops closed, work suspended, each curtain in every house drawn across and the streets deserted. Everyone seen outside, however low or high, wore some symbol of mourning, and in the great churches across the land the tolling bell sounded.

The Unwin Undertaking Establishment and the Unwin Mourning Emporium were, of course, also closed. Grace and the other store workers had toiled long and hard a full six days before that, and worried though she was about Lily, on arriving back at Edgware Road each night, Grace had been too exhausted to think about taking the long, dark walk across to the Kensington house to check that she was all right.

Now she stood on the Unwins' doorstep after speaking to Mrs Beaman, utterly dismayed. How *could* Lily have just run off without telling her? Was such a thing really possible? It was true that she did silly things sometimes, but she'd never shown any propensity for engaging in flirtatious or playful talk with young men, let alone getting to know one of them well enough to run away. No, the idea was unthinkable!

Grace walked back along the side passageway to the front of the Unwins' house, which was hung with all the trappings of mourning. A black-ribboned wreath of bay hung on the door and the hedges in the front were covered with black muslin. If the front door had been opened, an onlooker might have seen that the hall mirror was swathed in black and the royal hatchments (which the Unwins had absolutely no right to display) were similarly draped, for all the world as if the family had been closely related to Prince Albert.

The parlour curtains at the front of the house were closed, of course, but they shifted a little as Grace passed, and she suddenly saw a girl's face peering at her. The eyes of the girl locked with hers, and then the curtains moved again and the face was gone. It was, Grace was perfectly sure, Charlotte Unwin. Something about the expression glimpsed, something about the slippery deceitfulness of that swift disappearance from the window caused Grace further reflection. She felt certain she was being told a lie about Lily's disappearance; her sister would *never* leave without telling her.

She must go to the police to report her missing, she decided, although she'd be very nervous about doing so, for the police and the poor were at constant war in London and she couldn't imagine a peeler actually helping her. What else could she do? Advertise that Lily was missing in *The Times*, of course, if she had the fee – but Lily couldn't read. A better idea, perhaps, would be to ask the advice of James Solent. She'd been thinking about their last meeting lately, and how sincere he'd seemed in his wish to help her. Yes, being a man of the law, James Solent would surely know what to do about a missing person.

But when should she go? He wouldn't be at work that day, when the whole of England was mourning, and the following day was Christmas Eve and his chambers certainly would not be open then, either. It would be a day or so after Christmas, at the very earliest, before she could contact him, and Lily might be anywhere in the country by then.

A dismal tolling bell sounded from a nearby church and Grace shivered, partly at the sheer misery of the sound and partly through cold.

'Lily, wherever you are,' she whispered to her sister, 'take care.'

EVENING PARTIES FOR THE SEASON
in town and country
ATTENDED PERSONALLY
by Mr Henry Boot with his extensive collection of MAGICAL TRICKS, forming a brilliant and astonishing seance nouvelle.
A superior entertainment guaranteed.

Chapter Twenty-Two

On Christmas Day the Unwins supplied a plum pudding for those at Edgware Road who were not going home to their families, but Grace found herself so worried about Lily (was she eating properly? was she warm? was she being held against her will?) that she couldn't eat her portion, which ended up being divided between the stable lads.

On Boxing Day, designated as the day one gave to the deserving poor, the Unwins' female workers were presented with two linen handkerchiefs and a length of coarse material to make a work apron, while the men received handkerchiefs and a miniature bottle of whisky. These gifts were bestowed upon them by Miss Charlotte Unwin, pink-faced and perfumed in a full-length fur mantle, who reminded them that it was a wonderful thing that the Unwins were able to employ them, and said that everyone should pray that their luck might continue.

'May I ask if you have had any word of my sister?' Grace was bold enough to ask Miss Charlotte when she was handed her gift.

'I? Have word of your sister?' Miss Charlotte's eyes rounded in surprise. 'No, of course not. What an extra-ordinary notion.'

'I thought someone might have heard something,' Grace said, 'and as you had taken a kindly interest in her . . .'

Miss Charlotte shook her head. 'I have not heard a word, nor would I expect to. I told you she was a little over-friendly with a young man, did I not?'

Grace nodded.

'There, you see.'

'See . . . what?'

'See that once a girl has compromised her reputation in polite society, sometimes her only option is to leave it.'

'I don't believe that she –' Grace began, but Miss Charlotte had swept past her and away, for she was due to give out woollen vests at the Hospital for Fatherless Girls at midday and then attend a magic show.

Grace did not sleep at all that night. Perhaps if her

sister hadn't been how she was; perhaps if they hadn't always been so close; perhaps if there didn't seem to be something warped about the whole Unwin empire, she might have believed the story and would not now be turning over more sinister plots in her mind. But why would anyone want to take Lily away? What could possibly be gained from doing such a thing? Grace wrestled with the problem, tossing and turning and sighing, until even the placid Jane was moved to complain about her.

Towards morning, however, she suddenly believed she'd hit upon the terrible reason: the Unwins' number one interest was making money, and there was a sure way of doing this. Had they taken her simple, gullible sister to make her work as a prostitute?

One heard such tales – and close to home, too. Why, Mrs Macready had once told her of a poor unfortunate kept in the grimy cellars of the house next door expressly for the purpose of prostitution. 'Never allowed out to take a bit of air,' she had said. 'Always kept short of food, suffering from disease and chained up. The poor woman died in the end. When they found her body it had rat bites all over it . . .' Yes, the more Grace thought about it, the more she feared *that* was the answer.

Four more days elapsed before Grace was able to get to the Inns of Court. Scared of being turned away by Mr Meakers, she gave a street boy a ha'penny to take a message into the chambers and ask for Mr James Solent. After half an hour or so, he came out. They sat together on a bench in the grounds while Grace, embarrassed, tried to find the right words to tell him what she feared.

'I can assure you that nothing you tell me will go any further,' he said, sensing her reluctance to speak. 'When we met, I promised I would help you if I could, and I would still be happy to have the opportunity of doing so.'

Grace pressed her lips together. How to say such a thing?

'Have you fallen into ways of which you are ashamed?' he asked gently. 'Perhaps I can lend you a little money if it will help to remove you from temptation.'

'No! It is not that!' Grace said swiftly, shaking her head. 'Not I!'

'You are still working for the Unwin family?'

She nodded, then burst out, 'It's my sister – she's disappeared!'

'Disappeared?' James asked. 'From where?'

'She was working for the Unwins in their Kensington house as a maid,' Grace said. Then she faltered and began to cry before adding, 'And one day last week I went round to visit her and she'd gone!'

'I see. And when you asked where she'd gone, what did they say?'

'They said that she'd become friendly with a young man and had probably run away with him.'

'And you don't think this is true?'

'It is not!' Grace shook her head, agitated. 'My sister would never go off without telling me. She . . . she is a simple girl and sometimes easily led, but she would never just disappear.'

'But what could be more understandable than that she should meet someone and . . .'

'She would not!' Grace burst out. 'My sister is not a forward girl. She doesn't particularly like the male sex, for she . . . for we both had a bad experience and . . .' Grace stopped and swallowed, trying to close her mind to her ordeal, and for some moments could not speak.

'Well,' James said soothingly, 'let us think of other possibilities. I'm no admirer of anyone in the mourning industry – especially the Unwins, who seem to profit from it more than most – but why should they be implicated in your sister's disappearance?'

Grace looked at him. 'I fear they have taken her for immoral purposes,' she said, her face flushing pink. 'I have heard that there are houses where women are kept to satisfy men's desires. Perhaps they are keeping her at one of these against her will.'

James Solent shook his head immediately. 'No, no. I'm sure it's not that, for even the Unwins have a certain name to maintain and would not be connected with anything quite so scandalous.' He paused. 'It's alarming when our loved ones grow away from us, but I'm certain your sister is well and will contact you in her own good time.'

Grace, fighting back tears, was silent. She'd been quite sure that James would help her, but he didn't seem to understand.

'Thank you for listening to me,' she said when she'd gained control of herself. 'I must go back now, before the Unwins realise I've gone.'

'Will you let me know when you hear from her?'

'*If* I hear,' Grace said, 'though how I'll get a message from Lily when she can't even write her own name –'

'Your sister's name is Lily?' James asked with quick interest.

'It is. Did I not say so before?'

James put his head on one side and looked at Grace quizzically. 'It is not, by any remote and remarkable chance, Lily *Parkes*?'

Grace nodded. 'Yes. How did you know?'

'Lily Parkes!' James repeated, his voice rising. 'By all that's wonderful. And you are her sister.'

'I am.'

'Your mother – your mother is dead, I believe you told me. And her name?'

'Mama's first name was Letitia.'

James gasped. 'Your father was Reginald?'

'Yes,' Grace said in surprise. 'But I believe him to be dead also. I never knew him – I was born after he left.' She added, 'He didn't even know of my existence.'

James let out his breath in a great gust, then took both of Grace's hands in his own. 'Grace Parkes, you must prepare yourself for a shock.'

Grace burst into tears. 'Lily is dead! You have heard that she's dead?'

'No, not that at all! I don't know anything about your sister – other than the fact that the whole of legal London is talking about her.'

'Talking about my *sister*?'

'Talking about her, looking for her, speculating about the missing Lily Parkes and her mother.'

'But why ever should they be?'

'And they'll be talking about you, too, once it's known that you are the other living heiress of Reginald Parkes.'

Grace looked at James, mystified. 'What has this to do with my father?'

'Before I tell you,' James said, 'would you mind recounting the circumstances of how you came to work for the Unwins, for now I can only think that it is they who are behind Lily's disappearance.'

Grace looked at him, bewildered. 'It was merely that Mrs Unwin saw me at Brookwood the day I met you, and asked me to come and work for her as a mute.'

'And you told her what? Forgive me for being pedantic, but that's my training. I need to get the facts right and be sure about everything.'

It had just started to snow; large flakes fell gently and softly, and Grace brushed the sparkling crystals from her velvet jacket as she spoke. 'Well, I thanked her but said I wasn't interested, and then when our circumstances changed and Lily and I found ourselves on the streets, I was so distressed that I went to see her. I asked Mrs Unwin if she would employ us both, but she said that she could not, and I was about to leave when Mr Unwin came into the room and said that they would take me on as a mute and, out of charity, would offer Lily a position at their house.'

'Oh, I bet he did!' James said. 'And I bet he'd found out your full names by then.'

'I believe I had mentioned them. But what has this to do with anything? Why did you ask about my father? What has he done?'

'What's he done?' James opened and closed his mouth several times, then was moved to stand up and give vent to his feelings. 'What has he done?' he asked. 'He's died abroad and left you his complete fortune, that's all! You and your sister are probably the richest young women in the whole of London!'

There was a long pause when Grace could neither speak nor move; indeed she went so still that the snow settled on the brim of her black bonnet, so that it looked as if it was edged in ermine.

At last she said, 'You must be mocking me, sir, and it is not kind of you.'

'Indeed I am not. I promise I am not,' James said very sincerely, sitting down again.

'A fortune?' Grace asked. 'A *fortune*, you say?'

'Indeed. A king's ransom, I have heard.'

'And are you quite sure that it's my sister, Lily Parkes, who is being sought?' Grace asked, dizzy and confused.

'I am perfectly sure. The legacy is left to your mother and Lily, but as your father didn't know of your existence and your mother is dead, then you are her direct legatee.' He gave a great clap of laughter. 'We've looked at the advertisements often enough in chambers, speculated so much about where the girl and her mother might be, that I know the details by heart.'

'So the Unwins know all this, too,' said Grace.

'I rather think so.'

'And Lily *hasn't* run off with a young man.'

'Indeed not. The Unwins must be keeping her somewhere, grooming her in order to swindle you both out of the inheritance.'

'Oh, Lily!' Grace suddenly cried.

James was silent, thinking deeply for fully two minutes while the snow fell around them. Before he spoke again he took Grace's hand in his own. 'I will take advice about what to do,' he said, 'but in the meantime you must stay with the Unwins, keep a watchful eye on what goes on and play the mute.'

'That last part won't be difficult,' Grace said wryly.

'But I beg you to be careful. Together, the Unwins are a very powerful family. The cousin . . .'

'Sylvester Unwin?'

'Yes, he. He's extremely rich, fiercely ambitious and undoubtedly crooked – but there's talk of him becoming Lord Mayor of London. If crossed, he would make a formidable opponent.'

'You think he's involved, too?'

'Most definitely. The Unwins always work together.'

'But surely . . . surely you know what to do to stop them? Surely there's something that can be done?'

He shook his head. 'I'm sorry if I've given you an inflated idea of my powers,' he said, 'when actually I'm the most junior member of chambers and have as much authority as the man at the end of the street selling matches.'

Grace managed to smile a little despite her disappointment.

'No, this delicate matter calls for some cunning. I shall confide in one of the senior barristers and ask his advice.'

'How will I know what's happening? Shall I come here again?'

He thought for a moment. 'Would you be able to leave the house for a short while in the evenings?'

'Possibly,' said Grace.

'We must arrange a venue. Do you know the letter box at the top of Edgware Road?' On Grace nodding, he continued, 'I pass it each evening about eight o'clock; I could break my journey and wait there for you.'

'You may have a long wait – I may not be able to get out.'

'I'll be there every night for up to an hour until you *do* come,' James said. 'And together we'll decide what should be done.'

Grace smiled at him tremulously. 'I can't thank you enough.'

'It's my pleasure,' he said. 'This is a very renowned case and may help my name become known in the legal world. Besides . . .'

Grace looked up at him.

'Besides . . .' he said again, and then merely squeezed her hand and smiled until Grace had to look away, blushing. 'If you can, find time to go to Somerset House to get birth certificates for your sister and your-self. And – even more important – obtain your mother and father's marriage certificate.' He withdrew some coins from his pocket. 'You'll find that the certificates are one shilling each.'

'I cannot possibly take money from you!'

'Well,' he said, looking at her with mock sternness, 'I will lend you five shillings until you come into your fortune, and then you may pay me back – with interest if you wish.'

Chapter Twenty-Three

The following afternoon, just half a mile down the road, in imposing, wood-panelled offices, Miss Charlotte Unwin, accompanied by her mother and father, met the two most senior partners of that old-established law firm, Binge and Gently, in order to claim the Parkes' family fortune.

Miss Charlotte, well tutored about her new background, was looking slightly different. Not enough to cause the neighbours to gossip, but just subtle temporary measures that could be changed back later. The Unwins had no way of telling if there was anyone other than the sisters with knowledge of the general appearance of either of the Parkes parents, so to bring her complexion more into line with the skins of Lily and Grace, Charlotte's blooming complexion had become paler under a liberal application of face powder, and her hair treated with a mixture of glycerine, red wine and rosewater in order to render it darker. In addition, she was wearing a false switch of auburn ringlets on the crown of her head, which shook each time she burst into distracting tears – which was fairly often.

'My dear. Such a shock, I know!' Her mother produced a bottle of smelling salts from her crocodile-skin handbag and waved it under Charlotte's nose. 'But you always knew you were adopted, did you not?'

Charlotte sniffled tearfully.

'And now we shall take it slowly and go through all the correct procedures with these helpful and learned gentlemen,' she said, smiling gummily first at Mr Binge, then at Mr Gently, 'and then perhaps you and I can go away on a grand tour.'

'Can we go and find the place that my real papa lived?' Charlotte asked piteously.

'Perhaps, perhaps,' said her mother. 'We shall see. All in good time.'

'How quickly can we get the money?' George Unwin asked, and suffered a hard look from his wife. 'Our daughter is very sensitive,' he elaborated quickly, 'and we are anxious that things return to normal as soon as possible. She should not be subjected to too many disruptions to her customary routines.'

'Quite,' said Mr Gently, 'although you will appreciate that because of the large sum involved, there are certain formalities which have to be gone through.'

'Charlotte is such a delicate creature,' Mrs Unwin said, 'and that's why we must insist that publicity is kept to an absolute minimum. The fewer people who know, the better. And as for the newspapers finding out our identities – well, heaven forfend!'

'Indeed,' said George Unwin. 'The thought that our clients, colleagues and neighbours might find out about this is simply appalling.'

'We will do all we can to prevent that,' said Mr Binge.

'Although everyone in the city is talking about the case,' put in Mr Gently. '*Such* an unusual and exciting event, and such a very large sum of money.'

Mr Unwin only just prevented himself from licking his lips. 'What will happen next?'

Mr Gently looked down at the papers on his desk and shuffled them about a little. 'You say you have your daughter's adoption certificate at home?'

'Of course, of course!' cried Mr Unwin.

'It's just that we didn't stop to hunt for it,' said his wife. 'When my husband's cousin told us about the advertisement – only yesterday evening – we decided we must come here straight away.'

This, as with most things connected with the Unwins, was not quite true. Sylvester Unwin *had* rushed round the previous evening, but with news he'd heard on the criminal grapevine that a certain other party was also grooming a young woman and preparing a case in order to claim the inheritance. The Unwins had decided, therefore, not to wait for the false adoption papers to be delivered from the corrupt forgers who'd been employed by Sylvester Unwin, but to contact Binge and Gently immediately and beat the others to it.

'We don't take *The Mercury* ourselves,' said George Unwin. 'If Mr Sylvester Unwin hadn't seen it we might never have found out.'

Mr Gently looked at Charlotte, who trembled and burst into tears again under his steady gaze. She did this partly to deflect the questioning, partly to emulate Lily's own frequent outbursts and partly because she was terrified she would say the wrong thing and so lose her gig and driver.

When she had sniffed at the bottle of salts, delicately touched a lace handkerchief to her nose and partially recovered, Mr Gently asked her, 'Would you mind telling me again of your earliest recollections, Miss Unwin? We want to bring someone in to take notes.'

Charlotte looked rather taken aback at this but said she would do her best, and a clerk appeared carrying a stool and a sheaf of papers. He sat down at a respectful distance from the vast desks of the partners, while the new Lily Parkes sighed and gazed into the distance.

'The pity is, I remember so little of my past life,' she began.

'What about where you lived? Can you remember that, perhaps?'

'I do recall our house; a dear little cottage with a mulberry tree in the garden, quite near to a windmill. And I had a little whitewashed room upstairs, with a brass bedstead.'

'What about your mother? Can you recall her name?'

'Of course. It was Letitia,' said Charlotte, sadly and well rehearsed. 'And she had dark hair, like mine, and was very pretty. But I can't recall Papa at all.'

'Of course not!' said Mrs Unwin quickly. 'She wasn't much above two years of age when he went off.'

'Mama had a miniature of him on her bedside table, though.'

'And was there anything in particular about his appearance?'

Charlotte hesitated. 'It was quite a *small* miniature, but Mama used to say I was very like him.'

'And you lived in the cottage with the mulberry tree . . . ?'

'All on our own. And Mama always said that one day Papa would come back for us and we'd be very rich. We lived there until . . . until . . .' And Charlotte's face crumpled as if she were about to burst out crying again.

'Until her mother died,' Mr Unwin put in quickly for, having seen them often enough in rehearsal, he was beginning to weary of his daughter's outbursts. 'And then Mrs Unwin and I – being unable to have children ourselves – heard about the poor little orphan and took her in.'

'We claimed you for our own, my darling!' said Mrs Unwin, and she and Charlotte exchanged rapturous glances.

'But why did you change her name from Lily?' Mr Binge asked. 'The child was what – five or six years old? She was surely used to that name.'

'But I never liked it!' said Charlotte, looking pained.

'And, quite frankly,' said Mrs Unwin, 'I have always thought Lily to be a servant's name. We deemed it best to give the girl a completely fresh start.'

'But would you mind telling us,' put in Mr Unwin, 'how our Charlotte's natural father came by such a fortune?'

'Guano,' said Mr Binge.

All three Unwins looked mystified.

'Bird, er, droppings,' explained Mr Gently. 'A great amount of them which he discovered in the Galapagos Islands.'

Mrs Unwin was so dismayed by the subject matter that she could barely look Mr Gently in the eye. 'But why does anyone want that sort of thing?' she asked faintly.

'Fertiliser,' Mr Gently explained. 'It's a very valuable commodity. He found a veritable mountain of it.'

Mrs Unwin turned away, her face registering great disgust.

'Can you tell us anything else about your childhood, Miss, er, Charlotte?' asked Mr Binge.

Charlotte rattled off everything she'd learned from the real Lily and Grace: the bluebird tea service, the wedding bonnet, Mama's embroidered mottoes and the velvet-lined ring box all got a mention. When she stopped speaking and the clerk was dismissed, the partners informed the Unwin family that things appeared to be in order.

'And if you would bring in the adoption papers at your earliest convenience, I believe we can complete the formalities in a very short time,' added Mr Binge.

Both gentlemen then stood and, bowing formally to the Unwin family, gave their commiserations on the death of Lily's real father and their congratulations on the acquisition of a fortune, leaving the Unwins unsure about what sort of expression to allow on their faces as they left the offices and went home to open a bottle of vintage champagne.

Messrs Binge & Gently have announced that the young woman they have been seeking for several months has now come forward. Regular readers of this paper will know that certain persons were being sought in order to acquaint them with momentous news and it can now be revealed that the young woman in question was adopted by a London family.

Her adoptive family have asked to remain anonymous in order that she may appear in society without drawing indecorous and uncouth interest, and say that any begging letters will not be considered or acknowledged.

The Mercury

Chapter Twenty-Four

At the appointed time, by the letter box at the top of Edgware Road and under the light from the street lamp, Grace read through the newspaper article which James Solent had given her. When she'd finished, she looked up at him despairingly.

'It's the Unwins, isn't it? It's *they* who are saying that they adopted Lily.'

James nodded. 'I've made some enquiries to a friend of mine, a clerk at Binge and Gently, and it is them, I'm afraid.'

'They've claimed the money. Then they've won!' Grace said. She'd known, of course, that it was too wonderful to be true; that stories about poor girls coming into fortunes only happened in the fairytales she'd once told Lily.

'I wouldn't go so far as to say that they've won,' James said, 'although at the moment they certainly seem to have the upper hand.'

'But my *sister*!' Grace said, bewildered. 'I can hardly believe it. Why would she go along with this? How have they persuaded her to say she was adopted by them?'

'For money?' James suggested. 'Or perhaps they promised her some jewellery or other frippery.'

Grace began shaking her head immediately. 'Lily isn't interested in things like that,' she said. 'And she is too fond of me – and I of her – for us to ever pretend that the other one doesn't exist.'

'But something has made her lie.'

'She can't even *tell* lies with any degree of success. A child of four could find her out!'

'Hmm.' James thought for a long moment, then said, 'Perhaps they discovered that fact for themselves . . .'

Grace looked at him, not comprehending.

'Perhaps,' he explained, 'having discovered that

Lily wouldn't go along with the story they wished to perpetuate, they have employed someone else to be Lily for them.'

'You mean – an actress?' Grace asked.

'An actress. Exactly. Someone to take her part while the real Lily is kept out of the way.'

'Of course!' Grace said, and all at once realised the truth. 'But they don't need to employ an actress – they have their daughter!'

'The Unwins have a daughter?'

Grace nodded. 'A girl about the same age as my sister. They will have used her instead.'

'You've seen this girl?'

'I have. She behaved very pleasantly towards me. Oh!' Grace clapped her hand to her mouth. 'That's why she asked me so many questions about my mother and her circumstances. And Lily told me that she was as affable to her, too.'

'Oh, clever Unwins!' James said. 'She was trying to unstitch your past. To discover everything about your family that she possibly could.'

'But she seemed so very nice . . .'

James smiled wryly. 'Where money is concerned, niceness can be put on to order.'

'You don't think . . .' Grace hesitated, took a breath, began again. 'Do you think my sister is safe? They wouldn't have . . . have done anything to her, would they?'

James shook his head. 'I really don't think so. They

might kidnap someone, lock them away, but even the Unwins wouldn't stoop to mur—' He coughed. 'To anything worse.'

A violent cacophony of vehicle horns suddenly erupted from the encircling traffic and both James and Grace fell silent.

When the noise ceased and they could make themselves heard again, Grace asked, 'What can be done? There must be *something*.'

James nodded. 'Tomorrow I'll speak to Mr Ernest Stamford, the venerable head of our chambers, and acquaint him with the whole story.'

'Is there anything that *I* can do?' Grace asked anxiously.

'Just keep your eyes and ears open. Do you ever see people arriving at the funeral home and hear what they speak about?'

'Sometimes,' Grace said.

'Then it's possible that you may overhear something. My law clerk friend told me that the Unwins have yet to produce the adoption papers for Lily.'

'Because no such papers exist!'

'Quite. They'll be having forgeries made, of course, but these will need to look authentic and will take some time to create. If, when they get them, you were able to steal them ...'

'But wouldn't they just have more made?'

'They won't be that easy to counterfeit. And in the

meantime we'll be finding out more and gaining time in which to prepare our own case.'

Grace was quiet for a moment. 'But how much chance do we really have of defeating people as devious as the Unwins?' she said. 'Who's going to believe me over someone who's being hailed as the next Lord Mayor of London?'

'The truth is on your side,' James said, 'and we must trust in that.'

'I'll do what I can,' Grace said fervently. 'I'll look through keyholes and watch for messengers coming and going and listen in to conversations.'

'But you must take great care,' James said, catching hold of her hand. 'Remember that beneath the Unwins' air of respectability they are completely unscrupulous. Don't let them suspect for a moment that you know what's going on.'

'I won't,' Grace said.

James smiled, bent his head and kissed her hand before releasing it.

Grace didn't know what to think about this gallant gesture, so decided to think nothing at all. The Unwins, the inheritance, the whereabouts of Lily – all these filled her mind to the brim. There was little room for anything else.

James did not leave *The Mercury* with Grace, but put it on to a pile of rubbish left against a lamp post, where it was taken by a tramp and put inside his jacket as a form of insulation against the bitter cold. Grace did not, then, read the small advertisement in the personal column:

'Mrs Smith' urgently seeks 'Mary'. Last seen in Westminster Bridge Road, London, SW on 7th June 1861. If this date and address is pertinent to you, please contact: Box No. 236, The Mercury, London, regarding a matter of great importance.

Chapter Twenty-Five

'I was thinking,' said the widow, 'of having pine for my dear husband's coffin.'

'Were you indeed?' George Unwin said, sounding shocked to the core. 'Pine! Such a flimsy and insubstantial wood. I wouldn't say that it was at all suitable for a beloved husband.' He shook his head reflectively. 'If he was *very* dear to you, I fear that nothing less than polished oak will do. Of course, if he was not so important in your life . . .' His voice trailed off and the sentence hung in the air, unfinished, accusing.

It was a few days after Grace had heard the astonishing news about the inheritance, and she was once again standing in the red room, waiting to be produced as a living example of the type of conscientious funeral mute who might be supplied to enhance a leave-taking of this world.

The woman sighed. 'It's just that I find myself in some difficulties regarding the expense.'

'The expense should not be a consideration,' said Mr Unwin, sadly shaking his head.

'Have you considered the Necropolis train?' Mrs Unwin put in. 'Some of our more modern widows are finding it the very thing – and it can prove most economical.'

'A train?' said the widow. 'Certainly not. My husband couldn't abide the noisy things.' She sighed again. 'No, as for the casket wood . . .'

'Madam!' said Mr Unwin. 'I would be failing in my duty as a caring undertaker if I let you choose anything less than best-quality polished oak.'

'Oh dear, then, perhaps . . .'

Grace, hearing this with eyes lowered, hardly knew whether to rail aloud at George Unwin's deviousness, or applaud his ingenuity.

There being no funerals that day, she'd been embroidering another human hair brooch (the deceased's hair formed into a bay wreath and appliquéd on to silk) when she'd been told by Mrs Unwin to don bonnet and streamers and wait, looking tragic, in the red room. Now, as the Unwins and the widow went into the other room to reassess the question of wood, Grace took a good look around the red room, which she was seldom permitted to enter. She saw a substantial mahogany desk, some leather chairs and a tall cupboard standing slightly open. Above the desk were two large shelves, one of which was tightly filled with paper files bearing the names of the recipients of past funerals, the other holding trade periodicals and copies of the Bible. On the desktop there was a paperknife, inkstand and five wooden filing trays with details of Unwin funerals to be carried out over the next few days. There was no sign of any grand plan to defraud Lily Parkes of her inheritance. In fact, in the cold light of a London afternoon the whole thing seemed too preposterous to be true.

Grace pondered on this, then spent ten minutes or so quietly worrying about Lily before the Unwins returned to the room, the widow trailing disconsolately behind.

'If you don't wish to use the train, then having a mere *two* horses for the leading carriage looks rather paltry,' Mrs Unwin was saying as they entered. 'It seems to signify – if I may be so bold – a certain indifference on the part of the relatives left on earth.'

There came a murmur of protest from the widow.

'Last year, someone widowed in your very road chose to have four noble beasts to pull her husband's coffin to paradise, and they made the procession look quite magnificent with their feathery plumes and flowing manes, did they not, Mr Unwin?'

'They did! For they stood as symbols of the great love the woman bore her husband.'

'Oh dear, then. If you really think so . . .' the widow said.

Mrs Unwin turned towards Grace. 'And while we are on the subject of the funeral cortège,' she said, 'have you thought about mutes?'

Grace breathed in gently and stood, her fingertips touching, as still as a waxwork.

'I had not,' said the widow. 'I hadn't realised such things would be needed.'

'Mutes are very much in demand at society funerals,' Mrs Unwin said. 'They can come with hooded cloaks, or appear as Grace is now: with black bonnets and trailing ribbons. "Weepers", we call the ribbons – they symbolise the tears shed.'

'I see,' the widow said, staring balefully at Grace. 'But I'd not really –'

'They usually come in pairs,' Mr Unwin went on smoothly, 'and spaced each side of a front door can look very tragic. I think you'll agree that Grace here has a most profoundly heart-rending face.'

The widow sighed heavily and sniffed into a black-edged handkerchief, but agreed to two mutes. Grace waited to be dismissed, for she had more work to do on the hair brooch and she wanted to finish it before the daylight went. The widow was escorted to the front door, and Rose had only just closed it behind her when there was a sudden heavy knocking.

The door was opened again and Rose began a polite greeting, but this was cut short by Sylvester Unwin barging into the hall and heading straight for the red room.

'Got it, George!' he said, holding aloft a manila envelope. 'What we've been waiting for!'

Grace went hot, then cold. It was the certificate. It had to be.

She was dismissed in an instant, but instead of returning to the small sewing room, stayed close by in the narrow corridor which joined the public front of the house to the workrooms at the back.

'Good forgery?' she heard George Unwin ask.

'The best. Those men have cut their teeth on printing banknotes!' said his cousin.

There came the sound of an envelope being opened and Grace, her heart pounding, imagined a paper being unfolded.

'Looks sweet to me,' she heard George Unwin say after a few moments.

'Though what it *should* look like is anyone's guess,' said his wife.

There was a short silence when Grace presumed they were all reading the document.

'When are you going to take it?' his cousin asked.

'Close of business tonight,' George Unwin replied.

Mrs Unwin gave a little titter of delight. 'It shouldn't look too pristine, mind,' she said. 'Remember it's supposed to be some years old. Crease it; rub some soot from the fire on it.'

'Wise words!' George Unwin said jovially. 'That's wives for you.'

There was another short silence, as if the document

were being returned to the envelope, and then George Unwin suggested drinks all round in the back parlour. Mrs Unwin said she would leave that to the men – she had her girls to supervise – and quick as a flash Grace darted down the corridor and around the corner.

She went straight to the small sewing room, hung up her bonnet and cloak and picked up her embroidery. It was, perhaps, lucky that four of the Unwin girls were still working at the store in Oxford Street, so the only person in the workroom at that time was Jane. She was diligently embroidering initials on to a coffin pillow, however, and didn't even glance up as Grace returned.

Grace sat still and silent for a few moments, holding her work. What should she do? Could she let James know? How? If she did inform him, what would he want her to do?

And then the most frightening answer came into her mind: he would want her to steal the certificate!

Immediately she found herself shaking her head. No, she wouldn't dare do such a thing!

But if she didn't, came the voice from inside her, then was she prepared to stand by and let someone else take the fortune that her own father had made? Was she prepared to let Charlotte Unwin steal Lily's identity – and perhaps never see her sister again? To allow the Unwins to prosper unchecked?

No! She was not prepared for any of those things. And they would all happen if she didn't do something to stop them. Even if she were to fail in the attempt, at least she must try . . .

Coming to this decision and knowing it must be acted upon before she lost courage, she put down her embroidery and, taking a quick look at Jane to see if she had even registered her presence, went out of the room, down the corridor and (after listening at the door for a moment to make sure no one was in there) slipped back into the red room.

Oh, *easy*, she breathed, for the manila envelope was still on the desk. She took eight quick steps across to it, removed the thick white paper out of the envelope and read the top lines: *Notice of Adoption in the County of Middlesex.* Further down, Lily's name was inked in, and the names Letitia and Reginald Parkes cited as Lily's birth mother and father.

Oh wicked Unwins!

She didn't stop to read more, but (having the fore-sight to leave the empty envelope in its correct position on the desk) folded the certificate and pushed it inside her bodice. She turned towards the door – and then with a feeling of terror heard the voice of Sylvester Unwin calling for Rose to bring a decanter of port to the red room. Unluckily for Grace, Sylvester Unwin had decided to return to the red room and the larger fire.

Hearing his hated voice just outside the door, Grace froze, and then, seeing there was only one place to hide, she quickly pulled opened the door of the tall cupboard and got inside. She held it closed with trembling fingers.

Through the tiny crack between the doors Grace saw Rose follow Sylvester Unwin into the room. The maid spent a moment sweeping and tidying the hearth, then went out, and came back a moment later carrying a decanter of a rich red liquid on a tray. Sylvester Unwin spoke not a word of thanks to Rose, but took off his outer jacket and hung it on the coat stand, poured himself a glass of port and pulled a comfortable chair close to the fire.

Grace, breathing in as shallow a way as possible, felt faint with fear. She bit down hard on her lip to bring herself to her full senses, telling herself she could overcome this, that she could win – she just had to keep silent and still until he left the room . . .

But Sylvester Unwin did not seem inclined to leave the room; in fact, he seemed to be making himself at home, as if he intended to stay put for some time. Compelled to observe, Grace watched him settle into the chair; chest out, legs astride, self-important even in the simple act of sitting. After a moment he eased off his boots and leaned over to stand them at the side of the hearth, then removed his gloves, pulling first at the right one, and then the left, dropping each in turn on to the floor. He turned slightly and reached into his jacket pocket for a cigar, which brought his left hand into full view, and it was then that Grace, to her complete and utter amazement and horror, saw that this whole left hand was a contraption made of metal plates and rivets fastened to the stub of his wrist by canvas straps.

And then, of course, she knew the truth; the reason why cigar smoke and macassar hair oil set off a chain of memory which she didn't want to explore, the reason why her whole body cried out in revulsion whenever he was close. Sylvester Unwin had been the man in the church at the Welland-Scropes funeral, the man whose very presence made her feel nauseous. Sylvester Unwin was the man who had visited her in the night . . .

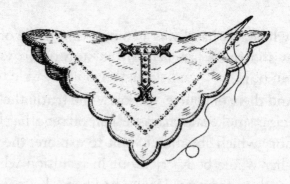

Chapter Twenty-Six

Again, Grace bit her lip, this time so hard that she tasted blood in her mouth and almost gagged at it. A hundred questions and a hundred sensations came into her head so that she felt she could hardly control herself. She wanted to leap out of the cupboard, shower blows on Sylvester Unwin, scream obscenities at him. She wanted to pick up the paperknife and plunge it into his heart! How she'd suffered because of this man. He'd taken her innocence, stolen her past and ruined her future – and now he was involved in a plan to take the inheritance which rightfully belonged to her family. How could such a man be allowed to live? She wanted to kill him where he sat.

And yet, as she stood hidden in the darkness, only just managing to restrain the fury inside her, she knew the impossibility of her situation. She did not dare to act upon her wishes. She had neither the strength nor the audacity, and was too terrified of the repercussions. A man of his size and strength would be able to overpower her in an instant. And besides, even if she had a knife or a gun to hand, to take someone's life in cold blood was an awesome and terrible thing. She was not capable of it!

Her heart hammered in her ears as she fought to control herself and stay absolutely still and quiet. She must keep calm, stay alert and wait for the opportunity to escape. Only if she managed to get out of the room unseen did she have a hope of beating the Unwins.

Sylvester Unwin, completely unaware of the presence of anyone in the room, tapped the cigar on to the desk with his mechanical hand. In his head he was calculating the likely amount that they would receive as a result of the fraud. The whole inheritance amounted to a hundred thousand pounds, someone had told him. A hundred and fifty thousand, another had said. Even shared half and half with his cousin, it would be a very acceptable amount. Enough for a new mourning store in one of the big industrial cities, perhaps, Manchester or Birmingham . . .

Thinking about the likely amount and the means by which it was being obtained, he turned suddenly to look at the envelope on the desk. He stared at it for a few seconds, then – his chair being on wheels – he moved a foot or so nearer the desk and stretched out his hand to pick it up.

Grace went icy cold.

He looked inside, then looked again, swearing incredulously. He threw it down and shouted a string of curses. He peered at the floor, opened drawers in the desk and then, blaspheming and shouting, ran from the room.

Grace didn't hesitate. She slipped out of the cupboard, left the red room and returned to the small sewing room, which was now empty. She picked up the piece of embroidery she'd been working on earlier, and then sat still for a moment to allow her mind to take in what she'd just seen and try to cope with the immensity of it.

It *had* been he. Of course! Hadn't she sensed that all along? He'd been the figure in church at the dignitary's funeral, the one whose attendance had brought her out in shivers. And in his store – she hadn't recognised him exactly, but something deep inside her had registered the horror of his presence. *His* had been the remembered acrid cigar smell and the scented hair pomade. *His* the aura of evil . . .

From elsewhere in the building she heard shouting and she quickly bent over her sewing, hearing the crackle of paper as she did so. The certificate! She must get rid of it as soon as she could.

But where to put it?

The fire was the obvious place, but, it being so late in the day, there were barely three poor coals smouldering in the grate and no flame to catch the thick paper quickly and burn it to ashes. Besides, it would surely be better to keep it – in order to prove its duplicity. What about her room, under her mattress? Thinking of this, she stood up and then just as quickly sat down again, realising that they'd be sure to search the servants' rooms – and that of Lily's sister first. They'd search everywhere. And then a possible exception occurred to her. Would they look in God's waiting room?

Immediately she went from the workroom and hurried down the stone steps leading to the cool chamber which that day contained the gentlemanly corpses of Mr Truscot-Divine and Mr Mayhew, both due to be buried at Brookwood the following day. They were quite ready for their ceremonials, lying in their coffins in their best suits, their arms neatly folded across their chests. The lids rested loosely on the coffins, for these wouldn't be nailed down until just before their interment. Grace knew this was to guard against them being buried prematurely (and, of course, to allow Mr Unwin the opportunity to relieve the corpses of any valuable objects).

It was fiercely cold in the room. One candle burned in a tin holder, and this flickered and guttered in the damp, creating shuddering shadows and a dark, morbid atmosphere. It did not deter Grace, however, and she picked the nearest coffin, which happened to be that of Mr Truscot-Divine, moved the lid and slipped the certificate inside and under his mattress. As she did so she could not help but be reminded of the other time she'd done such a thing: the sad addition that she had, some six months earlier, made to that other coffin in that other place. How strange that *that* moment was so inextricably bound up with this . . .

But it was no time for reminiscence, and, lifting her skirts, she quickly ran back up the stairs to the workroom. She could hear noise and confusion in the red room – the voices of both Unwin cousins and Rose, crying and protesting – and decided it might be wise to go and speak to Mrs Unwin and thus obtain some sort of alibi. She found this lady in one of the workrooms with Jane and two other girls, fashioning wax flowers into wreaths.

Grace dipped a curtsey. Over the last few days she'd found it extremely difficult to hide her hatred of the Unwin family and remain polite and deferential towards them, and now – in view of what she'd discovered about Sylvester Unwin – it was a struggle to sound normal.

'I've almost finished the bay wreath, madam, and didn't know whether to make a start on the pillow embroidery next,' she said, holding up the new piece of work she'd taken from the basket. 'Or perhaps you want me to begin something else?'

Mrs Unwin smiled falsely at Grace, employing a lot of teeth and gum, for she, too, was trying to act normally and as if not engaged in a mighty subterfuge. 'Do take whatever piece you want to from the work basket, Grace,' she said. 'How did you manage with the bay wreath?'

'Quite well, madam,' Grace said meekly. 'Would you like to see what I've done?'

'Indeed. You sew so very nicely – some of the girls would do well to try and emulate you.'

'Thank you, madam,' Grace said while the other girls stared at her resentfully. 'I'll bring it for you to see.'

The tiny embroidered bay wreath was brought in, examined and shown to the other girls – then suddenly thrust back into Grace's care when a distracted George Unwin flung open the door.

'It's gone!' he shouted to his wife.

Mrs Unwin turned to stare at him. 'What has?'

'The document! What d'you think?'

'But I saw it myself not half an hour ago. How could it have gone?'

'Never mind if it *could*, it *has*!'

Mrs Unwin suddenly remembered where they were, and that discretion was their byword. 'Not in front of the girls, in particular –' She stopped herself. 'Let us go to the red room.'

Mr Unwin left and Mrs Unwin followed him, silent and dismayed. Lately, she'd been unable to think of anything except the coming inheritance, which (she'd decided) would finance her retirement to a seaside villa. She'd had enough of the funeral trade, of pretending concern, of giving sympathy when she didn't feel any, of feigning interest in the vexing question of whether to have red roses or pink carnations in a wreath. She sometimes found herself longing to say to grieving relatives, *'What does it matter? They're not going to see them, are they? They're dead!'*

As Mr and Mrs Unwin shut the door behind them, the Unwin staff gravitated as one to the far end of the workroom, all the better to try and hear what was going on. The voices of all three Unwins were raised, which made eavesdropping easier.

'Where in the name of hell is it?'

'If I knew, I'd look there!'

'It must have been taken by outsiders.'

'Perhaps a draught from the window?'

'What, took it out of its envelope? Don't be ridiculous, woman!'

'Can't whoever made it make another?'

'No time,' said Sylvester Unwin. 'The other faction is right behind us.'

There was a moment's silence and then George Unwin said, 'It must be an inside job. Get everyone together, and we'll search all the rooms.'

The whole Unwin staff, including the blacksmith and ostlers, were then gathered together in the hall and told that something important had gone missing and their rooms were to be searched. This was carried out in a very short time, for their rooms contained nothing but a bed and a chair, and none owned more than one change of clothes.

As the other workers, pretending concern, enjoyed the drama of the occasion, Grace fought hard to keep her composure. She was certain that the servants would be questioned next, and perhaps searched, and although no one would find anything on her, she feared greatly that it would be Mr Sylvester Unwin who'd do the searching. If he did so, if he as much as touched her, then she knew she wouldn't be able to control herself any longer. She might not be capable of killing him, but she would not stand there and be pawed by him. She would be tempted to bite and scratch and maul him. And then, of course, the game would be up.

'No one has left the building within the last hour, have they?' Sylvester Unwin asked.

As everyone shook their heads, Mrs Unwin did a quick headcount. 'Not as far as I can see,' she said.

'So if the missing document is not hidden in the building, then someone must have it on them.'

'Hang on.' George Unwin pulled out his gold pocket watch and, shielding the engraved words *To Thomas Perkins from his loving wife*, clicked it open. 'Someone *has* left the building. Two people actually. Tomorrow's cadavers have gone off to Waterloo Depository ready for the morning train.'

'Well, *they* haven't taken it!' scoffed his wife.

There was a moment's silence and then George Unwin said thoughtfully, 'They might have. I went down to the cool room earlier to make sure all was in order, and noticed that one of the coffin lids was slightly displaced.'

'You're saying that a corpse got up and stole the certificate?'

George Unwin gave his wife a withering look. 'I'm saying that someone put it in the coffin to get it away from the house.'

Hearing this and feeling quite faint with horror, Grace looked at the faces of the other girls and tried to copy their more innocent, interested expressions. She had long known, of course, that the London Necropolis Railway always collected any coffins destined for a Brookwood funeral the night before the event, but in the stress of the moment hadn't remembered this.

'Now what?' asked Mrs Unwin.

'Now we must go after the coffins,' said Sylvester Unwin. 'Where is it they're going, exactly?'

'The coffin depository, just by Waterloo station in Westminster Road,' said George Unwin.

'And whose corpses will I be looking for?'

'Mr Truscot-Divine and Mr Mayhew,' Mrs Unwin answered. 'In polished cherry wood and oak respectively.'

'Or what looks very much like oak,' George Unwin murmured. He turned to his cousin. 'Do you want company?'

Sylvester Unwin shook his head. 'You stay here and search again, in case we've got it wrong,' he said curtly. 'Besides, my driver's outside in my gig and there's only room for me.' He pushed the nearest servant. 'Go and get my jacket, girl.'

Everyone began dispersing, whispering to each other and trying to work out what was going on, while

Grace went back to the sewing room, pale and trembling. Now what should she do? If she let things take their course, then the certificate would be retrieved by Sylvester Unwin and everything would be as before.

She could not let that happen. No, somehow she had to finish what she'd started: she must hail a hackney cab and try to get to the coffin depository first.

FOGS During the continuance of a
real London fog - which may be
black, or grey, or more probably
orange-coloured - the happiest man
is he who can stay at home.

Dickens's Dictionary of London, 1888

Chapter Twenty-Seven

When Sylvester Unwin went into the street where his gig and driver were waiting, he couldn't find them, for a thick London fog had rolled up and, although the horse and trap were but a few feet away, they were lost to his vision.

'What-ho!' Sylvester Unwin shouted. 'Where the devil are you?'

'Here, sir!' the driver said, and coughed as the damp and murky air hit the back of his throat.

'Damn you, man! Have you moved?'

'I have not, sir!' The driver waved his whip. 'Here I am, sir, sitting in the gig and waiting just where you left me.'

Sylvester Unwin stretched his arms out in front of him and endeavoured to peer through the gloom. The fog was banked up and in some parts looked more substantial than in others, one moment appearing grey, then muddy brown, then a thick and putrid green. Occasionally a thin ray of sun shone through and turned it a pale yellow. No matter the hue, however, it rendered one almost blind, clung to clothing, seeped into limbs and chilled flesh to the bone.

'It was right as rain here up to an hour ago – then it came off the river. A regular pea-souper,' said the driver.

'Keep talking so I can find you!' called Sylvester Unwin.

'Here, sir! Straight ahead!' the driver shouted several times, and finally Sylvester Unwin's outstretched hand touched the side of the gig and he hauled himself on to the seat beside the driver.

'Damn fog! Damn city!'

'Where is it you're wanting to go now, sir?'

'Waterloo station. Quick as you like,' Sylvester Unwin replied.

'I don't know about *quick*, sir,' the driver said doubtfully. He adjusted his scarf so that it covered the lower part of his face and became a makeshift mask through which to breathe. 'And I shouldn't think there would be trains running tonight. Not in this.'

'I'm not getting a train,' growled Sylvester Unwin. He breathed in deeply and began coughing. 'Leave off the chat. Just get me there as damned quickly as you can.'

'Do you want to pay for a link boy?' the driver asked, for he could see, ahead of them, boys waving flaming torches and walking before vehicles to help light their way.

'Get two,' came the reply. 'Just get me there.'

'Aye, sir! Link! Link!' the driver called into the impenetrable darkness, but the nearby boys were already taken and eventually, after Sylvester Unwin swore that he'd strangle him with his bare hands if he didn't get going, he flicked his whip.

The horse obediently set off, but his eyes could no more penetrate the pall than those of human eyes, and the creature immediately stumbled upon a wooden crate which someone had discarded in the middle of the street. The horse righted itself, but it had injured its foreleg and its orientation had gone – as had that of the driver – so after some confusion and a wrong turning, the horse found itself lost in the murk and trying to climb a set of slippery marble steps up to a front door.

'Stupidity!' Sylvester Unwin roared as the gig's wheels stuck on the bottom step. 'What d'you think you're doing?'

'Can't see a thing, sir!' the driver apologised. 'Worst fog I've ever been in.'

'So what if it is. Get back to the road and get going. Find some link boys! Pay them double!'

Halting, swearing and shouting instructions by turn, Sylvester Unwin began his slow progress towards the building more commonly known to the workers on the Necropolis Railway as the Stiffs' Storehouse.

*

Grace left a full ten minutes after Sylvester Unwin, partly because she couldn't bring herself to leave the relative safety of the funeral parlour and partly because she greatly feared being in close proximity to the man who had ruined her. Somehow she felt that the evil which emanated from him might still be able to harm her.

It was thinking of Lily, however, of *her* present and unknown plight, that finally spurred Grace into action. Looking out of the window and seeing a dense fog, she obtained a length of white muslin to tie around her face and filter the air being breathed, for one thing she could remember Mama telling her was that to go out in a thick London fog was dangerous to the lungs. The muslin obtained, however, the question came of how to get out of the funeral parlour. Should she make some excuse, tell the Unwins she felt ill, pretend she was going to a hospital or some such thing? But supposing they didn't allow her to go?

She frowned, steeling herself. Why ever should she worry about the Unwins? If she got the certificate back, then she might never have to see any of them again – at least not as their employee. If she didn't get it and they stole the inheritance, then how could she ever work for them, knowing what she did? Could she really go on with the pretence that everything was normal simply to keep a roof over her head?

No, she would just *disappear*, she decided, so this was what she did, bidding farewell to no one and slipping out of the front door unseen.

Entering the world of fog was like being transported to the land of the blind. People groped their way along the street, coughing as they breathed the fog into their lungs, tapping canes in front of them, holding out their arms like sleepwalkers or – if they were lucky enough to secure the services of a link boy – grasping his shoulder while he lit their unsteady progress along the pavement. Grace quickly realised that there was no point at all in taking a hackney cab, for having gone no more than fifty yards she came across two such cabs which had lost their way in the grey gloom and had tangled with an omnibus. All three vehicles were missing one or more wheels and now stood at a standstill, lop-sided and broken. In the road nearby stood two carthorses, left to feed quietly from nosebags until the fog lifted.

Grace edged past the big houses that fronted Edgware Road as quickly as she could, using their railings as markers and guides. She was conscious of the necessity for speed but this seemed near impossible, for one could only fumble along, apologising to those one bumped into, tripping over dogs and occasionally finding oneself down a dead-end alley or back at the place one had passed not ten minutes before. Children ran by, playing at ghosts, hooting and wailing and frightening those of a nervous disposition, and some people simply sat themselves down to wait in convenient doorways until the fog lifted a little and they could find their way home. On reaching Oxford Street things became easier, for the windows of the shops were lit with lamps and each provided a small haven of brightness in the gloom. Passing the Unwin Mourning Emporium, Grace even saw Miss Violet, her smile as cheerful as ever, greeting a customer who'd come in out of the murk, although the rest of the store was practically empty.

She hurried down Bond Street, ignoring the elegant shop windows, hearing every now and again the shrill whistles of the peelers as every petty crook and pickpocket in London tried his luck. Many shops suffered when the fog was thick, for the thief would come in boldly, take the nearest thing and disappear back into the fog before the shopkeeper could take a step to apprehend him. Several times running feet pounded past Grace followed by futile shouts of 'Stop thief!'

From Bond Street, Grace went to Piccadilly, and then down Haymarket towards the Strand. She was on her old ground now – her watercress-selling ground – and made use of her knowledge of the alleyways for shortcuts, although the closer she came to the river the worse the pall of fog hanging over them became. Once she was accidentally knocked to the floor by a market trader who wheeled his barrow into her, and once she came across a man who'd tumbled unknowingly into a cellar and was calling plaintively for someone to rescue him. She dared not, however, spare the time to stop and help.

As she neared the Strand there was a decision to make, for Waterloo and the Necropolis station were on the other side of the river and she didn't know whether to try for a ferry boat or to head for Hungerford Bridge, still some distance off. This little iron bridge had recently been bought out by a consortium wanting to use it for trains, however, and she didn't know if it was open for pedestrians. If she got there and it was closed, it would mean a long walk downriver to cross at London Bridge and this would delay her considerably. After an anguished moment trying to decide, she made her way to the waterfront to see if there were any ferries going across.

As she had feared, there were none, so – becoming very anxious – she made her way to the Sailors' Rest to look for a ferryman. She found a dozen or more men 'resting' in the tavern, all roaring drunk, and went from one to the other, asking if anyone would take her across the river for a matter of life or death. She was refused throughout the tavern, with much jeering and derision, and was despairing that she'd have to go to London Bridge after all, when a ferryman, younger than the others and sober enough to appreciate a pretty face, said he'd take her across for two shillings.

'Though I don't promise we'll get there, mind,' he said, slurring his words.

'I'll give you another shilling if we do,' Grace said recklessly, mentally thanking James Solent for the loan of his money.

'Very well. And if we is run down by a barge, then that's too bad for us.' He gave a bellow of a laugh.

'Though I feels luck in me bones today, so I think we'll survive.'

Grace had now reached a state of mind where she was ready to risk all. As she saw it, she would travel across the river in fog and either they would be run down by a barge, or they would not. Subsequently she would get the certificate, triumph over the Unwins and find Lily, or she would not. It was all in the lap of the gods.

She climbed on to the boat, settled the white muslin more firmly around her nose and mouth and closed her eyes. With a violent shove which sent the boat rocking sideways and sent stinking water over her skirts, they set off.

The ferryman's method of avoiding other boats seemed to be to put his head down and go as quickly as possible, cutting up the water with short strokes of his heavy oars.

'I goes like old Nick, as fast as can be,' he said to Grace. 'If I gets into trouble, I quickly gets meself out again.'

Grace was so frightened that she kept her eyes closed the whole way across, and so missed seeing the other two craft on the water: a huge coal barge that was so mighty and untouchable that it sailed regardless, and the small coracle of the old man who rowed the river day and night, fog or no, searching for drowned bodies in the water to relieve them of their clothes.

After landing safely and paying the ferryman his

dues, Grace found her way to Westminster Bridge Road fairly quickly, getting lost once but luckily discovering a peeler with a lantern at the York Road junction who was directing anyone who'd become disorientated. Reaching Waterloo and the ornate gated entrance to the Necropolis Railway, she saw a man sitting in an office and checking over some paperwork, but he was only watching out for hearses and didn't notice Grace as she slipped through the iron gates.

The coffin depository had been built as a normal warehouse for goods in transit and only later had been transformed, with sober paint and fittings, into a holding bay for the dead. This had proved necessary because London traffic, especially in the mornings, was so bad that a body setting off five miles away could often take more than two hours to reach Waterloo, thus causing some to miss the train and their own funerals. It was for this reason that the Necropolis Company insisted that all bodies destined for burial at Brookwood should be collected, ready for boarding as it were, the evening before.

Grace had been inside the depository before, and knew what to expect. What she didn't know was if Sylvester Unwin had got there first. If he had, and had already removed the certificate, then the game was over and she had lost. If he had not, then there was hope.

The iron door to the warehouse was wide, enabling a coffin to be carried in on two undertakers' shoulders with ease, and it took some strength for Grace to push it open. Inside, rows of sturdy shelves held three layers of coffins in a similar layout to that of the coffin van on the Necropolis train. There were about thirty coffins which had been collected from the various undertakers around London, and also two empty ones, which Grace had been told were kept to accommodate victims of road-traffic accidents or bodies fished out of the nearby Thames. There were a few candle lanterns about the place as a mark of respect to the dead, but generally the place was not well lit, for no visitors were likely.

Grace was shaking with cold by the time she went into the depository, for the riverwater and fog had seeped into her crêpe clothing and caused the heavy material to cling to her clammily. Quickly looking round, she could see that there was no live person in there, and it didn't seem as if any coffins had yet been disturbed, for certainly no lids were lying to one side. Perhaps she *had* arrived first.

She hurriedly moved among the shelves, looking up and down, straining to read the brass nameplates in the dim light. All she could remember from the glance she'd given to the coffin at the Unwins' was that its occupant had a double-barrelled name – and she found three of these here. One coffin named a woman, however, and one had a flag folded on its top denoting that its occupant had been an officer of the armed forces – she'd seen no such flag at the Unwins'. It had to be Mr Truscot-Divine, at the end of the warehouse, on the top shelf.

Grace stood on tiptoe and, taking a deep breath,

prepared to slip her hand into the coffin. It was then that she heard, with absolute horror, the voice of Sylvester Unwin from outside, sounding very irate because they'd had to go right up to London Bridge to cross the river.

'Open up, you watchman, and quick about it!'

'Who's there?' came the response.

'Unwin! I have a last-minute addition for a coffin going to Brookwood!'

This not being too unusual an occurrence – for a grieving widow would sometimes want to have a last letter or some such thing put in with her husband – there was a grating noise as the outside gate was opened. By this time Grace was running hither and thither like a terrified animal, unable to find anywhere to hide. Apart from the coffin shelves, the depository was blank and featureless; the door she'd come in at was the only opening, and there were no windows to clamber through.

And then she remembered the two empty coffins. These were soon located, for although they were a conventional coffin shape they were but temporary things made of cheap corrugated cardboard, and were on the lowest shelf just inside the door. Grace quickly ran to the nearest one, climbed inside and pulled the lid over herself. There she lay in complete darkness, striving not to move, shiver or scarcely breathe.

For a moment there was silence, and then Sylvester Unwin crashed through the door, holding a lantern aloft. He stood for a moment, looking around him. Grace, of course, could not see him, but sensed that he was close in the same way that she had sensed his nearness on other occasions: because his proximity caused such terror as to render her faint and nauseous.

Perhaps it was this terrible fear that made her reckless, for she had a sudden urge to confront him, to show him that he could not go through life trampling down those less fortunate than himself. She would not be a silent, faceless victim a moment longer!

So she sat up.

There was a swish as her coffin lid fell to the floor and Sylvester Unwin wheeled around in considerable fright. Grace, seen in the dim light, her head draped in white muslin, made a formidable apparition, for some wisps of fog had penetrated the building and propitiously formed themselves into a mist about her, causing her to look mysterious, terrifying and other-worldly.

Filled with rage, yet clear-headed and fully aware of what she was doing, she pointed at her enemy and cried, '"Vengeance is mine, sayeth the Lord!"'

Sylvester Unwin screamed in terror, clutched his heart and fell to the floor, dead.

Chapter Twenty-Eight

'*Dead?*' James Solent repeated. 'Sylvester Unwin dead? I don't understand. When did he die? How?'

Because of the fog, James had been late getting to their usual meeting place – in fact, he had nearly decided that he wouldn't go at all, for he'd felt sure that Grace would never venture out on such a night. About eight o'clock, however, a light breeze had blown up and begun dispersing the fog, and by nine o'clock when he was just about to leave the spot, the air was almost clear. Suddenly Grace appeared, running towards him, breathless and crying.

'He's dead because I killed him!' Grace said, sobbing. 'I didn't mean to, but I did.'

'You mean you . . . you stabbed him?' James asked in dismay.

'No.' She tried to quell her sobs. 'No, not that.'

'Then how?'

'I . . . I was in the coffin depository.'

James looked curious. 'What's that?'

'It's a warehouse at Waterloo where the coffins go before they catch the train to Brookwood.' James still looked puzzled, so she added, 'You see, he brought the forged adoption certificate to the funeral parlour this afternoon, and I took it and hid it in a coffin . . .'

James's face was a picture of bewilderment.

'They started looking for it and realised it must be with the bodies, but they were at Waterloo by then. So Sylvester Unwin went after it, and I went after him but got there first. I was hiding in an empty coffin and I sat up and he saw me and . . . and I think he died of fright.'

As she spoke, she watched James's face nervously for his reaction. Was he going to tell her she must go to the police? Perhaps, as a representative of the legal profession, he would insist that he took her there himself. And then she would be locked up for ever and never see Lily again.

'You were hiding from him – so why did you sit up in the coffin?' James asked, endeavouring to understand.

Grace swallowed, her mouth dry. 'I hated him so much, I wanted to frighten him.' Then she corrected herself, saying, 'What I wanted to do was kill him, although I didn't really think he would die. But . . . he did.'

'But why did you hate him so much?' James still looked puzzled. 'Because of the inheritance? Because of what he's stealing from your family?'

Grace shook her head. 'Not that. It's something else. Something he stole which was . . . was even more precious than money. And he stole it from me, and from my sister, too.'

James looked at her closely, and then he offered her his arm. 'I can see there is more to this than you are telling me,' he said. 'There's a seat in a little garden along the road. Shall we perhaps walk to it and sit down for a moment?'

Grace nodded and they walked along the dark street in silence until they came to a paved garden with a stone horse trough and a small wooden bench.

'Do you want to tell me the whole story?' James asked, placing Grace on the seat and then sitting down beside her. 'You don't have to, but you might feel better for sharing it.'

Grace was silent for a long moment, trying to get her feelings under control, then sighed and said that she would tell him everything.

'Lily and I were in an orphanage after our mother died,' she began, 'and were reasonably happy there. When I was fourteen we were moved to a training establishment where she was to be taught domestic work, and I was to learn to become a teacher.' She paused, dabbed at her eyes with a handkerchief, then went on, 'We were told that our accommodation and training were funded by a wealthy and important man anxious to give working girls a start in life, and that we were very lucky to be there.' She shuddered and, after a little while, continued in a small voice, 'Unfortunately, this man believed that if he funded the training of a girl, it meant that he could . . .' here she stopped and took a deep breath '. . . could visit her bed.'

James took her hand at this, but Grace shook it off, saying he must hear the full story before he offered sympathy. She closed her eyes, the easier to speak.

'I had a child,' she said in a voice little above a whisper. 'And it died. The day . . . the day I first met you at Brookwood, I wasn't there to mourn my mother. I was there with the sole purpose of burying the little thing.'

She paused again, and this time when James took her hand she was so grateful for the comfort of it that she didn't take it away.

'I couldn't tell anyone.'

'But no one could blame *you* for what this man did,' he said gently.

'Wait,' she said. 'There's one more thing you should know. The baby I birthed – I couldn't afford to give him a proper funeral, or even a coffin, so I put him in with someone else who was about to be buried.'

'I have heard this is sometimes done.'

'The coffin I chose . . .' she hesitated, and then said in a rush '. . . contained the body of your sister.' She looked at James anxiously. 'I only chose her because she sounded kindly. I felt that she wouldn't mind having my child with her.'

James didn't speak for a time, then merely said, 'You poor girl.'

'I didn't know then that my aggressor was Sylvester Unwin, but I do now. And later I found out that he had violated Lily, too.'

James nodded slowly. 'He kept several institutions going and there have been rumours about his conduct in girls' homes. Last year two complaints were made against him.'

'And was he charged with anything?'

'No, because unfortunately the accusations were dropped. Whether he paid the girls off or frightened them into not pressing the charges, I don't know.'

Grace sat back on the bench, breathing deeply, for it had been difficult and painful for her to say what she had.

'And so . . . so the adoption certificate remains in the coffin?'

She shook her head. 'No, I have it here. I tiptoed around his body on the floor and retrieved it.'

'That's excellent news!'

'But what will happen?' She looked at James fearfully. 'Will I be accused of murder?'

'Of course not,' he said, shaking his head, 'because you didn't murder him.'

Grace turned an anxious glance on him.

'Well,' said James slowly. 'He went into a warehouse and had a heart attack, that's all. No one can discover the circumstances because there's no evidence – and anyway, who could tell whether or not his heart attack occurred because of your actions at that precise moment?' He looked at her searchingly. 'I trust no one saw you?'

'No one,' said Grace. 'I was terrified and hid behind the door for five minutes or so, until his driver came in looking for him, and as he went in, I crept out. I was probably halfway down York Road by the time he found the body.'

'Very well. That's it. That's all we'll say on the subject. The matter will never be mentioned between us again.'

Grace looked at him with apprehension. 'I don't have to go back to the Unwins, do I?'

'Of course not!' he said, smiling. 'And I shouldn't think you've had time to go to Somerset House for the birth certificates, have you?'

Grace shook her head. 'I have not. And now I've spent the money you gave me.'

'That's of no account. I've been there and obtained them myself.'

Grace caught her breath. 'And is everything as you hoped?'

'Indeed. The certificates are completely unambiguous: your father and mother, Reginald Parkes and Letitia, née Paul, were married in April 1840. Your sister, Lily, was born in –'

'Lily!' Grace echoed, for in the last couple of hours she had hardly been thought of. 'Where is she?' She gave a sigh. 'How am I ever going to find her again?'

'We *will* find her,' James said with certainty in his voice. 'I promise.' Grace smiled at him gratefully and he went on, 'So, Lily was born in 1844 and you, Grace, in 1845, if I remember correctly.'

Grace nodded. 'That's right.'

'Your father's name is given on both birth certificates, but on yours it's written that he's in foreign parts.'

'Do you have them with you? Can I see them?'

'Not at the moment, because they're with Mr Stamford.'

Grace's expression brightened.

'I've acquainted him with your circumstances and he's most interested.' He thought for a moment. 'No, interested isn't strong enough a word – he's *ecstatic* at the thought of being connected with the famous Parkes case and with thwarting the Unwins at one and the same time. And to see Mr Stamford ecstatic is a strange and unusual thing.'

Grace managed to smile at this. 'What will happen next?'

'Mr Stamford has spoken to the partners at Binge and Gently, and they've called the Unwins to their offices at midday tomorrow. Now that we have the forged certificate, we'll go there, too – before the Unwins. I intend to go to Mr Stamford this very evening to acquaint him with the latest happenings. I'll say we have the adoption certificate, but not speak about how it was come by.'

'And will the fact that we have this help us?'

He nodded. 'It will. Had the Unwins handed it over, they might have got away with it. But now they're under suspicion, the certificate will be checked and double-checked – and someone will also verify that there never was an original at Somerset House.'

Grace's eyes widened. 'You said tomorrow. But the Unwins have two funerals to conduct. The bodies are already waiting at the warehouse.'

'I'm afraid that's of no consequence,' James said. 'The Unwins have not been invited to Binge and Gently as much as been summoned. Besides, they'll be eager to go along because they'll believe it's the final hurdle before getting the money.'

'They will have heard of the death of their cousin by then.'

'I don't think that will affect them too much,' James said dryly. 'If I know the Unwins, it'll just mean more money for those who're left.'

They sat for some moments longer on the bench, each busy with their own thoughts (Grace's very much on Lily and her possible whereabouts) until the initial glow of excitement wore off and the intense cold began to cause her to shiver alarmingly.

James immediately stood up and offered her his arm. 'What am I thinking of? Come, I must get you to warmth and shelter straight away.'

'But I've nowhere to go,' Grace said. 'Unless . . .' She thought of the last awful lodgings she'd stayed at with Lily – the warehouse in Southwark – and shivered anew.

'Then leave it to me to find you somewhere comfortable,' James said, hurrying her along the street.

The traffic, earlier stalled by the fog, was flowing freely now, and with the aid of a peeler they crossed Hyde Park Corner and went towards Mayfair. As the streets grew more elegant and the buildings smarter, Grace looked down at her clothing.

'Where are we going?' she asked in alarm. 'Look at me! No halfway decent lodging house will take me.'

'You aren't going to lodgings,' James said. 'An heiress doesn't sleep in lodgings.'

'*Am* I an heiress?'

James nodded. 'Remember, you are your mother's legatee.'

They had reached a hotel by then: a famous, mirrored, sumptuous hotel on the edge of Park Lane. James whisked them through the swing doors, and, while Grace hung back, embarrassed, he went to the front desk. A business card was shown, she heard the name 'Mr Ernest Stamford, QC' and also the word 'heiress' and the manager immediately materialised. He bowed her towards the central staircase, not seeming to notice what she was wearing.

'I shall see you in the morning, about ten o'clock!' James called, and was gone before she could properly thank him.

Chapter Twenty-Nine

G race stood at the window of her hotel room, looking at the vast expanse of Hyde Park spread out in front of her. It was a crisp day with frost in the air, the sky a clear blue. There were clouds of steam coming from the nostrils of the dray-horses pulling the omnibuses, and the people, huddled into their winter clothes, had a pinched look about their faces.

Grace had hardly slept. Of course not; she was too fraught and anxious about what she'd done and besides, the room she was in was so grand she'd not wanted to *sleep* in it, she'd wanted to walk around it, touching the curtains, sliding her hand over the polished furniture, stroking the thick blankets and patting the cloud-like pillows. And when she had finally lain down she'd felt compelled to go over, again and again, the strange and bewildering circumstances by which she'd come to be in such a wonderful place.

She turned from the window and sat down on a sofa. Before her, on a low table, stood a frosted-glass bowl full of fruit: apples, oranges, peaches and grapes. A whole bowl of fruit, just for her. She didn't feel she could eat it right then, but she must certainly take some away, she thought, and she picked up two apples and put them in the pockets of the petticoat she'd slept in, then topped this with two oranges and stood up to look at herself sideways in the long mirror. She smiled – she looked ridiculous, as if she were wearing a donkey's panniers! She took the fruit out again – just in time, it seemed, for there was a tap at the door which made her start in panic. She knew she shouldn't have been allowed in such a place; they'd come to throw her out! Worse, the Unwins had discovered what she'd done. Another tap came, and Grace quickly climbed back into the bed and pulled the bedclothes up to her chin.

'Come in,' she said in a voice so tiny that no one could have heard it, then cleared her throat and said more loudly, 'Come in, please!'

A maid entered the room carrying a bucket of coal to make up the fire, followed by another ready to open the curtains and tidy the room, and a third with a large jug of hot water, which she carried into the bathroom. Their duties accomplished, all three surveyed Grace with as much interest as she surveyed them, for the news that they had someone important staying – an heiress, no less – had circulated below stairs in an instant.

'Will you be wanting your breakfast now, madam?' one asked, and it was all Grace could do not to look behind her to see who was being addressed, for she'd never before been called madam.

'Yes, I would, please,' Grace answered. 'Where should I go to collect it?'

'We'll bring it to you, madam,' came the startled reply. 'And what would you be wanting to eat?'

'What is there?'

'There's sausages, rissoles, bacon, black pudding and devilled kidneys,' said the first girl, counting them off on her fingers. 'With eggs done anyways you wish.'

Grace's mouth began to water. She nodded. 'Yes, please.'

'Which, madam?'

'I have to choose?' she asked in confusion.

'Well, I suppose not,' said the maid, her eyes widening. 'Not if you don't want to, madam.'

'Then I'll have everything,' Grace replied recklessly, thinking how Lily would have loved to sit in bed eating sausages with her.

Of course, when the food arrived on white china

plates covered with silver domes and accompanied by toasted bread in a little wicker basket, Grace was too overawed to eat very much at all. She managed a small amount of scrambled egg and a quarter piece of toast, thickly buttered, but could not manage any of the meat stuffs. Feeling guilty about what she'd wasted, she threw the sausages into the fire, left the rest of her breakfast under the silver domes and was pleased to be in the bathroom (a gleaming white-tiled room which – incredibly – was just for her) when a maid arrived to collect the trays.

Her washing water was almost cold by this time, but she was used to this and it didn't stop her making full use of the washbasins and large, soft towels provided. She washed herself, and then her hair, with a pink soap which smelt wonderfully of roses, and rinsed it with copious amounts of water from the taps. These only gave out cold water, alas (for the hotel's hot-water system had not quite been perfected), but it seemed miracle enough to have as much washing water as one wanted merely at the twist of a tap. Kneeling in front of the fire to dry her hair, she decided that while the fairytale that her life had turned into seemed highly improbable and might disappear at any moment, she was going to make the most of it.

She pushed her hair into shape (for she didn't have as much as a comb with her), then looked at the only clothes she had to wear: the limp, half-dead-looking mute's clothes, stained and dusty and damp from her exertions of the day before. She shuddered; how could she *ever* put on those dreadful garments again? But she'd have to if she wanted to leave the room. She found some hairpins on the dressing table and managed, after a fashion, to pin back her hair, when there was another tap on the door.

Dressed in no more than a towel, she fled to the bathroom calling, 'Come in!'

One of the maids wheeled in a leather suitcase on a trolley. 'A gentleman brought this case for you, madam,' she heard. 'He sends a message to say – begging his pardon and please excuse his presumption – that you may wish to avail yourself of some of his sister's clothes.'

Grace peered around the bathroom door.

'He said he was worried that you might not have anything right for the season,' she continued, 'what with you being new to town and all.'

Grace hid a smile. How kind of James; how thoughtful. 'Thank you. And please thank the gentleman very much,' she added.

'He left a message to say he would be pleased to see you downstairs in about half an hour,' said the maid before departing.

Grace opened the suitcase and found that it contained several gowns and matching mantles which she presumed had once been Susannah Solent's. Looking quickly through the garments, which were all of a style and elegance befitting a young lady, she found a gown, tucked and pearl-buttoned, in a vibrant shade of turquoise. She shook some creases out of the skirt and hesitated a moment about the whys and wherefores of putting on a dead girl's clothes, but finally came to the conclusion that as Susannah Solent had been such a nice person, she surely wouldn't mind.

Dressing and looking at the final result in the mirror, Grace almost laughed at her altered appearance. She'd been in black for so long – and before that, only in drab, washed-out colours – that to be in such a bright shade made her feel like a completely different person. There was a matching turquoise bonnet, too, with white flowers sewn around the brim, and she crammed this down over her curls and hoped that she had chosen well for the day ahead. The only thing to mar this stylish outfit was the fact that she had no elegant shoes, so was forced to wear the black lace-up boots she'd been given by the Unwins.

James was waiting downstairs in the reception hall, and sprang up as she appeared on the staircase.

'You didn't mind?' he said, after complimenting her appearance. 'You didn't think it was too presumptuous of me to send clothes in?'

Grace shook her head. 'I could not have come out in my mute's clothes. I really could not!'

'Then what would you have done if I hadn't turned up with those?' he asked, amused.

'I would have had to cut down the room's curtains

and fashion something to wear!' she said, laughing.

There were some hackney cabs already waiting outside the hotel and on a porter summoning one, James helped Grace in and tucked a travelling rug around her. As the driver whipped up the horse and Grace leaned back on upholstered cushions, the magnitude of what might happen that morning suddenly washed over her, so that she began trembling.

'My dear girl, are you cold?' James asked.

'Not cold.' Grace shivered. 'Frightened. For they will know by now, will they not? About . . . ?'

'About him?' James gave a meaningful tilt of his head and she nodded. He brought out a newspaper from under his coat and asked in a normal conversational tone, 'Have you seen the news this morning?'

She shook her head nervously. 'I have not.'

He unfolded *The Mercury*. 'One of London's top businessmen has been found dead. Chap who owned a mourning warehouse in Oxford Street.'

'How . . . how did . . . ?' But Grace felt herself panting with fear and could not finish the sentence.

'See for yourself.' He smoothed out the newspaper and held it in front of her.

Grace saw the words SYLVESTER UNWIN – SUSPECTED HEART ATTACK, and was able to breathe again.

'Shall I read it to you?'

'If you wouldn't mind.'

James read, '*To the considerable shock of the city of*

269

London, Mr Sylvester Unwin, owner of the famous mourning emporium in Oxford Street, was found dead yesterday evening in the depository belonging to the Necropolis Railway, next to Waterloo Station. It was thought that Mr Unwin (cousin of George Unwin, of the Unwin Undertaking Establishment) had gone to the warehouse as a favour for his cousin, to insert a love token into a coffin for a grieving widow, when he suffered a heart attack. Mr George Unwin said that this thoughtful deed, undertaken on a desperately foggy night, was a typical act of kindness on the part of his cousin, and it was both poignant and tragic that he should die in its implementation.'*

James glanced at Grace, who had her eyes tightly closed, and asked in a low voice, 'Shall I read you his obituary?'

'No,' she said. 'Thank you, but no. I don't want to think about him – and what he's done – ever again. I'm glad he's dead.' She opened her eyes. 'Is that very wicked of me?'

James shook his head slowly. 'No, I think not.' One of Grace's hands lay on top of the rug, and he moved his own to rest upon it.

She smiled at him tremulously. 'Lily will be glad, too,' she said, and offered up a prayer that one day soon she would be able to tell her about it.

Just before eleven o'clock, Grace was sitting on the edge of her leather chair in one of the interview rooms at Binge and Gently. She'd been introduced to both partners, and also to James's own celebrated head of chambers, Mr Ernest Stamford, QC, who was famous not only for his astute counsel, but also for his lavish facial hair – his mutton-chop whiskers and vast curling moustache.

All parties had questioned her closely about her relationship with the Unwins and how she had come to be working for them. Mr Binge, in particular, had wanted to know everything she could remember about her mother. Sometimes he questioned her so aggressively that she felt he did not believe her stories, and at one point he asked if anyone could vouch for her to prove that she was who she said she was.

'For instance, is there anyone who can verify that you and your sister were using the names Grace and Lily Parkes a year ago, before the inheritance was advertised?' he asked.

After a moment's thought, Grace nodded. 'We were living and using those names at Mrs Macready's lodging house in Seven Dials.'

'Seven Dials?' queried Mr Binge, raising his eyebrows. 'Can one rely on the word of someone who owns a Seven Dials lodging house? Is the woman still there?'

Rather reluctantly, Grace shook her head. 'The house was condemned.'

'Exactly!' said Mr Binge.

'But I know where Mrs Macready lives,' said Grace. 'I can find her.'

Mr Stamford interposed, 'According to one of my clerks, the woman in question – Mrs Macready – had a lodging establishment in Seven Dials for over twenty years. She is known as an honest woman.'

'Hmm,' said Mr Binge.

A little before midday, seeing that Grace was becoming increasingly anxious, James escorted her on to the terrace to take the air.

'I don't care very much for Mr Binge,' she said to James as he led her outside to a sky heavy with snow. 'He doesn't seem to believe anything I say.'

'You must try not to take it personally,' James said. 'At some stage your father appointed Binge and Gently to oversee his affairs, and they have to ensure that his exact wishes are carried out and his money goes to the rightful persons.'

'But is it necessary for them to be so severe?'

'Mr Binge is just doing his job,' James said gently. 'We are like a small court of law here. We are trying to discover the absolute truth.'

When they had paced along the small terrace for ten minutes or so, they went back into the office, where, the closer the arms of the mantelpiece clock came to midday, the more agitated Grace felt, until she thought she might faint, or be sick, or do some other such thing to disgrace herself. At five minutes to the hour, Mr Gently showed her, James and Mr Stamford into an anteroom, where they were to wait while the Unwins were interviewed. There was a comfortable chaise longue here and the gentlemen bowed her towards it, but Grace felt too nervous to sit down and, after asking Mr Stamford and James to please excuse her, could only pace the floor in a restless fashion.

Supposing it all went wrong? In London there wasn't much that couldn't be fixed for a bribe, and who was to say that Binge and Gently weren't in league with the Unwins? Supposing Lily had been sent away somewhere and they never saw each other again? How was she going to survive the winter without a room or money of her own? What about the night she'd already spent in the hotel? Could she be flung into a debtors' prison for staying there without the means to pay for it?

Grace might have shared some of these worries with James, but after a few moments he was called out of the room by an official who said that his presence was urgently needed elsewhere, and she did not dare to address Mr Stamford on what he would surely think were trivial matters. Besides, he was busily doing *The Times* crossword, pencil in one hand and twirling his moustache with the other.

At twenty minutes past midday, Mr Gently came into the anteroom and asked if they would go back into the main office. Grace, quite terrified, looked down the corridor along which James had disappeared, hoping for his return, but was disappointed. Mr Stamford, however – a calm, solid presence – offered her his arm, and she was glad to take it.

In the office sat Mr and Mrs George Unwin and Miss Charlotte Unwin. The two ladies were in black fur, Mr Unwin was in full mourning, and all three of them looked immensely startled at the sight of Grace. This was especially true of Charlotte Unwin, whose powder-pale face became quite ashen.

'Mr and Mrs Unwin, Miss Charlotte Unwin, may I present Miss Grace Parkes?' said Mr Gently, as if they'd never met each other before. 'Miss Grace,' Mr Gently went on smoothly, 'now you can be reunited with your sister.'

'She is *not* my sister,' Grace said. 'That is Charlotte Unwin.'

'But . . . but . . .' Charlotte Unwin wavered, thought hard about her gig and her footman, and rallied. 'Yes, I am Charlotte Unwin *now*, but before I was adopted by my dear Mama and Papa here, I was Lily Parkes.'

'You never were!' said Grace fiercely. 'How could you say such a thing? I only have one sister and that is Lily, and you are not her!'

'How dare you contradict my daughter!' Mrs Unwin bristled, glowering at Grace. 'I took you to work at our establishment out of the goodness of my heart! Is this how you repay me?'

'You employed my sister, too!' Grace said. 'But where *is* Lily?'

'What are you talking about?' Mrs Unwin threw up her hands. 'The poor girl is demented!'

'Mrs Unwin, can you tell me your story again from the beginning?' Mr Binge asked. 'Right from the adoption of er . . . Charlotte here.'

'Certainly,' said Mrs Unwin, 'it's quite simple. When Mrs Parkes – Mrs Letitia Parkes – died, she left a child, a daughter named Lily.' Here she indicated Charlotte. 'We knew the girl's father was abroad, believed dead, and so we adopted her and made her our own. Here she is now, fully grown, a fine young gentlewoman whom we have long nurtured and loved.'

George Unwin shook his fist at Grace. ''Tis a wicked, wicked thing you are doing now, trying to prevent our dear girl from taking what is rightfully hers.'

'Indeed it *is* mine!' Charlotte Unwin burst into tears. 'Mama always used to tell me that Papa would make his fortune abroad and then we would be very, very rich.'

'She said that, did she?' Mr Binge interposed.

'She did! We were living in a dear little cottage in Wimbledon then, and though we were poor, every day Mama would make tea in her special teapot with bluebirds of happiness on it, and we would talk about what we would do when we came into money.'

Grace stared at her. 'You only know all this because of what Lily and I have told you!' she cried furiously. 'And where *is* my real sister? What have you done with Lily?'

'I don't know what you're talking about,' said

Charlotte Unwin disdainfully.

There was a silence, a stand-off, with all parties glowering at each other, and then Mr Stamford coughed slightly to draw everyone's attention to himself. 'My client, Miss Grace Parkes, has the birth certificates for her and her sister,' he said. 'What hard evidence do you have, Mr and Mrs Unwin?'

'We have an adoption certificate,' said Mr Unwin, and he exchanged a meaningful glance with his wife.

'It's just that — silly me — I've mislaid it at the moment,' put in Mrs Unwin. 'And, you know, with the terrible shock of our dear cousin's death only yesterday, I haven't yet been able to find it.'

'We *will* find it, though,' said Mr Unwin.

There was a pause just as long as a heartbeat and then Mr Stamford said in a jocular tone, 'Well, as it happens you don't have to worry, because — what do you think? — by some strange coincidence we have the very thing here!' He waved a document in the air. 'At least, it *says* adoption certificate at the top.'

The silence that followed this statement was longer and more profound as all three members of the Unwin family stared at the certificate, each wondering how on earth Mr Stamford had managed to get his hands on it and what this might mean.

Charlotte Unwin began crying. 'I'm telling you the truth: I am Lily Parkes! Mama — my real mama — had a miniature of Papa by her bed, and she always used to say how much I looked like him! It was painted by someone . . . someone whose name I can't quite remember but . . .'

And then the door to the office was unceremoniously flung open and Grace heard a voice shouting, 'No! Mama painted it herself!'

She looked around to see her sister – her dearest, real sister Lily – standing there, with a smiling James behind her. She rose, and Lily saw her and ran towards her, in her great eagerness tripping over the rug and almost falling. And then the sisters were in each other's arms.

'It's Mrs Beaman we have to thank,' James began to explain just a little later.

Grace and Lily – the latter having just managed to quell her sobs – were now sitting side by side, arms around each other, on the chaise longue in the small waiting room. They made a strange pair: one girl elegant in turquoise blue, the other in a stained apron over a dingy grey cotton frock with no shoes on her feet.

'Mrs Beaman, the Unwins' cook?' Grace asked in surprise.

'The very same. Apparently when you, Grace, went to the Unwins' home after Christmas wanting to see Lily, Mrs Beaman felt so sorry for you that she decided to go to the police and tell them the truth: that Lily had been removed from the house against her will.'

'Oh, how kind of her!' Grace cried.

'Well, it was partly kindness,' James said, 'and also the fact that George Unwin hadn't been too generous with his bribes. He seemed to think that ten shillings might cover the matter from beginning to end.'

'And where has Lily been all this time?' Grace asked, looking anxiously at her sister and hoping she hadn't suffered too much.

'In a hospital . . . an asylum in a Manchester slum,' James answered.

'Oh, Lily, was it too awful?' Grace asked.

Lily considered. 'It wasn't *that* bad,' she said. 'There were lots of children there . . .'

'Children whose relatives wanted them out of the way,' James put in in a low voice.

'And I looked after some of them and told them stories. But I really missed you! And I kept asking when I would see you but no one took any notice of me.' She shot a look at Grace, gazing in admiration at her fashionable gown and bonnet. 'But you look so very grand and ladylike now . . . are you *sure* you missed me?'

'Of course I did!' Grace answered, hugging her closer. 'Every minute.'

'Mrs Beaman reported the matter,' James went on, 'and then when the police at this end started their investigations, two of them eventually went up to Manchester. They spoke to some chaps there, and between them they found out where Lily had been placed. They brought her back to London yesterday, and one astute peeler recognised her name and realised who she was. He got in touch with Binge and Gently and, well, you know the rest.'

'I do, and it's all wonderful,' Grace said, smoothing her sister's matted hair.

'They said you might come and see me, and I used to spend all day at the window looking for you but you never came,' Lily said pathetically.

'Dearest Lily,' Grace said, 'for some of that time, I didn't even know you were gone! And when I *did* find out, they told me that you'd run off with a groom.'

Lily pulled such a face at this notion that James and Grace both laughed.

When Mr Stamford came into the room some fifteen minutes later, he looked very pleased with himself.

'Mr and Mrs Unwin, together with Miss Charlotte Unwin, are to be charged with grand fraud,' he said. 'It's obvious that Sylvester Unwin was implicated in the plan but, as we know, the Lord has already meted out *his* sentence.'

Lily looked around at their serious faces. 'What does all that mean?'

Grace took a deep breath. 'I have a lot to tell you.' She addressed Mr Stamford, 'Does my sister know about Papa and the . . . ?'

Mr Stamford shook his head. 'We haven't told her everything. We thought that might be better coming from you.'

'What?' Lily asked, seeing everyone was looking at her.

'I'll tell you everything when we get to the hotel,' Grace promised, for she was feeling tired and drained.

'Binge and Gently now have all the relevant documents in their possession,' said Mr Stamford, 'including the fake adoption certificate. It only remains for you to produce an affidavit signed by someone who – at least six months ago – knew you and your sister as Grace and Lily Parkes.'

'That will be Mrs Macready,' Grace said. 'I believe she's living with her son in Connaught Gardens.'

'Then perhaps tomorrow morning my clerk here,' Mr Stamford said, indicating James, 'could go with you to ask if she would kindly append her signature to the necessary papers. It will then only remain for a trust fund to be set up.' He paused. 'I presume you don't have a bank account?'

Grace shook her head.

'Then a joint one will be opened for you and your sister, and money transferred as and when you need it.'

Lily frowned, yawned and looked at Grace. 'Are we rich? Is it Papa?'

'It is Papa, and I rather think we are going to be quite rich, quite soon,' said Grace.

At Rest

Chapter Thirty

'Will we take a hackney cab?' Grace asked James, looking out of the hotel reception area into the damp greyness of the morning. She was wearing a dark-green velvet mantle with matching fur muff and bonnet; the colour complementing her hair and making her eyes shine with an amber light.

James laughed. 'How quickly you've become used to your new-found wealth,' he said. 'Two nights in London's best hotel, breakfast in bed – and now a demand that I call a hackney cab to take you to Connaught Gardens.'

'Oh really, please don't think . . .'

He laughed again and shook his head. 'I'm only teasing; of course we must have a cab.' He spoke to a porter, who went to find one. 'Where's your sister this morning?'

'She's gone back to bed,' Grace said. 'Or what I should really say is that she hasn't yet risen, because we hardly slept at all last night. We stayed awake for hours, chatting and exchanging stories and talking about what we were going to do. And I'm sorry to say that Lily ate every piece of fruit in the bowl.'

He laughed, and then grew more serious. 'Did you tell her about the unfortunate demise of . . . of that certain gentleman?'

'I did,' Grace said as they got in the cab. 'And I told her that I'd discovered who he really was, too.'

It had been a memorable night for the two girls: a storytelling session to end all storytelling sessions, during which they'd both laughed and cried so much it was hard to tell which emotion had predominated. Grace smiled, remembering. 'But anyway, Lily couldn't come out with me today because she hasn't any shoes.'

'Ah,' said James, handing over a small envelope, 'then it's just as well that Mr Stamford has advanced me ten pounds so that you may buy any little necessary items for yourselves.'

Grace took it and thanked him, her heart full. It was impossible to put into words, she thought, how it felt to be riding with a young gentleman in a hackney cab through London traffic with ten whole pounds tucked inside a green velvet muff. She could not shake off the feeling that at any moment someone was going to come along and say it was all a mistake.

They were directed to a tall terraced house in Connaught Gardens where Mrs Macready was living, and it was she herself who opened the door to them, gasping at the sight of the distinctly different Grace.

'Dear child!' she said, then stood back to take a better look at her. 'Well, haven't we gone up in the world! Aren't we la-di-da now we're away from Seven Dials!'

Grace laughed. 'Indeed we both are!' she said, admiring Mrs Macready's lace-trimmed day dress.

They were invited into the parlour, where Grace introduced James and explained why they'd come. Mrs Macready's eyes grew round with amazement as a brief synopsis of the tale unfolded, and she readily agreed to sign the papers that James had brought with him.

'Of course I'll sign to say they were with me,' she said. 'Two nicer girls I never had under my roof in all my life.'

As James thanked her and began preparing the papers, Mrs Macready looked across at Grace and winked, pressing her index and middle fingers together to indicate that she and James made a fine pair.

Grace didn't react to this, hardly knowing *how* to. She'd grown very fond of James, but had not dared to think that an educated young man such as he, with prospects, from an excellent family, might consider her a suitable friend – especially since he knew the very worst things about her there were to know.

Mrs Macready signed *Jane Ebsworthy Macready* in a slow and careful hand. This was witnessed by James, and the document was sanded and rolled. Following this, Mrs Macready kissed Grace heartily on both cheeks and made her promise to visit again soon.

Grace was just about to get into the waiting hackney cab when the older lady beckoned her back. Grace, anxious to get back to Lily, thought of pretending she hadn't noticed, but then excused herself to James and ran back up the steps.

'Is there something else?'

'Well, I've been thinking about it, and it worries me, you know,' said Mrs Macready.

Grace looked at her enquiringly.

'Because she came again and said it was her dying wish to find you. And that puts a bit of an obligation on a person, doesn't it, knowing someone's told you their dying wish.'

'I suppose it does,' Grace said, still baffled. 'But who are we speaking about?'

'Mrs Smith, or whatever her right name is.'

'Oh!' said Grace. There were some parts of her life that would, it seemed, never go away.

'She came round with her daughter and she begged me to help find you. Of course, by then you'd told me that you worked for the funeral people, and I could have said where you were, but I didn't because I thought she might be up to some mischief.' Grace was silent, waiting for whatever was coming. 'Looking at her, though, I could tell she didn't have long to live, and I'm thinking that she can't do mischief to anyone now, seeing as she's so near her end. So it's up to you, dear.'

Grace nodded, recalling again the saddest, most pitiful day of her life.

'She might be dead by now, of course – and then again she might not.'

'Where does this Mrs Smith live?' Grace asked.

'A house named Tamarind Cottage in Sydney Street. Not a bad area.'

Grace nodded. 'I know where that is. I remember it from my cress-selling days.'

'So will you go to her?'

'I don't know.'

But actually Grace had already made up her mind. She had overcome Sylvester Unwin, and triumphed over the rest of that family; she would now face Mrs Smith. And when she had seen Mrs Smith and dealt with her, then she would have confronted all her demons.

Getting back into the hackney cab, she asked James if he would tell the driver to stop somewhere in Oxford Street, so she could buy a pair of shoes for Lily and some for herself, too.

'And then I shall walk home,' she added, 'to enable me to take the air and reflect on things a little more.'

'There!' James said. 'You are bored already with being driven around in hackney cabs.'

Grace laughed. 'Indeed I am not! But things are

285

happening so fast that I need some time to think about what we should do next.'

'Then of course you must have some time,' James said, and he bade the driver stop at the top of Regent Street – for he said that was where the most exclusive and fashionable ladies' shops were – and promised to call on Grace and Lily later, at the hotel, and bring them details of some more permanent places where they could stay.

Grace went into the first shoe shop she found, where she was faced with yet more imponderables. She couldn't remember ever having a brand new pair of shoes before, so found herself entirely dazzled by the type, quality and variety on offer. Joyfully taking up each new pair she was shown, she ended with seven pairs standing on the counter before her, all in different coloured leathers, and was about to pay for them when it suddenly came upon her that she was being ridiculous. She didn't know how much money they had yet and if she spent it stupidly they might find themselves poor again. She must be careful! Apologising to the shop worker, she bought just two pairs of shoes in identical plain black (but with shiny leather bows on, for she didn't want them to look like mourning wear) and had them wrapped.

She began to walk towards Sydney Street – hurrying now, to get the next part of the day over with as quickly as possible – and coming to Tamarind Cottage, found it a neat terraced house with a small garden in the front. The door was painted red and it had a well-polished brass lion's-head door knocker.

Grace knocked, not quite sure how she felt about meeting Mrs Smith again. She rather hoped the lady would be out – but then this would only delay something which seemed to be inevitable. Besides, facing Mrs Smith now, she told herself, might be good practice for facing the Unwins in court.

There was no sound from inside the house and Grace, after waiting perhaps a minute, turned to go, giving the lion knocker one last half-hearted tap before she did. As she quickened her step to go out of the front gate, however, the door opened and, to the intense surprise of both young ladies, Grace found herself facing Miss Violet, the assistant from the Unwin Mourning Emporium.

'Miss Violet!'

'Miss Grace!'

The two girls smiled at each other questioningly, and Grace spoke first. 'Surely it's trading hours. Why aren't you at the store?'

'It's closed for three days as a mark of respect,' Violet said. 'Mr Unwin is . . .'

Grace nodded swiftly. 'Yes, I heard.'

Violet looked at her quizzically. 'And you . . . ?'

Grace cleared her throat nervously. 'I came here to speak to a Mrs Smith.'

Violet nodded, but a sadness crossed her face. 'Mrs

Smith is the name my mother used sometimes.'

Grace hesitated. 'Is your mother dead?' she asked gently, and then noticed the black band around the girl's upper arm.

Violet nodded again. 'A week back. The funeral was yesterday; just a small one.'

'Not an Unwin?'

'Certainly not an Unwin!' Violet said spiritedly. 'I might work there but I don't espouse their ways. But I'm very curious as to why you've come to see my mother.'

Grace made several false starts trying to explain, stopping and hesitating, and in between these attempts, Violet ushered her through to a small parlour and bade her sit down and take some tea.

'I understand your mother very much wanted to see me,' Grace said eventually. 'She knew me as Mary.'

Violet, knowing well what this meant, looked at her in surprise. '*You* were one of her Marys?'

Grace nodded and blushed. 'I was. And I believe you and your mother went to my old landlady, Mrs Macready, in order to discover my whereabouts.'

Violet's eyes widened still further at the mention of the landlady's name. 'You are *that* Mary! So you met my mother last June? At Berkeley House?'

'That's right.' Grace nodded. 'But Mrs Macready didn't know the circumstances and, because she suspected some sort of swindle, didn't tell your mother where to find me.' She took a deep breath. 'I've just seen Mrs Macready again, however, and she was very eager that I find your mother. She said she wished to speak to me urgently.'

'She did,' Violet said. She sat down on the sofa next to Grace. 'In fact, my mother made me promise to keep looking for you, and said that if I ever found you, I was to tell you something very important. The truth.'

'The truth!' A spasm of fear crossed Grace's face. Something had been wrong with the child she'd birthed! It had been crippled, maimed, horribly disfigured in some way!

'It's not a bad truth,' Violet said, seeing the way Grace's mind was working. She hesitated, then glanced at the clock on the mantelpiece and seemed to make up her mind about something all at once. 'Will you take a walk with me?'

Grace wondered for a moment if she had misheard. 'A *walk*?'

'Yes. I'll explain everything on the way, I promise.' Violet gathered up her mantle, bonnet and gloves, showing Grace her only concession to mourning on her outer clothes – a spray of purple flowers around the bonnet's brim.

'We must go towards Bloomsbury,' she said.

Once safely across the road, past the big hotels and shops and heading towards Russell Square, Violet took her arm.

'I'm sorry if I seem strange and mysterious, but this is the last thing I shall ever do for my mother and I want to get it right. Mother said I should take you, and explain carefully, and then everything would be up to you.'

Grace did not reply to this, for her mind was a mass of questions.

'After my father died, my mother became a midwife in order to survive,' Violet explained as they passed by two ragged children squabbling over a cigar end. 'She was one of the first women to train properly. She attended women at home, mostly, and also worked at Berkeley House two days a week in order to help those less fortunate. She told me once that she thought she must have delivered a thousand babies.'

Grace nodded, trying to keep calm in order to understand what was being said and not to jump ahead of herself.

'Of course, not every baby survived, and some mothers died, too – childbirth is such a perilous business. Some women lost many infants before they had a live birth. One woman in particular lost five babies one after the other, and at the final death was so devastated that her husband thought she would lose her mind.'

'Poor woman . . .' Grace said softly.

Violet went on, 'The very next day, a young unmarried girl came to Berkeley House. She was friendless and alone, with no protector nor family, and she lived in a slum. She had nothing prepared for the birth and no money put aside for the child's requirements.'

She looked at Grace searchingly. Grace, mouth dry, nodded at her to go on.

'My mother feared that this girl's baby wouldn't survive for – although born healthy – its birth weight was low and it had various other small problems that the girl would not have been able to afford to have treated. She felt that if she let the girl take the baby home, she was almost pronouncing a death sentence upon it. So . . . so she did something she should not have done.'

Grace, fearing and longing for what might come next, gave a little cry, stopped walking and turned to face her.

'She took the baby and gave it to the poor woman who had lost five of them,' said Violet.

'No!' Grace cried hoarsely. 'She should not have done that!'

'She knew she shouldn't. She knew she was doing wrong,' Violet said pleadingly, 'but she said that at the time, it seemed the right and proper thing to do.' She looked at Grace. 'That baby would not otherwise have survived its first few months.'

Grace thought about trudging around the cold streets with a baby, about having nowhere to bed it down at nights, about having no food all day bar a crust of bread. 'But what about the poor girl?' she asked with a sob.

'Yes, what about the poor girl?' Violet sighed. 'My mother couldn't forget her and it played upon her mind. Once she knew that she was going to die – for she had been diagnosed with a cancer some months previously – she began looking for her.' She turned her gaze to Grace. 'Looking for *you*, and when she didn't find you, she made me promise that I would take over the search.'

'She should never have done it,' Grace repeated in a whisper.

'No, she should not,' Violet agreed.

Walking on, they reached the edge of Russell Square and entered a street with attractive, white-painted villas, vines and greenery climbing about their fronts. Violet beckoned Grace to follow her down a small alleyway. 'She knew it was wrong. But she told me to find you and tell you, and let you make up your own mind about what to do. She left me a confession which is signed and witnessed and would stand up in court. It would be possible for you to claim your child back, and I promised her that if that's what you wanted, I would aid you.'

So saying, she stopped by the iron railings which enclosed someone's back garden and gave a view into a nursery: a splendid room with painted ships on the walls, a rocking horse and building bricks scattered about. In this room a woman – Mrs Robinson – could be seen, carrying a child about seven months old on her hip. The child – a boy – was bonny, sturdy of limb and robust with health. Grace uttered a little cry, and then gazed at him with such love that it seemed she might draw him to her side by the sheer force of her affection.

'I hoped we might see him,' Violet said. 'My mother used to come this way in the mornings sometimes just to look at him, to prove to herself that she'd done the right thing. He's a child who is very much loved and wanted by his family.'

Grace gave a sudden cry. 'Then . . . who was it I took to Brookwood Cemetery?' she asked in distress. 'Was it someone else's dead child?'

The corners of Violet's mouth lifted a little. 'No,' she said, 'it was a penny loaf.'

'*A penny loaf?*'

Violet nodded. 'Mother said it was about the right weight and shape.' She could not prevent a smile then. 'So whoever's coffin you chose has a loaf of bread to see them through to paradise.'

Grace turned towards the nursery window and continued staring at the child, now seated on the floor with his mother, playing with the bricks. She could indeed see that he was greatly loved, and loved back in return.

She sighed deeply. There would be much to think about in the coming months and many decisions to be made; about finding somewhere to live, about doing the best she could for Lily, about choosing what she was going to do with her life, and about what might happen between her and James. This was one decision, however, that she didn't have to think about.

'I would not take him away,' she said to Violet, her

293

eyes still on the baby. 'I couldn't do such a thing.'

Violet turned to her. 'That's what I so hoped you'd say. But are you quite sure? You don't have to make the decision now.'

'I am sure.' Grace nodded. 'I don't need any more time. It would be cruel to take him away, and break at least three hearts.'

Violet, who had tears in her eyes, took Grace's hand and squeezed it. 'I'm sure you have made a good decision, and the right one.'

'I don't want my child to learn about heartbreak so early in his life,' continued Grace.

'I don't think you'll ever regret it,' said Violet, keeping hold of Grace's hand.

'But sometimes, perhaps, you and I can come for a walk down here and . . .'

'Admire the gardens!'

'Yes, admire the gardens,' Grace echoed.

The two girls looked at each other, and then Violet offered her arm and they walked on.

My Inspiration for
Fallen Grace

There are lots of different elements in *Fallen Grace*, which makes it difficult to pin down my main source of inspiration. Perhaps the idea for it first began with my interest in Victorian funeral practices; not only all the paraphernalia that surrounded a death – the glass carriages, the mutes and feathermen, the horses with black plumes – but the customs of giving out black gloves or jewellery to the chief mourners as mementos, the sending of black-edged mourning cards and so on. Alighting on this as the background and theme for my book, I satisfied my curiosity by finding out more and more fascinating things to use in the novel.

After theme come characters, of course, and my inspiration for Grace was found in Mayhew's *London Labour and the London Poor* (see Bibliography). Here, amongst the true and traumatic reports of impoverished Londoners, I discovered several examples of young children selling watercress; bunching it up on icy winter mornings and selling it for next to nothing on the streets. This, I decided, would be the way that my main character earned money.

Then I needed villains! I found several examples of that much-maligned fellow, the Victorian undertaker, in popular fiction of the time. Undertakers never had good press! George Unwin, the epitome of these scoundrels, required a partner, so I gave him a cousin, Sylvester Unwin, who, as well as being involved in the funeral trade, was also a do-gooder. (I discovered that some Victorian gentlemen were only too ready to shoulder the task of rehabilitating fallen women, even to the point of taking them into their own homes.)

I already knew about the beautiful and evocative London cemeteries, but then I came across the Necropolis Railway, a steam train which ran from Waterloo station in London to Brookwood Cemetery in Surrey. This railway is the link which meanders through the different elements of the book and pulls them all together.

Mary Hooper

Do you want to know more?

Contact Mary on www.facebook.com/maryhooperfanpage

Some Historical Notes from the Author

The Brookwood Necropolis Railway

The cholera epidemic in London in the late 1840s resulted in nearly 15,000 deaths and greatly increased the problem of burial in the capital. The disposal of London's dead had been a problem for some time with church graveyards becoming so overcrowded that plots had to be dug up and reused over and over again. Cremation not being an option in those days, the idea was mooted for a vast cemetery outside London which would provide a burial ground for Londoners for many years to come.

The site chosen in Surrey (far enough from London not to endanger the health of those in the capital) could be reached cheaply and conveniently only by railway. There were objections to it at first. The Bishop of London, for example, considered 'the hustle and bustle' connected with railways inconsistent with the solemnity of a funeral. There was opposition, too, from the wealthy, some of whom found the idea of their relatives being conveyed for burial with the lower classes offensive – for it was intended that even the poorest would be able to afford both the fare and the reasonable cost of interment at Brookwood, and thus be saved the shame of having their dead buried in a paupers' burial ground. The bishop and other objectors having been given assurances that the first-, second- and third-classes of mourners and their respective coffins would be kept apart from each other, and that there would be segregation as regards to religion, the Brookwood Necropolis Railway was finally established in 1854.

At this time, travel by train was still a novelty – the first regular passenger service was only introduced in 1830 – but it was to become immensely popular. During the 1840s, the Industrial Revolution was well under way and by 1851 some 6,800 miles of track had been laid. In 1863, after much clearance of poor housing to make way for it, London's first underground railway opened.

I have used the invaluable *The Brookwood Necropolis Railway* by John M. Clarke for all sorts of basic information about the line, such as the price of a mourner's ticket and the segregation of the classes, but for the purposes of the plot have used dramatic licence when describing the layout of the trains (which would not, for instance, have had corridors). The Necropolis Train ran from Waterloo in London to Brookwood in Surrey until about 1941, although burials still continue in the cemetery today and there are regular guided walks –

some of which are specifically centred on the Necropolis Railway – around its beautiful grounds.

Death and Mourning – the Victorian Way

Some churchyards in London had been full since 1665 (the year of the Great Plague) and by the time Queen Victoria came to the throne many had been locked up. Purpose-built cemeteries were proposed, the first of these being Kensal Green Cemetery, near Paddington. When the Duke of Sussex, Queen Victoria's uncle, died in 1843, he said in his will that he wanted to be buried at Kensal Green amongst ordinary Londoners, and this boosted the popularity of the new cemetery enormously. This spacious, park-like burial ground was swiftly followed by six others on the fringes of London, including Highgate Cemetery, which became quite the most fashionable place in London to be interred. Highgate not only had catacombs (underground passageways containing shelved compartments on which coffins could be stored), but an Egyptian avenue leading to the marvellous Circle of Lebanon, where 20 large family vaults lined a path which ringed a magnificent ancient cedar tree. On Sundays, well-to-do Victorian families would promenade along the glades and avenues, visiting their departed loved ones.

It was Queen Victoria who, after Prince Albert's death, fanned the cult of mourning. Initiated by the queen and then the aristocracy, it was imitated by the newly rich industrial and trade classes and spread downwards to the poor. Once the poor were wearing mourning, it meant the upper classes had to redouble their own efforts to demonstrate their social superiority, so that during the second half of the nineteenth century, the wearing of black became such a cult that no one dared defy it. Upper-class women travelling away from home would always take care to pack the correct mourning wear in case they suddenly found themselves in the company of a newly bereaved member of the royal family.

In his book *Mourning Dress*, Lou Taylor attributes the spread of mourning clothes partly to the proliferation of the newly published fashion magazines, which gave details of the latest fabrics and accessories and advised on mourning etiquette. On Prince Albert's death, upper-class families slavishly followed the queen by going into full-mourning, then half-mourning and quarter-mourning, perhaps hoping that others would think they were affiliated to the royal family. For such an important death as this, a society lady would alter her whole wardrobe for a year. To encourage sales, crêpe manufacturers and mourning businesses (there were at least two vast warehouses in Regent Street selling nothing but) put it about that it was unlucky to keep mourning wear in the house between deaths. The rules grew even more complicated and far-reaching. For example, in 1881, a magazine advised that a second wife, on the death of her husband's first wife's parents, was obliged to wear black silk for three months.

Victoria and Albert

Queen Victoria came to the throne aged 18 in 1837, following the notorious Regency period, during which the royal family had become unpopular. She married her cousin, Albert, in 1840, and though the marriage was stormy, it was genuinely loving and they went on to have nine children. Their union was held in high esteem and the ordinary people of the empire were encouraged to aspire to it.

Some British subjects, however, weren't keen on Albert, firstly because he was foreign, and secondly because of the influence he and his family had over the queen. Albert was initially constrained by his position as consort (which didn't involve any official duties), but he soon took responsibility for running the royal household and involved himself in several public causes, including trying to improve the status of the poor. He was also instrumental in organising the Great Exhibition of 1851. The British remained slightly suspicious of Albert, but sincerely mourned him when he died of typhoid, aged 42, in December 1861.

Following his death and Queen Victoria's edict that the nation make a respectable mourning, London became engulfed in black as, out of respect for the prince, the ordinary man in the street struggled to obey his queen's wishes and clothe himself and his family for several months at least in the most decent black outfits he could afford. It is said that even London's railings, painted green before 1861, were painted black after Albert's death. It is generally agreed that Queen Victoria took her mourning too far by staying away from London and wearing widow's weeds for the rest of her life. Overwhelmed by Albert's premature death, she more or less retired from public life and thus become unpopular with her subjects, who felt neglected.

Victoria reigned for 63 years – longer than any British monarch so far – until her death in 1901. During her reign she restored the nation's respect for the monarchy, became a symbol of the spirit and identity of the nation, and also strived to improve the conditions of the poor by such measures as introducing basic education for all and limiting the working day to ten hours.

The Victorian Poor

Henry Mayhew, a journalist, interviewed hundreds of ordinary Londoners and published the first volume of *London Labour and the London Poor* in 1851. This provided first-hand details of what life on the streets was like for those at the very bottom of society.

There were countless ways in which the poor earned money to keep themselves alive, including bird- and dog-duffing (changing the colour of birds and animals by painting them), and placing heavily sedated small animals together in a box as 'Happy Families'. Children would collect and sell birds' nests, hunt in sewers for lost objects, collect 'pure' (dog dung) for the tanning trade, catch rats for dog-versus-rat fights and sift through muck in rubbish yards – anything to earn a penny or two. There were armies of small boys and girls aged six and upwards selling any small and cheap commodity: watercress, oranges, lemons, sponges, combs, pencils, sealing wax, paper, penknives or match-es. Some of these children were sent out by their parents as a way of supplementing their own earnings, but there were also a great many orphans and unwanted children living completely independently of any adult care and struggling mightily to survive.

Some of the details that Mayhew gives are heart-breaking. For example, he tells of the small children whose mother died of starvation and whose eight-year-old sister had to care for them; of a woman who lived on tea and bread, using the same tea leaves over and over again; of a boy who had no shoes or clothes of his own and so could only go outside when his older brother was indoors.

For many, living conditions were pitiful, overcrowd-ing was rife and starvation was just around the corner. A room in a tenement building could cost two shillings a week and this might be occupied by two or more families; those that couldn't get into a bed at night having to find space on the floor. There was no sanitation or running water, the rooms stank and the mattresses were usually running with bedbugs, fleas and lice. If someone in the family died (an all too frequent occurrence), their body might be left lying in the same room with the living for several days until enough money had been collected to bury them.

The authorities strongly disapproved of the overcrowded houses and rookeries (mean tenements where the very poorest lived cheek by jowl with each other, as rooks nest together in tall trees), so the decrepit boarding houses in the worst slums were gradually demolished and new roads and railway lines cut through. This did not help the situation as far as the lodgers were concerned, however, since those displaced had no choice but to move along to the next road and lodge there, thus causing new overcrowding.

Workhouses were universally feared and hated, but were an effort to solve the problem of extreme poverty in London. Hundreds of charities were set up during the Victorian era with such names as The Association for Befriending Young Servants, The Industrial School and Home for Working Boys, The Home for Deserted Destitute Children and The House of Charity for Distressed Persons. More than two million pounds was spent annually by these organisations in trying to relieve poverty, though sadly they were merely scratching the surface, and very little difference was made to the lives of the truly poor.

Charles Dickens

Charles Dickens was the most popular novelist of the Victorian period and is still so popular that his works have never gone out of print. The theme of social reform runs through his work and the publication of many of his books in magazines in serial form meant that he could adapt the story as he went along to suit the whims of the public. His characters are extremely memorable, so much so that they often take on a life of their own outside the books.

It is known that Dickens held a dim view of undertakers and the funeral trade, and it was he who coined the term 'Dealers in Death'. He was not a supporter, either, of Prince Albert, and Peter Ackroyd says Dickens was not at all pleased when Albert's sudden death meant that he had to postpone the six readings he was to give in Liverpool and return to London.

Dickens's popular novel *Great Expectations*, with the thwarted and spiteful bride, Miss Havisham, was first published in serial form in the magazine *All The Year Round* up until August 1861, so I have drawn its publication out a little longer to fit my own story.

Oliver Twist, arguably Dickens's most famous novel, is partly a criticism of the new Poor Laws and also an exposé of the treatment of orphans in London. Dickens selected the steps on London Bridge to be the setting of the brutal murder of Nancy, the girl who befriends

Oliver, by Bill Sikes, the most evil character in the book. The steps immediately became a tourist attraction, and even nowadays on a walking tour of Southwark one will be told about 'Nancy's Steps'.

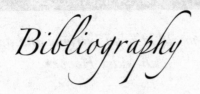

Bibliography

Ackroyd, Peter, *Dickens*
Mandarin Paperbacks, 1991

Arnold, Catherine, *Necropolis: London and Its Dead*
Pocket Books, 2006

Clarke, John M., *The Brookwood Necropolis Railway*
The Oakwood Press, 2006

Curl, James Stevens, *The Victorian Celebration of Death*
Sutton Publishing, 2000

Dickens, Jnr, Charles, *Dickens's Dictionary of London, 1888: An Unconventional Handbook*
Old House Books, 1993

Mayhew, Henry, *London Labour and the London Poor (1851)*
Penguin, 1985 edition

Picard, Lisa, *Victorian London*
Phoenix, 2005

Taylor, Lou, *Mourning Dress: A Costume and Social History*
Allen and Unwin, 1983

White, Jerry, *London in the 19th Century*
Vintage, 2008

The Times newspaper
24th December 1861